TAZ

TALES OF A RASCAL POOCH

Michael J. Dibden

Leigh - never forgotten

Michael J. Dibden

The episode in life in which Taz featured spanned over a decade in which Michael and his family lived in Yorkshire, on a hill, in a cottage dating to the 1750s, and yes, with a Staffie called Taz. This is all based on true stuff.

 Michael spent his childhood up to no good on a smallholding on the English south coast. Aged 16 saw him flogging cameras on the high street, before working overseas on a sheep farm, then volunteering in a charity shop full of weird nicnacs and old clothes, before (yawn) drifting into software engineering.

Having travelled extensively, Michael today lives with his family and a dog called Bonzo on a small farm in the warmer climes of the Mediterranean, with an added passion for cycling in the mountains, distance running and open-water swimming.

A Note of Thanks

In writing this memoir-inspired claptrap, I will admit to being on the receiving end of a generous level of support and assistance, from composing the initial idea into a viable outline, through numerous redrafts into what you read here today.

First off, none of this would have possible without the love and support of Nicky and Michelle, as the coinheritors, I guess you could call them, of many of these anecdotes.

On the practical front, a big round of applause is owed to Adam, Tra, Linda, Jason, Bayram, Hassan and Kate, who each spent precious time trawling through various drafts and shaking their respective heads at what I then thought was a passable manuscript. And from a literary and professional standpoint, Sarah's guidance, critique and endless encouragement made a significant impact in bringing Taz's story to light, and is therefore to be plied with a generous heap of sincere gratitude.

As for the wicked caricature of Taz on the front, the talented Can Kosk is the one who gets my applause.

You've often heard it said that behind every guy is an even better gal, well on that I do concur. Lily, I salute you for kicking me for so long to pen Taz's story. Thank you.

PART I – From Captive to Coddled

PART II – The Rural Rascal

PART III – Livin' the Life of an Adolescent

PART I

From Captive to Coddled

Paws, Mud & Poo

By 'eck, me nuts were nearly frozen!

It was a particularly cold Yorkshire February, and my crown jewels were being hammered into tiny solid marbles by a biting wind blowing right up my wotsit. Existence for me was an outdoor wire cage in some bloke's backyard. It was like a bloody great birdcage really, but obviously much bigger and stronger and supposedly well-suited to housing dogs. On that I would have to disagree. Life in a cage was, well, not all it was cracked up to be.

My then owner, Guy, was a fairly roguish sod. To be honest, he was more interested in stuffing his wallet from exploiting my tackle than anything close to being a responsible dog owner. He wasn't a particularly nasty arse-kicker type or anything, just about as endearing and attentive as a sack of shit. I was fed, I was caged and I was put to work. That was it, just a business relationship, plain and simple.

For a year or so I was caged inside an old breezeblock, tin-roofed garage, but then he got himself hitched to an old hag who immediately banished me from the confines of the house or anywhere connected through bricks or mortar. It was at that point I was exiled to a life outdoors.

After six months I was finally put up for sale. Guy had seemingly lost not just another battle to the old hag, but the whole war too. Whilst I'm sure Guy wanted to keep up the business side of the arrangement, I'm guessing he just wasn't up for being on the losing side of what could have been a long and drawn out conflict. Also, apart from the necessity of daily feeds and our *business trips*, he rarely seem bothered at my existence.

I was ready for a change of scenery too, and for the prospect of defrosting my extremities. It was also an unsettling time, ya know, better the devil and all that. But I had hope – life surely had to be better than being caged, especially when it was pissing it down. So, awaiting prospective new owners or not, I was mostly pretty pissed off and a tad cranky before anyone even bothered turning up in response to the advert he'd gone and placed in the local rag.

Then, one Thursday lunchtime, I think, or maybe a Wednesday, dunno, some boring-arsed looking suit turned up to gawp at me. Apparently he'd come for a 'viewing,' but looking, as he did, like some office wimp and definitely not hardened Staffie owner stock, I didn't rate his chances. The suit, as in the actual apparel rather than the bloke, was, I jest not, far too bloody perfect. It was a sort of medium-light grey in colour, and oh so very handsomely clean.

'Ha, come 'ere twat, let me at ya!' I woofed towards his ugly mug.

There were unheard discussions afoot. Not exactly sure what, so I pressed an upturned earflap to the cage bars and listened carefully... Hmm, whilst I took it to mean I'd soon be on the move, I wasn't sure if it was gonna be good news or not. I really didn't have a sodding clue to be honest. He could've been some axe-killing nutjob, or worse still, some weirdo with a doggie fetish – urgh, yuk!

After some through-the-bars inspection and more hushed discussion, Guy looked sideways at The Suit and half laughingly said, 'Nah, he's not aggressive or owt, it's just that my wife fuckin' hates 'im, so he's just gotta go.'

Bloody charming. As a proud and honoured member of Clan Staffie, that kinda hurt. But there again, life in a cage wasn't great either. I rarely went anywhere or even saw anyone else, fellow canine or hooman, except, that was, for droppin' ma drawers for cash as was the nature of my occasional part-time employ. Life was, on the whole, as boring as crap, so, perhaps a change being on the cards was gonna be a good thing.

Something then started to happen...

The obligatory current/prospective owner chitchat was complete, and Guy waltzed over to my cage and promptly released the catch. He then attached me to what I had presumed was formerly an anchor chain of a small tugboat. So yes, I was out, I was free… well, free in terms of the confines of the yard anyway, but still. So, I guessed it was time for some closer inspection by The Suit. Having been forewarned that this day would come by the old hag indoors (a.k.a. Guy's 'better half,' yeah right), I attempted vague pleasantries with The Suit. I didn't gnaw on his ankle, knees or nuts; in fact, I played as 'nicely' as I knew how. However, that lovely clean suit just kept calling, ya know, just beggin' for my attention…

It was yucky cold rather than icy cold, so the yard was mostly mud, with just the odd wisp of grass struggling to survive here and there, oh and added piles of doo-doo I had dotted around for good measure. Whilst some were new and pretty smelly, even one still slightly steaming in the cold air, others were so old that they were covered in white furry mould like discarded sugar-frosted doughnuts. The Suit then came over and sort of half bent down at the knees in order to greet me. He seemed genuine enough, not some nasty git just after a fighting dog from which to earn a few quid on the side – I might have been handy in a ring, but really wasn't bothered about chasing down such dodgy career options.

I returned his greeting the best way I knew, and firmly planted all four muddy/shitty paws right smack on the crisp white shirt he'd worn under that lovely suit. Down he went. Splat. Gave me a soft landing at least.

'Gotcha, cocksucker!' I yapped with delight at a face registering absolute shock.

According to the book, I knew hoomans enjoyed being licked by dogs. We dogs do that too, lick each other that is. But I'm told it's somehow a tad different. So anyway, I licked The Suit's face, his ears and his slightly snotty nose, whilst continuing to distribute slapping's of mud and shit, quite literally, all over him.

Guy quickly grabbed me by the collar, unclicked the anchor chain and then shoved me forcibly back into the cage. Oh crap, not a good sign. Had I gone too far? Had that meant a prospective new owner crossed immediately off the list? Damn, I was only being friendly.

Off Guy went towards the house, with The Suit in tow. More words were exchanged, but yet again I didn't hear them. I did, however, see 'something' pass from The Suit to Guy – probably it was the business card of The Suit's lawyers. Guess he wouldn't be taking me. Fair do's. But, hmm, what if instead he were to sue Guy's butt for a wodge of cash and thereby manage to ruin the old hag's holiday plans to boot. Maybe it wasn't a bad ending to the day after all.

Time passed slowly for the rest of that day, and the next, and the next. And so life soon returned to its normal monotonous state of gloomy caged boredom.

~ ~ ~ ~

Some days later the kitchen door opened. The Suit was back. Bloody hell, I hadn't bargained on that.

The office garb had been noticeably replaced by old jeans and a dodgy-looking former Christmas jumper (best guess, poor sod). Me, I looked around for a second bloke holding aloft a signed court order in one hand and a dogcatcher's pole or dart gun in the other. I saw no one else.

I was therefore dumb-as-fuck-founded when The Suit waltzed over and said, in his soft 'n' posh southern nancy voice, 'Now then Taz, you are coming home to live with me now. I hope that's okay with you fella?'

'Whoa, what the heck?' I barked, 'Really? You're shitting me, aren't ya?'

Although trying to play it cool, I was given away by my bloody tail which I forgot was set to auto-wag. I wasn't sure at that stage how fluent The Suit was in Dog, or if my northern dialect would cause confusion to his tender southern ears and by default, limited brain size as I'd been told about these non-Northerners, but I gave it my best.

6

'Yeah, whatever tough guy, I'm up for it,' and then I followed it with 'C'mon then, let us out, you short-arsed Muppet-hugger.'

Well, I didn't want to appear too overly keen and all happy puppy like. After all, I had my big bad Staffie reputation to consider. He probably only heard 'Woof, bark, woof, growl' anyway, so I reckoned it didn't matter one crap what I actually said.

Still slightly agitated at the thought of heading off to either a decent new home, or perhaps the veterinary clinic, or even another cage for all I knew, I bade farewell to Guy with a hearty 'Fuck off and die!' and then promptly farted as loud and as long as I could muster in the general direction of the old hag, who I noted was giving me the finger by return from the open kitchen doorway – proving once again to the world what an abominable creature she really was.

Guy then helped The Suit bundle me into the back of some hairdresser-styled mini 4x4 Japanese shitty light blue excuse for a Jeep, and that was that, I blew the joint and never once looked back. All I hoped was I had well and truly left behind my caged life of misery, albeit swapped for adventures completely unknown...

The Arrival

Driving home after a stressful week at the office with some brute of a dog in the back was, to put it mildly, an uncomforting experience. But what was perhaps more unnerving was the prospect of introducing him to Penny, my good lady wife of almost five years. Okay, so both of us were experienced dog owners, both together and in our respective former lives I guess you could have said, but neither of us had any tangible experience racked up handling muscular dogs like this Staffie I had just adopted or bought or rescued; well anyway, somehow acquired.

Any feeling of foreboding could was largely attributable to having not actually explained in advance any details as to 'what' we'd ended up adopting. It hadn't been a conscious decision either way to be honest. Penny had been away visiting her mum some six-plus hour's drive away on the south coast when I'd heard at work about this dog, Taz, being in need of a better home. It wasn't a rescue per se, just a fully-grown dog belonging to a colleague's neighbour, and the word was such that this dog badly needed rehoming, as well as feeding, grooming, and above all, loving. It was all I really knew, but it was enough. For some time we had talked about finding another dog, and we weren't at all breed or age-specific in our planning. So when I heard about this opportunity, I just called Penny on the spot from work.

'Whatever, however… Just go see the dog, and if you think we could improve his life, well, that'll be enough. You know best,' was the gist of the response.

The dog, as I then found out, was a 20 kilogramme Staffie that was aptly named 'Taz.' More formally known as the Staffordshire Bull Terrier, they are a well-known breed, but for mixed reasons. Whilst self-confessed muscle nuts, they are mostly just a people-friendly version of the Pitbull, or so I had gathered from a bloke at the office, but without the antisocial arsey nature or penchant for chomping postmen or the neighbour's kids. The breed had apparently started out in 19th century Britain as a small, fast fighting dog, but were best known as faithful companions renowned for their intelligence, courage and love of children (playing with, not eating I hasten to add).

However, had I acceptably accomplished the mission I had been tasked? As the saying went, only time would tell.

Off we drove, Taz and I, and soon left behind the bright city lights of Leeds, heading west across and up into the Pennine hills of Yorkshire, the backbone of England as it was known. Taz, our newly acquired mutt seemed fairly settled in the back. Well, at least there were no alarming noises, no drama or scuffles emanating from his direction as I drove. All appeared satisfactory.

Then, after perhaps ten minutes I felt the need to urgently open my driver's side window. It was February and admittedly it was bitterly cold, but more's the point I had felt as if my own premature demise was fast approaching. The car was in need of a serious rebalance between oxygenated breathable air and a dangerous noxious gas buildup due to excessive doggie bum-burps.

My opening line, 'Christ, was that you Taz?' I asked into the drivers' rear-view upon sensing the latest waft of something disgusting permeating through the car towards me.

No response. Perhaps he felt some degree of shame or guilt. In hindsight, I was perhaps just being a bit overly optimistic.

'So, you're Taz then? Right?' I tried.

I thought we'd better start getting acquainted on the journey, hoping it would make our arrival at the cottage somewhat less dramatic for all concerned.

Then I said, 'So, my name is Michael and I'm gonna be your new dad' That too was met with silence.

I ploughed on, 'We are heading to your new home. So, we, that's my wife Penny and I, live in a really old cottage right up on top of a hill. It was built hundreds of years ago and has fields all around where you can run about… I reckon you're gonna love it there. What do you think?'

I don't know if I expected some instant human to pet bonding kind of moment, but the continued silence was unnerving. I rabbited on; 'You'll have your own room, your own garden… and no cage, promise. And we'll feed you every single day, take you for long walks, and we'll all have great fun together, you'll see.'

The words were greeted with utter silence, that is, apart from yet more farts. He was obviously trying to slowly kill me, or perhaps I was in some weird murder-suicide plot.

Overall, not a great conversationalist. It held the promise of a tiresome and seemingly long journey home. Whilst I was obviously excited, I was also nervous too I'll admit. Taz certainly wasn't the type of dog either of us had been accustomed to — our previous being an excitable young long-legged Brittany Spaniel named Lucy, ergo, nothing at all like the brute I'd gone and found.

I seemed to talk aimlessly through my nerves at what was perhaps just a dark void. Yeah, I know dogs don't *actually* talk, but like all owners, one hopes or assumes that they understand everything you ever say to them. Period.

I told him about my job, how I worked in a huge open office of a national financial institution, that it was as dull as dishwater, but that it paid the bills. I also told him about the work-related move up to Yorkshire from the south coast of England, Dorset in fact.

In summary, I talked and talked and talked… pretty much for the whole hour I drove Taz to our home.

But, eventually we arrived. It was showtime. Time to see if I had judged Penny's forbearance accurately or not on the matter of our canine acquisition. Penny might have been a tall, slim, bottle blonde with a cracking smile and a zany, forever humorous outlook on life, but she was also a woman who spoke her mind, often with succinct clarity I might add, and I did wonder if I was about to be on the receiving end of some of that clarity.

~ ~ ~ ~

Tired from my long drive back up a very long motorway from what had been an enjoyable visit with my aged yet delightful mum, I was relieved to see Michael arrive home safely shortly after me, having just driven the car up our steep stone driveway outside the cottage, and pretty much on time too. The security lights popped on automatically, momentarily dazzling him, yet again. He really needed to move them. It was yet another task on that forever list; you know, the list that anyone refurbishing an old building has going and is seemingly never-ending.

Having recovered from his temporary blindness, I witnessed him regain focus as he saw me standing there in the open doorway, waving like a kid at a train station reuniting with family after a long summer spent at Aunt Mildred's place. It was another exciting new chapter in our life together, and so much so that I found myself stood there clapping my hands in anticipation at meeting our new family member. Admittedly I'm a sucker for animals, although I still had no idea what awaited me in the back of Michael's car, apart from some youngish dog in need of a better life. But that was enough info I reckoned; we'd do what had to be done.

'Welcome home love,' I greeted Michael as I always did when first in the door from work.

'You too. Good trip? How was Mum? Been home long?' he enquired almost rhetorically, not particularly waiting for any of his questions to be answered. He then took a rather visible yet involuntary gulp as he opened the car's rear swing door.

Suddenly, and certainly unannounced, some dark lump simply launched itself up the steps towards the cottage and towards me. At the end of a hefty looking chain was Michael, being similarly launched in my direction like some forgotten ragdoll. Immediate thoughts of doggie cuddles with our new puppy dissipated like air from a just popped balloon. This was not a very reassuring start. My immediate thought was how bloody strong he was, the dog, not Michael!

I could feel my face turn from what was probably something akin to wondrous delight to something bordering acute horror.

'What the heck is "that" Michael?' I shrieked.

'Err yeah, that's Taz love, he's our new pooch,' he replied, trying to sound far more confident in his actions than he obviously was.

I looked down the steps at him and said, 'I'm sure he's lovely really, but crikey, he's not exactly of the cuddle variety, now is he?'

I know dogs can get all overexcited in new surroundings, but this one might take some convincing. I just hoped that 'it' knew at least some basic rules about being a house pet. If not, I reckoned Michael could be joining him, banished to the garden shed, or perhaps they'd both stay in the car – I hadn't quite decided that far.

'So, Michael, this is the "young rescue doggie" you mentioned on the phone,' I stated accusatorily, 'Am I correct, or did you just stop by the zoo on the way home and grab whatever was in the first cage on the left?'

After giving my husband my best Paddington stare with a lingering look that I was pretty sure hit home, I looked down and saw this large smelly beast slobbering and licking my faux-fur-lined pink slippers. Delightful. I didn't know what it was, other than a dog, obviously, but me being me I knew he wasn't to blame for turning up to ruin my Christmas slippers right on my very own doorstep.

'You'd better come on in then Taz,' I said softly to him. And that is about as much as I recall of that rather surreal event. What was beyond doubt, however, was Taz had well and truly arrived.

~ ~ ~ ~

'Well, that was one seriously crappy loooong journey,' I thought to myself.

I was never a dog famed for conversation. I don't usually mind a bit of banter, but for fuck's sake, The Suit talked almost all the way – serious, I mean, he didn't stop, although in fairness I hadn't much of a clue what the heck he was saying either – bloody Southerner. He said his name a few times. I didn't get it. It was something like 'My Ball' or 'My Cool.' But nah, I reckoned he'd just be 'The Suit' to me.

Being in the back of the little Jeep thing gave me time to think at least, to try and take stock of what the heck was going down as a new chapter in my sorry-arsed life was obviously just beginning.

The Suit was a slim, neat sort of geezer. My guess; he was in his early thirties, but obviously an office wimp and mildly posh-like. But worse still, he was an out-and-out Southerner. Incidentally, I noted the swapping of his boring office wear for a pair of respectably dirty, but still boring, unfashionable old jeans that didn't quite fit. Perhaps he'd only had the one suit, and it was getting cleaned after I'd well and truly fucked it over big time with my mud and shit dance, or perhaps he just had more smarts than I'd credited him with? Jury was still out on the fella. Minus the actual suit, he had seemed like a decent enough chap though. There was no shouting, kicking or beating, so far, and that was certainly a good sign. Just wish I could have understood him a bit more, even though he assured me it was apparently English, but still…

The nancy little car was okay – it had a heater of sorts at least. However, I did note that The Suit's window had remained at least partially open throughout much of the journey. Perhaps my involuntary butt-trumpeting was not to his liking. We drew to a halt after about an hour. The car had stopped on a sort of small hill, with two lights blazing through the windscreen at us. The Suit then cut the engine and pulled on the handbrake. It was truth time.

It was then that I met Ms Noodle. The Suit's tall lady wife did say her name a couple of times, but she too was a Southerner. Bugger. At the time I thought she said her name was Poodle, or something with a 'P' anyway, but with the accent I went with 'Ms Noodle' for the foreseeable, and after that I guess it stuck.

Ms Noodle was obviously the hooman boss-lady of the cottage, and quite obviously The Suit's better half. She was tall and athletic looking – which is how I believe one describes skinny hoomans – and was topped off with shortish, spikey blonde hair, which I later learnt was chemically induced, and multiple large dangly earrings I had taken a fancy to chewing on at some later point. She was also wearing some weird soft shoes on her feet that looked like very small pink sheep with a foot jammed up each respective butt. Overall she had looked okay to me, seemed friendly enough, and certainly a full ten points up on the old hag at Guy's place. Yep, could have done a heck of a lot worse, I thought to myself.

'So then Ms Poodle-Noodle, where's my place then?' I respectfully barked up, having quickly completed a negative scan for any cage or shed at the end of their driveway.

Hmm, a spark of recognition in those kind eyes... I reckon she may even have understood a bit of Dog; now that really would have been cool.

'You'd better come on in then Taz,' she said a tad nervously as she went to lead the way inside what I presumed was the old cottage The Suit had been banging on about.

Bugger that. Pleasantries aside, I barged past her and went straight in to explore my new digs. With no obvious through route, I didn't get far past the front door when I halted, not quite knowing where the heck to go, of course. Still on a short leash, I soon found myself being led by Ms Noodle through two small rooms and then directly outside into what was clearly a backyard, and all in a little under four point three seconds.

'So, Taz,' Ms Noodle opened with, 'This is our back garden, and now it's gonna be yours too. How do you like it?' she asked rather excitedly.

'It's all right I guess, seen worse,' I replied indifferently, yet secretly grinning coz I saw it had real grass at least.

I was then gobsmacked at being 'asked' by The Suit if I would care to have a slash and/or a dump. Hmm, okay, now *that* was weird. Could it have been some southern house-welcoming ritual? I reckoned I'd just play along, and so of course I let rip, as was my custom. Wow, it was a full eight-seconder too, almost a record, and one that I great pride in by the way. Back to the question in hand, I managed to oblige on both counts, which seemed to please both hoomans no end. Weird fuckers.

It was then that I became speechless for close to the first time in my relatively short, bitter and unceremonious life. Ms Noodle opened with, 'Right then young Taz, all done?' and took the lead once more and walked me back *into* the house. 'Yes, that's right. We don't live out here in the cold, not even you my friend. Come on then, follow me,' she said.

Note the 'into' bit: blimey, now that was certainly a change I was gonna take some adjusting to. And walked too. Most weird. I wasn't shoved, dragged, thrown or pushed, just gently led.

But then the door was promptly shut behind me the second my tail was clear. Bang. Bastards! Was that it? Was it all some ploy all along to lock me up yet again? Tough lad I might have been, but I was admittedly scared shitless at that point. My tail, which was always fairly long and liked to bruise bare legs at will, was nowhere to be found, having been swiftly auto-retracted to a position of safety, and thereby protecting the crown jewels from any unforeseen attack.

A quick scan up, down, left and right… hmm, nope, no cage in sight. Good, okay so far. Then, something caught my eye…

'What the heck's that?' I squealed.

There was a big red fluffy blanket folded neatly on the floor against a wall which had some large flat white metal thing on it. If you'd never seen a dog pinch itself, then you should have been there to see me.

'What – the – holy – fuck?' was about all I could come out with in response.

Perhaps noticing my rather confuddled expression, Ms Noodle simply stated, 'This is yours Taz. This is your bed. Oh, and yes, this is a heater. It'll stay on for you all winter long.'

A bed? A heater? Dumwotsitted I was, but I quickly managed to regain some level of composure and woofed back a casual, 'Yeah, well, thanks Poodle-Noodle. This'll do nicely,' whilst shouting 'Fuck yeah, fuck yeah…' over and over in my head.

Opposite the bed was a bowl of clean water. There was no floating crap or unhealthy murkiness I might add. And to top it all, next to that was… a bowl of food! Had I unknowingly snuffed it and entered Doggie Valhalla, or was this what 'being rescued' was all about, just as I had read about a month before in Woofers Weekly? Either way, I was rather liking it, and seriously liking it at that.

After a couple of nervous minutes of having my every move watched, the hoomans walked towards the interconnecting door that we'd come thorough not ten minutes before. Presumably somewhere between 'my room' and the front door was the rest of the cottage where they hung out.

'Okay then, we'll let you settle in then Taz,' were Ms Noodle's gentle parting words.

The door was then calmly shut and they were gone. Just like that.

It was suddenly quiet. Very quiet indeed. But bloody hell was it nice and warm though. I had food, I had water, it wasn't raining or windy or cold, and my arse wasn't bruised from an evening kicking either. Overall, I reckoned one could get used to such a life.

~ ~ ~ ~

Time passed, which gave me time to think. First impressions? Well, yeah, pretty comfy I had to say, all things considered. I had the small room they left me in all to myself. It was an old kitchen by the looks of it; although there was no longer a cooker, it still had large kitchen-style cupboards down one wall, under an old stainless steel sink and a few more slapped up on the longest wall. Each had solid hardwood doors, but the ones I could reach all had special little bloody plastic locks on them, so I might as well have been stuck in a smelly old horsebox rather than a kitchen stuffed with food, or so I had hoped for at least.

However, admittedly, the room I had been given was real cosy. That wall heater thingy stayed on, just as promised, which, fair play to the hoomans was pretty sodding considerate. It was one of those flat, white, thin metal board contraptions screwed to the wall and gave out a low heat yield but at a very low cost (apparently, as I had later learnt; as if I really gave a single shat about such stuff). All I knew is that it was right smack bang next to my special blanket. At a stretch I could even raise my hairy old butt high enough to 'sample the exquisiteness,' an action that afforded one fuck of an interesting and rather gratifying sensation to the old nether region. That was an unexpected bonus I'll admit.

Then, quite late at night, The Suit reappeared.

'Okay then lad, time to see if we can't try once more before bedtime,' were his words.

'Do what mate?' I replied, 'What the heck am I supposed to do now?'

The questions fell on deaf ears, and I found myself led outside once again. Then I got it. Ah yes, it was obviously time for another supervised pee or poo. Wasn't entirely sure of the legality of these goings-on, not with some bloke keeping me tethered so my every action was witnessed, checked and cheered on from close quarters.

'Oi, turn yer back at least will ya? Can't a dog get a bit of privacy around here, or is this "your thing"? Eh, eh, is that it matey, is that it?' I muttered as I laid a slimy big turd just next to a fancy trimmed heather bush.

As much as it seemed a bit bizarre, The Suit seemed satisfied and, additionally, I noted that Ms Noodle too signalled her approval from behind the adjacent window with two 'thumbs up' and a rather large grin slapped on her cheery face. Hoomans can be seriously bloody strange at times.

So, business having been duly attended to as commanded, and yes, still firmly tethered by the lead, The Suit and I retreated back indoors. This time the door was shut, and then also locked and bolted.

Fuck! Trapped again. However, now I was trapped *inside*, with the warm air and my new blanket, and not *outside* with sweet fuck all – cue big cheeky grin.

Ms Noodle then popped in to say 'Goodnight' (yet again).

That was followed by a parting 'Night then matey. We're off upstairs. Sleep well,' from The Suit.

Just before they went, Ms Noodle plugged in a funny little lamp into a socket right above where I guess a cooker would have once been. It made some rather strange light shadows and shapes in the room that spooked me out a little at first. I guess somewhere in their hooman's Reference Guide to Doggie Creature Comforts was some unfounded shit that us dogs were scared of the dark, hah, as if. The butt-heater seemed permanently switched on though, so a little light was nuffink to put up with. Tell you what though, it was entertaining just lying there on my blanket playing shadow puppets in the lamplight with my best friend, Timmy the Todger.

On that note, I awoke suddenly in the wee hours on what was a very long first night…

'Holy crap! What if they had some video-link camera setup?' I thought scarily to myself having remembered what I was doing not half an hour before.

Cleanliness Is Next To Dogliness

In terms of my 'getting used to such a life,' well, let's just say that I did... in time. I mean, you wouldn't believe the crap they put me through at first. Talk about undignified, I ask ya.

After that inaugural night of warm blissful butt-squeaks, I was up and about all nice and early, all ready and raring to see what Day One had to offer in what was, after all, a whole new chapter in life. I had plenty of ideas, but all completely baseless. In reality, I hadn't a clue as to what it would entail.

The Suit was the first to enter my room, followed close behind by Ms Noodle, who apparently had completely forgotten she'd only seen me just six hours previous.

'Morning Taz. Have you got a cuddle for your new mum?' she squealed. So, I was guessing all the 'How can I cuddle "that"?' shit had clearly just been a short-lived 'have a go at the hubster' ruse. Looked like yours truly was gonna be in favour after all. Cool!

Not wanting to seem overly amenable at the start of Day One, I stared back blankly at the tall blonde nutjob. I wasn't used to such demonstrative girlie tendencies and was naturally weirded out just a bit. With a bewildered expression slapped firmly in place, I simply and quite honestly responded with... 'What the heck's a "cuddle" lady?'

Well, this 'cuddle' thing turned out to be a mixture of head scratches, back-stroking, body squeezes and tummy rubs, but all seemingly delivered at the same time, and with continuous infantile noises emanating from the provider, that being Ms 'Nutjob' Noodle. The overall purpose of the 'cuddle' experience somewhat stumped me though. It didn't hurt at all, and was sorta fun. Also, Ms Noodle seemed noticeably very happy before, during, and after said event, so I just did the decent thing and went along with it.

The cuddle session was followed by my first scrutinised wee of the day, before we all withdrew quickly back into the warmth of the cottage, with no argument heard from me. Then, my shiny and obviously ever-so-newly purchased grub bowl was filled with birdseed, plus lukewarm water added apparently for good measure.

'Wait. What?' I hollered, 'I'm no fuckin' vegetarian! Where's the meat? Oi lady, look, four legs not two! Do I look like a bloody pigeon to ya?'

Nothing came back from all of that, nothing except daft hooman grins from both of them. There seemed zero nutritional variance on offer though, so I gave it a go coz I was well-famished after all the excitement of the move. However, as much as I hated to admit it, the birdseed was actually passable on the taste front, even though it looked like shit; taste-wise, not in literal terms. It certainly wasn't quite the bowlful of fat old pork sausages ladled in thick cold gravy I had been holding out for, but it was still passably tasty nosh all the same.

I couldn't resist one more jibe though. 'So, I take it the sausages and gravy get served up for lunch instead around here then...?' That too was met with blank looks exchanged between them and me. Not that I ever ate like that at Guy 'n' Hag's gaff, but it was worthy of a try. Nothing ventured, nothing gained, right?

Guessing the answer well in advance, I mumbled 'So, that's a big fat "No" then' disgruntledly to myself and returned to pecking away at the birdseed.

~ ~ ~ ~

Michael and I had not owned a dog in quite some time, at least not since moving up to the wild open Yorkshire Dales from the sunny South as was required for the job. However, it was admittedly quite satisfying to have a dog about the place once more. Our previous pet was an adorable young Brittany Spaniel. Lucy was her name. She was a young, playful, forever bouncing, long-legged spritely individual who uncontrollably licked each and every visitor that dared turn up at the front, or even back door. Unfortunately, she also howled every minute of every hour of every day that we weren't there with her. So much so, I eventually felt forced to sign her ownership away to a pet rehoming charity in order that she could hopefully find more suitable lodgings. As heart wrenching as it was at the time, we both knew it was the right thing to do, for her at least. It was also deemed a necessity in order to put an end to the neighbourhood declaration of open hostilities in what had amounted to an uncomfortable domestic battleground against neighbours on both sides who seemingly never ever went out.

But that was all part and parcel of a life we'd moved away from a couple of years previous. I still really missed the South. I certainly missed my family, my friends, and even my old job in the hospital laboratory, and of course I certainly missed the halfway decent weather of the south coast too. Hillside life in the Pennines was great, a real change and quite a tonic to be honest, but climatic differences alone sometimes made it feel literally worlds apart.

And so, Taz had suddenly become our newest family member overnight. Time would tell the degree to which he'd brighten up our lives, but I personally thought having another dog would help alleviate a few remaining feelings of unsettledness on my part.

To say that Taz the Staffie was in any way similar to Lucy the Brittany, except for commonalities of snout, number of legs and a tail, I'm sure could have formed a valid court brief under the Animal Descriptions Act, presuming there was such a thing. Lucy was cute, she was loving, she was skinny and she was tall, and always smelled of sweetness, in a lovely cuddly doggie type of way. Taz, so far as I could tell from his first few hours in situ, was a short, stocky, solid lump of muscle, bone and attitude, whose most famed attribute would have to be his constant ability to generate noxious bodily gas at will, and who was, based on guesses as to his regular articulation, one grumpy short-arsed son-of-a-bitch, literally.

Suffice it to say, Michael and I held 'discussions' when we retired to bed at the end of that interesting first night having brought Taz into our home. We did, however, agree that whilst it was most probably going to be a serious 'challenge' for all concerned, that Taz would stay on for the foreseeable to see if he and us could make the arrangement work. But with regard to Item One on the agenda, we were in total accord… that smelly lump was in urgent need of decontamination before anything else.

~ ~ ~ ~

'Arrrgghh…!' I woke suddenly from the most peculiar of dreams.

Whilst sleeping next to a heater was certainly great for my butt, it also had me dealing with all sorts of weird nightmares. After being left to my own devices for much of that first morning, both The Suit 'n' Ms Noodle came in to see me, but I noted both wore rather strange and determined looks, although I wasn't at all sure as to the reason or purpose.

I was feeling good. The birdseed had stayed down, the bed was well-comfy and the heater did its thing. So, apart from one particular nightmare that involved eight pink cats, life was pretty much as sweet as one dared hope for after the ruckus of the house move just the day before. The air in the little room was a bit ripe though, but I put it down to my last meal at Guy's and the dodgy-looking meatballs the old hag had thrown at me, literally. All that having brewed for some 18 hours seemed a logical explanation for my attempted annihilation of all living creatures, or so I reckoned. Wasn't overly bothered personally as all quite normal in my book. Ms Noodle's face said otherwise. I even thought she was gonna upchuck all over me at one point. Bless her, what a southern softie.

After regaining her composure and somewhat adjusted to the atmosphere, Ms Noodle was the first to speak, 'Now young Taz, we have something very… [said extra slowly] …special lined up for you.'

The Suit said nothing, but scuttled quickly out the back door, but not before giving me a strange sideways glance, followed by a distinct nod to

Ms Noodle. 'I'll get the stuff ready then. Give me three minutes,' were his instructions.

Perplexed hysteria washed across my face. I tried in vain to fathom the meaning of such an odd statement.

Lo and behold, The Suit reappeared within the aforementioned timescale and duly clipped on my lead (again). However, he was notably wearing welly boots, old trousers, had his sleeves rolled-up, and a firm yet not unsympathetic smile, or was it a smirk? What the heck he was up to I really had no idea, but guessed that I wouldn't have to wait long to realise my fate.

The Suit looked at me square in the eyes and said 'C'mon lad, out we go. Nothing to worry about.' That was it... when one was told 'not to worry,' the opposite was usually much nearer the mark in my experience.

'What you got in mind Big Man? What you two up to then?' I asked with more than a twinge of growl in my woof. The Suit just semi-smiled back at me, and gave the lead a gentle tug.

Rather than my normal approach to exiting a building, as in 'let's get the fuck outta here,' that morning I gingerly placed one paw in front of the other as I reluctantly followed The Suit. It was a coolish but bright and sunny winter's day, and the centuries old natural flagstone slabs that separated the cottage from the raised main garden had changed since my last poo 'n' pee adventure. It had been hastily set out like a carwash, with hose, bucket, brush and other... such... stuff...

Oh crap. Was this another of those semi-lethal activities that hoomans forced their pets to endure, according to Derek the Doberman?

Yep, it was definitely *not* a carwash, nope it was worse, it was... a soddin' dogwash!

My tail auto-retreated, my ears immediately dropped, and my heartrate exploded bigtime. Being a dog not a duck, I was never much of a water freak, and so I started to panic about things like how long Staffie's could hold their breath.

Ms Noodle, I noted, was bravely stood off at a safe distance, but did her bit by shouting words of encouragement. 'Oh Taz, you'll be just fine.' she said, 'In five or ten minutes it'll all be over, just you see.'

My mind raced in overdrive, 'all be over?'

As I stood there trying to work that bit out, my world exploded... the faded old blue garden hosepipe that had, up until then lain innocuously still, suddenly came to life and shot a jet of cold water right up where the sun don't shine.

'What the holy mother of fuck was that for Mister?' I shrieked, whipping my soggy butt out of the direct line of fire, whilst straining at the leash that had been shortened by The Suit's left boot and thereby curtailing my immediate escape plans.

Protesting as best I could, I was soon soaked from snout to tail and from the top of my head to the pads of my paws. I couldn't really comprehend what the crap was going on, but I seemingly had no option due to The Suit's welly-booted feet firmly plonked either side of me, forcing me to stay put and endure said abuse.

The water stopped as suddenly as it had started. Of course, being of canine disposure, my immediate impulse was to 'do the doggie shake,' but the bastard still had me held so darned tight that even that was out of the question. Hmm, should I have just bitten the fucker and had done with it, assuming I could reach one of his legs?

The Suit looked down at me and firmly said, 'Don't worry lad, it's for your own good.'

'Are you totally nuts?' I woofed back up at him, 'Let me try this on you and see how you bloody well like it!'

Then the foam started.

That was something I really had *not* been expecting... Bloody foam everywhere, and I mean everywhere!

The Suit covered every morsel of my shorthaired being with, apparently sweet-scented, crappy cleansing foam. Out of the corner of my eye I spotted the source of this dire stuff. A tall narrow plastic container was emblazoned with a single word I was unfamiliar with, but comprised of two known smaller words, 'poo' and 'sham.' And what a sham it was too; them pretending this was supposedly something akin to an agreeable experience. It didn't help that Ms Noodle was by then laughing hysterically, taking bloody photographs too, which all added to the indecency and shame of the whole episode.

So, this 'poo of sham' was rubbed into every external area of my body. I remember feeling invaded, assaulted, degraded... and clean. Uh, the horror and humiliation. I was bred from fighting stock for fuck's sake, had they no decency?

Soon after, the soapy shit was rapidly removed by another session with the garden hose, to which I responded with a loud but ignored, 'Aww c'mon! That's enough... sod off will ya?'

I just hoped to hell nobody else could see me. I did a quick 360, or as best I could manage, bearing in mind my restricted positioning. Was the cottage overlooked? Could any other dog, or worse still a cat, bear witness to my hour of shame? I could have died right there and then, or left with a memory scar that hung like a heavy chain around my neck for years to come.

Then, the hosepipe finally stopped.

'Okay. You're all done Taz,' The Suit proudly announced.

With that, the lead was clicked off and I suddenly found myself set free! Now, consider, if you will, three points of certitude with regards to that moment. First off, I was completely loose, set free from a torturous and unexpected incident, so instinctively I bolted forward, reaching terminal velocity in a little under 23 nanoseconds. We Staffie's are not famed for our track speed, but by crikey, we can move like a fuckin' bullet when the need arises, and that moment certainly qualified as such.

The second point was that I was wet, very wet; soaking bloody wet even, having been forcibly half-drowned, foamed and then the other half also drowned, all whilst being held against my will, I might add. As a woofer, the overwhelming urge was to shake, shake, shake… and of course run for my damned life.

Thirdly, the question was simple, to where should I run? I was in a strange land, in a high-walled garden with two Muppet's who seemed warm-hearted one minute, and oppressive brutal tyrants the next.

The net result was the most peculiar dance ritual imaginable. I sort of shook, and ran, and jumped, in a roughly circular motion all around the garden like some sort of demonic bull at his inaugural rodeo, not really having a clue what the heck it was supposed to do once the bucking chute gate was unlatched.

'Fuck you!' I barked. Then I threatened him with, 'I'll get you Mister!' and then, 'Just you wait!' followed by 'Never again!'

All of these were barked out sporadically during my frenetic, uncontrolled tearing around and around the garden.

Both Ms Noodle and The Suit stood and watched, apparently highly amused at my fury-filled pirouette-on-the-run display. The only break in their joyous entertainment came when I went crashing into a bed of suddenly rather squashed white snowdrops.

'Be careful Taz!' shouted The Suit at that point, 'Calm down lad.'

'Sod off!' I replied, and carried on regardless on yet another round of the garden.

As the nutritious value of the birdseed began to wane, I commenced a gradual slow down, much to my own dismay. Actually, I really wasn't done, I had way more in me… but my battery charge was dangerously close to being depleted. Calm I was not. Knackered I was. I eventually came to a halt somewhere around the middle of the lawn. I stood there, panting like a lunatic. I eyed up my tormentors, but didn't say a dicky-bird – just stood there, panting, and of course farting.

~ ~ ~ ~

A loveable lunatic. Yes, one day into our adventure and that's how I would describe Taz. Whilst Michael had certainly surprised me with the breed, it didn't take me long to become strangely attached to him; Taz I mean. Yes he was rude, crude, and boisterous, but there was some loveable quality in there, although admittedly it wasn't inherently obvious at surface level.

We just stood there. I looked at Michael, and he back at me. Then we both burst out laughing as we looked at the strange lunatic little beast that had just come to the end of the most bonkers runaround we'd ever witnessed. I'd hopefully captured some great shots though, holding the camera aloft as it clicked away on auto whilst Michael had tried, and failed, to calm Taz down a bit. Eventually it happened, but that was probably more due to his energy levels than any slight element of control either of us had over the situation.

'Taz…, calm down, calm down,' I said softly, trying to bring some semblance of order and peace back to proceedings. 'If you'll just stop for a moment, I have something very special here for you,' and held out a chewy bone-shaped snack in my right hand, whilst hunched down, knees bent so to be more at his level. He very slowly approached, warily watching my every move. I guess after his surprise 'shampoo and set' it was going to take a bit of time and bribery to regain whatever trust Taz had in either of us.

~ ~ ~ ~

Ms Noodle was calling my name, notably employing her soothing 'I'm really your very best friend' type of voice. She then picked up two objects which she held forth in outstretched hands, one at a time. First, in her right hand, was a sort of bone-type-looking-thing. Not an actual bone, I guessed that much, but it was intriguing all the same. As my breathing returned to within non-lethal levels from my spontaneous and rather exhaustive runabout, I slowly ventured to within sniffing distance, but not close enough for either of them to clip the bloody lead back on. Trust was in short supply at that point after the hosepipe affair. Hmm, the bony thing seemed innocuous enough, and so I simply sat there and then proceeded to stare at it, as ya do.

One whole minute passed.

Ms Noodle obviously wasn't gonna chuck it my direction either, so I stood up, lowered my haunches and stalked forward, ever so slowly. With no alert signal registering on my 'hoomans are total shits' inbuilt threat-monitoring receptors, I was eventually able to gently grab said bone-thing from her outstretched hand and retreat quickly to a safe distance.

Now, dunno how one would describe it, but it was weirdly nice. It turned out to be a sort of bone-shaped arrangement of dried cowhide or pigskin — tasted bloody lovely in fact. These humans were clever little shits sometimes. Whilst inside I was feeling that some sort of 'Thankyou' was perhaps in order, I was still too livid from the 'wash' to let any gratitude show either. Therefore, neither of them heard my silent 'Well, ta for that, I guess.'

Of course, being a Staffie, I scoffed the whole thing in less than four minutes, which seemed to rather upset Ms Noodle I noted. She was busying herself referencing the packet it came from, which presumably stated some crap like 'hours of contentment for your doggie' or some other such bollocks. Nope, a quick chew, a few bites with my Staffie jaws and that was that. Gone.

'Oh look love, he really did enjoy that, didn't you Tazzy-wazzy?' she exclaimed towards The Suit.

My observations were confirmed. The woman had well and truly lost the plot. 'Tazzy-fuckin-wazzy' indeed. Bit rich that, coming from 'Ms Poodley-Noodley-Woodley.'

So,… just what was she holding in her other hand? That one looked like a dead doll, having had its vertebrae surgically removed from the state of it too. It was something I hadn't recognised, but in for a penny, in for a pound… I wandered forth, slowly and still very warily, in order to investigate.

'What the heck is it?' I asked.

I then got close enough to have a sniff and confirm its status; inedible, that much was evident. So nope, not food. It felt both softish and hardish at the same time too. The middle bit was like a thick rope, with a large hard knot tied at each end.

'This is called a "ragger" Taz,' explained The Suit.

'It's a toy. You can play with it!' exclaimed Ms Poodle-Noodle, 'We got it especially for you,' she added, seemingly very happy with herself over said purchase.

'Err, so? I questioned, 'Just what the heck am I supposed to do with it?'

It didn't taste of anything, and it didn't seem to do anything either. But when I snatched it up and launched it across the lawn just for the sheer hell of it, Ms Noodle let out a holler of delight (very weird). I then moseyed on over to retrieve it, all casual like, and threw it back across towards where they still stood; same result, another squeal from Ms Noodle, and this time with an added 'Bravo. Great throw!' from The Suit.

The hoomans seemed amused at least and, curiously, I was kinda too. I'm not saying I was ecstatic, bound over by emotion and all that rah-rah shit, but yeah, it did seem sorta fun. It seemed to make the hoomans laugh like billy-o if nothing else, and if there was one thing I'd learnt over the years, it was that happy hoomans fed ya loads, and they don't tend to kick yer butt then either.

As a former cage dweller, up until just a day before, I had fuck all experience with 'toys' of any kind, so I really wasn't that au fait on the do's and don'ts, let alone the whole point of the exercise. Whether there were other moves with the 'ragger' I would have to learn, time would tell, but for the next 30 minutes or so I stuck with that same old pick it up, throw it; pick it up, throw it, type of routine.

It was cool, but pretty sunny that day at least, and I was soon fully dried off and comfortably warm at the end of my inaugural ragger session. I had food in my belly in the form of a well-chewed pretend bone thing, and had been watched by two passive but weirdo hoomans that, okay, had their moments (i.e., the hosepipe), but seemed generally kosher on the whole. I also seemingly had a garden that I had by then judged to actually be all mine. Oh, and I had the ragger toy thing...

In summary, I'd gone from caged to relative comfort in just about one day, and that had to be a result in anyone's book, foam or no foam.

Cottage Rules

Even as a lifelong pet person, having a dog around the place after an absence of a few years still required a degree of readjustment. It's not that far removed from having a small child all of a sudden; everything literally changes overnight. Of course, it's all very exciting in the lead up to the new arrival, such as heading out to shop for those all-important stainless steel bowls for water and food, making sure you have a suitable lead and collar, trying to suss out the differences and suitability of all the canned food versus dried varieties, checking that your car is pet-compliant, that the garden is appropriately fences, the house is pet-ready, and more importantly, making sure you, the prospective 'new parents,' are also suitably organised and up to the task. As self-assured experienced former pet owners, we reckoned we had it all pretty much sussed, that both the cottage and ourselves were adequately ready, having been 'ready' for a while in fact, just waiting to find a pet, or as in this case, one to more or less find us.

The annexe at the back of the cottage had been chosen as the 'pet room.' It used to be our kitchen before we created a large kitchen-diner during a period of extensive and very messy renovation of what was once a formal dining room. Years ago, that one room would have constituted the entire ground floor of one of the cottages, prior to the adjoining of cottages Three and Four. Whilst it was always a lovely room, with its large inglenook fireplace and oak beamed ceiling, it was always deemed too 'formal' and, sadly, rarely even used. The large old solid oak table and Edwardian carved chairs just went to waste, rather than having been put to daily use. Particularly in old cottages where there aren't many rooms, any area left unused is always a crying shame. However, since the room's renovation and makeover, it had been very much used on a daily basis as a functioning kitchen, coffee lounge and daily dining area, as well as for occasional entertaining, a day room, and even as a study-office when work followed either of us home.

But the room set aside for Taz was the old and much smaller former kitchen. It housed the wall-mounted gas central heating boiler, the washing machine, and an old food freezer. The old kitchen's cupboards were still there, but instead used to store anything from washing powder and bulk food supplies, to a full range of tools and equipment necessary for life in a two and a half century old cottage under constant chunk-by-chunk renovation.

The ultra-flat, ultra-low-consumption electric wall heater was an absolute bargain, and brought about a much-needed level of basic comfort to what was always such a cold annex room, and especially so for our newest member of the family. However, the prior acquisition of a collar and lead was an unmitigated disaster I'll admit, having not quite bargained on nabbing a pet with the sheer strength of a demented lion cub. And so, that first weekend necessitated a quick trip to town to upgrade said items for more appropriately constructed apparel that was better suited to maintaining basic control of our not-so-wee beastie.

Other than that, the cottage itself hadn't been particularly difficult to rearrange, as most ornaments were already above paw level, or so we had thought. Certain rapid response corrective actions were taken here and there as we came to see the folly of our plans during those first few hours and days, and of course Taz delighted in pointing out every little thing we'd missed.

Like children, pets need firm boundaries, dogs especially. They respond, mostly, to rule-based commands and work best within pre-set confines, or so the theory goes. No point having a lovely home if it faces partial destruction within a few short hours of a new pet arriving, no matter how well-intentioned or cute they may seem. House rules, or cottage rules in this case, had to be discussed, agreed, set and reinforced until they became accepted and adhered. Well, that was the principle at least.

Later that first day I set forth on a personal mission, to develop, agree and introduce said set of 'cottage rules' to Taz.

~ ~ ~ ~

From cage to relative comfort, yep life had finally spun me a bloody good'un. Even me nuts had started to defrost after far too long sat in that damned cage which, even with the few bits of wood and cardboard Guy had used to cover the most exposed side, left plenty of opportunity for the cold Yorkshire winds to freeze my nuggets to the size of small marbles — and I'm talking those tiny teeny Oxblood Peewee marbles that were worth fuck all in a primary school playground game of marbles.

Relocating from cage to cottage required one heck of an adjustment on a scale that I hadn't really anticipated. It was by no means an easy time I can tell ya. After the external bathroom capers with the hose, followed by the runaround session with my new ragger, we had all ventured back indoors. With the hoomans having retreated to their armchairs, television and bowls of comfort snacks, I made myself at home snuggling into my cosy new blanket bed by the heater. Happy enough that I'd sussed out some aspects of this new lifestyle, I reckoned I mostly knew what was in store from that point onwards, or so I thought. Yeah right — naïve was not the bloody word.

Once I had my paws wiped for me (what?) — Fuck me, I wondered if I was expected to do that bit myself in future? — it was sanctioned that I could venture further indoors, beyond the limit of what was termed 'Your [my] room.' Ms Noodle looked a tad concerned at this point, I have to say, watching my every move like a hawk, but one wearing tight jeans and fluffy slippers. That delighted the mischievous in me. It's always good to have the upper hand, or at least make them 'think' so. The Suit had been lurking in the shadows I noted. It was immediately obvious that 'indoors' was ruled by Ms Noodle, whilst 'outdoors' was The Suit's domain, and both now mine too of course. It was all new territory for me, so I took consent having been granted as a sign of good faith by the hoomans. However, I also got the feeling that one sly shit behind the three-seater could instantly reverse my supposed good fortune.

Ms Noodle then proceeded to 'show me around' the living room. It was pleasant enough, perhaps a bit over-cottagey for my taste, but hey, I hadn't paid for it so what the heck, right? How to describe the room? Well, there was a low ceiling (for hoomans anyway, not me, I was just fine with it) with two whopping great polished ship's beams running end to end. There was no central hanging light I noted. I guessed it was coz of the restricted height, favouring instead black iron carriage-styled wall lights and small ornamental table lamps such as on the large wooden television cabinet and on the music cabinet. Not that I gave a crap really, I was more interested at looking for stuff purposefully kept beyond my immediate reach, for that was obviously where all the best stuff had been moved. There were these huge deep window shelves covered in shitloads of photographs and nicnacs from all their travels. With such massively thick walls, the window shelves' depth could easily accommodate a stretched out kitten. Hmm, I immediately wondered if I should have that theory tested out?

'Now young man,' began Ms Noodle.

I looked around with a full head spin, saw no other person or animal befitting the 'young' bit and so replied, 'Oh, guess you mean me, d'ya lady?'

'So, this is our living room,' she said very slowly, as if I was fuckin' stupid or summat. 'This is where we relax, watch television, and talk,' she continued, again as if I was a two-year-old hooman, not three in doggie years, which was, by my reckoning, fully-growed-up!

'Is this my room too now?' I asked excitedly. The sudden keenness had obviously reflected in my eyes, as an immediate corrective statement was put forth; 'and no, this is not *your* room too, this is *our* room.'

Bugger.

Trying to ignore the veiled insult, my mind drifted to take in more of *their* room. It was then that one outstanding, mind-blowing, and mega-bestist feature hit me – a whopping great flat-topped cast iron wood-burning stove, set deep into a huge inglenook fireplace topped with yet another beam – yowser! My first thoughts were that any self-respecting pooch could nicely warm up his dangly bits sprawled out in front of it. But then I really wasn't sure if I would ever see such a prospect, thinking that first visit might just have been a cursory 'newcomers orientation tour' granted only for the sake of politeness.

Ms Noodle walked on through a narrow set of half-glazed double doors to the left of the fireplace, 'and this is the kitchen Taz,' she stated, but immediately tagged on, 'and please note, this is also *our* room, not yours.'

The kitchen was obviously where the hoomans prepared and scoffed their grub, whatever that was – probably not birdseed would've been my guess. From what I could see, the large wooden table and surrounding chairs were in obvious need of gnawing. But that was as much as I could see from the doorway, coz mutt-features here wasn't actually allowed 'inside.' See, I was only permitted to 'look' into their room, not physically enter. That fact had some clarity added by way of The Suit keeping a firm grip on my collar and his foot blocking my entrance. There was one of those goldy-coloured carpet-joining bar thingies separating the two rooms, and that was the apparent demarcation line.

'Now, I must warn you Taz,' Ms Noodle continued, 'we have a strict rule of "No pets in the kitchen," so no going past this line. Ever! Got it? That is, unless you are specifically invited in by one of us.'

'Fuck off,' I laughed, 'You gotta be joking, right?' I retorted.

The sternest of looks on both their faces said they were bloody serious. What the heck they thought I was gonna do in there was beyond me, perhaps invite seven friends in for Sunday roast cat-poo parcels, and then proceed to barf it all up in unison?

Ms Noodle, however, seemed adequately persuaded that my solemn agreement had been granted. The Suit less so – shrewd old git. In order to augment Ms Noodle's case, additional pressure was piled on by The Suit with the simple words; 'Enter here equals dead dog. Kappeesh?'

With thoughts of persecution and torture should my paws ever cross the gold bar threshold from living room (occasional permitted territory) to kitchen (don't even fucking think about it territory), I took it the rule was not gonna be particularly flexible. At that point in the proceedings, a small, silent involuntary 'pfffftt' seemed appropriate, as it happened. As to my own personal viewpoint on said ruling, the jury was still out. I wasn't gonna commit either way – not that I'd let on with regards to my future intentions, so I just woofed a quick 'Yup, whatever' and hoped they would leave it at that.

Ms Noodle then asked me to turn around.

I obliged, albeit a little wary.

Suddenly she was down at my level, and notably on all fours.

'Woah, misses… what the…?' I shrieked.

Tail retreated, ears dropped, I was instantly troubled by this sudden turn of events. Oh crap, not some threesome hooman fetish to follow the hosepipe up the butt experience and all that sham of the poo stuff?

'Aww gawd,' I whined nervously.

Long story cut short; clothing stayed on, hands stayed put – phew, okay, so that was a bloody relief at least. In fact, all Ms Noodle did was to get down at my level so as to facilitate direct communication between hooman and well, 'me.' With eyes looking right through to the back of my skull, Ms Noodle, very 's l o w l y' explained another of her 'Cottage Rules.'

'Taz,' she started, 'there… will… be… no… pooing… inside… my… cottage! Got that Mister? Not anywhere.'

'You're addressing me, I presume?' I asked all nonchalantly like. She looked blankly back at me. Okay, so I guess she didn't mean The Suit then.

Talking of The Suit, he again decided to throw in his manly two pennyworth. 'To put it in the simplest terms possible,' he started, 'you even attempt a dump indoors and you're out. That'll be it, gone, history, and no second chances. Clear enough?'

Hmm, personally I just laughed inside. What a knob, offering up such a challenge so early on. Idiot.

I guess he saw the slight lack of appreciation in my eyes, as The Suit continued to explain by way of rather graphic actions. Taking a dump behind their prized furniture, or anywhere else in fact that wasn't outside in the garden, was 100% not kosher at any time, night or day, from that point onwards, and right up until the end of the planet's existence, or mine; whichever happened to occur first.

It was all well and good in theory, but I didn't commit either way on this rule either, no siree. Having a crafty dump in forbidden places was part 'n' parcel of the challenge of being a rascal house pooch, so no way was I signing up. Instead, I just stood there, farted (again), and bowed my head in mock capitulation. It seemed they bought it anyway. Suckers!

The standoff, or rather stare-off, lasted just a few seconds longer than comfortable. All three of us then remained on the big rug in front of the wood burner. Ms Noodle then looked across at me. Shit, I felt another 'rule' coming on.

She decided it was best to employ the old 'show and tell' pedagogical methodology. So, rather than simply stating the next rule, she lifted up the toy ragger given to me earlier and then, looking me square in the eyes said, 'Ragger *yours*, cushion *not yours*.'

Next, she turned and picked up a small green ball with some never-ending white stripe synonymous with a daft hooman game apparently called 'tennis,' and repeated the same mantra, 'Ball *yours*, figurine *not yours*,' and so on and so forth with a few more examples that I needn't bore you with.

Naturally I presumed this stoopid rule incorporated an element of flexibility, after all, it seemed more of a dare if I was honest. Breach of contract was inevitable and a pretty likely occurrence on a regular basis if not a downright certainty before that very first weekend was out.

I cocked my head to the right, and looked straight past Ms Noodle towards the sofa. 'You sure about them cushions?' I barked questioningly, 'They do look rather shaggable.'

I looked at Ms Noodle and then across to The Suit, and then back to Ms Noodle, hoping for a response from one of them, or both. Zero, nope, nothing, nada.

'You sure?' I asked once more, followed by 'Look, they have tassels at each corner, oh and so do those dangly big rope thingies on all the curtains too. How the heck am I supposed to tell the sodding difference between them and my ragger thingy? Same shit, innit?'

Familiar blank expressions returned their answer. Even at that point I could envisage reparations demanded somewhere down the line in the form of withheld food or privileges withdrawn for flagrant infringement of this bastard rule alone.

After a couple more minutes allocated for these primary Cottage Rules to apparently sink in, we all traipsed back to 'my room.' Ms Noodle then proceeded to open one of the wall cabinets and took out a box of some hooman food labelled 'basmati rice.' She then placed the box down right next to my food bowl, the one that had earlier contained that birdseed stuff.

My bad, she obviously hadn't finished explaining that last rule, and that was it, off she went again... '*Your* food, Taz, *your* food' whilst pointing to my bowl, and then '*our* food' as she pointed to the box of rice.

Even though not permitted entrance to the hooman's kitchen, I gathered that the remaining cupboards in 'my room,' being their old kitchen, were still partly used for occasional food storage of the boxed or canned variety. It was then explained that my food would be 'given' twice daily by way of direct placement into my shiny new metal bowl. That was it, period. No food seen, stored, or found elsewhere was to pass my lips, not if I had any hope of seeing my next birthday, apparently, or any beyond that.

To clarify, The Suit yet again felt the need to back up Ms Noodle's explanation with his own bit, '*Your* food will be found in *your* bowl. Food taken or scoffed from elsewhere will mean a swift kick up the bum. Simple.'

Not much subtlety there, but guess he was clear enough. And yes, of course there's was an unspoken 'however' brewing in my mind. What sort of dog did they think I was?

Then the back door was opened and my ragger promptly thrown out on to the lawn. I immediately dived after it – seemingly the only logical thing to do after the apparent conclusion of the boring, never-ending lecture that formed part of my compulsory 'Regulations 101' course. Enough with the bloody rules was all I could think.

As I lay there on the lawn, ragger in gob, I contemplated my first 24 hours of cottage life. On balance, so far so good. Accommodation was well-up to scratch and the nosh was okay too. The rules seemed a little archaic, but admittedly it was mostly what I would call 'agreeable.' I just had to try and remember; 'keep out the kitchen,' 'no crapping indoors,' 'no scoffing ornaments,' and 'touching the hooman's food could induce a serious butt-ache.' Being a dog, I wasn't apparently required to 'sign' anything official, so bugger it, that surely meant they weren't legally binding either by my reckoning.

Of course, I let it be seen that I intended to play along nicely, ya know, making it all seem like they had won the day. However, all along I was screaming within, 'Bollocks to ya both, and to yer bloody rules!'

Flap's Away...

The cottage was built somewhere around 1750, having assumed that nugget from scrawled ownership records and letters dating back to 1754 found in with the property deeds, suggesting that the property was constructed a few years previous. At that time it was a row of four cottages, providing tied accommodation to estate workers of a nearby large ancestral home. I don't recall the exact historical details, but I do remember that one of the Bronte sisters once worked as a teacher at the house, which was indeed pretty cool.

1750. That's a seriously long time ago. I mean, we are talking of an era when Robert Walpole, the First Earl of Orford, was Prime Minister of Great Britain just five years previous, having served under both King George I and King George II, and who subsequently died some ten years after the cottages were built. It was also a time when the 'small town' of Manchester, over the other side of The Pennines, had a population of just eight-thousand souls, compared to today's sprawling city of over half-a-million, and the average life expectancy in 18th century Britain was just 30 years of age. If one then considers the comparative fledgling histories of other now established democratic nations such as America and Australia, then it's not difficult to appreciate just how darned old the cottages actually were.

Construction likely took place employing estate workers from the 'big house,' toiling endlessly in what would likely have been pretty rudimentary conditions, and all for a pittance in wages and some very basic accommodation thrown in. Situated on top of an exposed hill, the sweat and graft of the workers in their baggy trousers, tough leather boots and Yorkshire flat caps must have made for an arduous life.

As for us, Penny and I purchased what was already by then a knocked-through double cottage, having been made into a single dwelling a few years previous. The other two cottages in the row had remained as single residences. The already partial renovation had made it an interesting project to take on and indeed a charming place to live. With so much history entwined in the very fabric of the building, everything in terms of its restoration and modernisation was an adventure in itself. The external walls were some 50 centimetres thick, that's an astonishing 20 inches in old money, of mostly huge blocks of locally quarried Yorkshire stone. There were certainly no cavity walls filled with EU-compliant, fire-retardant insulation materials back then.

Whilst there were no particular issues with earthquakes around those parts, there were, however, some pretty fierce storms to contend with, often blowing a howling gale that would knock inattentive sheep over should they venture far from the drystone walls that surrounded most fields; but I can tell you straight, that cottage never creaked, never groaned, never moved, not once. It was well and truly solid by any definition of the term.

And another solid element, shall we say, was Taz. Staffie's are pretty much famed for their muscular disposition, having stout, solid bodies that are not unknown for being tested against physical barriers put in place to contain them in one place or another. Their skulls are notoriously tough, as we came to witness all too often. On one such occasion, just after we first acquired him in fact, our new cottage companion decided to demonstrate his physical robustness in a rather unexpected fashion.

In keeping with the thickness of the walls, the cottage was accessed by thick old hardwood external stable-type doors, and by that I mean split doors that enabled the top half to be opened independently of the bottom half, which could still remain firmly shut and bolted; an advantageous feature when it came to airing the cottage on a warm late spring day. The old doors were lovely, but had become quite warped over the years, and so much so that they let in some roaring and unwelcomed draughts. We later upgraded two of these old doors for more modern versions that better protected the cottage from the cold winds.

Being originally two cottages plus an annexe, we in fact had one 'front door' and two 'back doors,' with one of the back doors leading off the kitchen-diner of what was cottage Number Three, and one that led from the annexed extension at the side of cottage Number Four, the room where Taz lived, and both doors led directly to the back garden.

~ ~ ~ ~

Them first couple of days livin' with Ms Noodle and The Suit were well-mad, I can tell ya. What, with that hosepipe blasted up me jacksie, trying to get my noggin around stoopid cottage rules, and being force-fed birdseed. Whilst still 'finding my paws,' so to speak, I really hadn't much of a clue as to what was what, how the heck the hooman's rules would actually translate into daily life, and to whereabouts the limits of my new territorial boundaries extended.

Beyond the door to my room at the back of the cottage was a smallish garden, surrounded by a pretty tall moss-covered old Yorkshire drystone wall which I reckoned I could have tackled with relative ease should the need have arisen to escape the confines of my new gaff. I had pretty much guessed that everything 'within' the walls was essentially 'my pad,' my domain, my world where I could rule supreme – well, can't a dog dream a little? I knew by then that indoors was most definitely Ms Noodle's queendom. Whilst The Suit may have *thought* he was boss there, I knew the truth really. But the garden I reckoned was mine, all mine. Well, weekdays at least.

Back on Day Two of my residency, I was sat there with the winter sun coming through this weird small door/window thing which some nice hooman had conveniently placed down at my level, close to the bottom of the back door. What a considerate thought, eh? As I'd moved there in late winter, around mid-February I think it was, I remember how bloody cold it was on top of that blowy old hill. Now, whilst I consider myself a pretty tough sort of pooch, if truth be known that heated 'doggie room' was bloody lovely compared to my former life freezing my nuts off in that cage stuck outside of Guy's place. The weekend afternoon sun was sublime though, and slowly I started to doze off as my bits warmed to a new level of comfort... Suddenly, something caught my eye, and instantly I was 100% awake and staring out of the door/window thing.

'Was that a... a fuckin' cat...?' I half asked to myself.

What the heck? It bloody was too! And the damned thing was taking a stroll across *my* garden... Yep, just ambling across the lawn like as if it owned the sodding place.

Now, I obviously wasn't gonna put up with that sort of crap, not on my watch and not on my patch either, newly acquired or otherwise. In my best manly Staffie gruff voice, I barked out a series of very angry and menacing expletives.

'Get the fuck outta here!' I woofed being a prime example. It was a genuine attempt on my part to put an end to the invading moggy's antics.

Arse. It had about as much effect as barking at a fridge, hoping that the door might suddenly swing open in order to facilitate scoffing the odd slice of strawberry cheesecake. The feline invader had no doubt heard me, that much I had gathered coz it stopped, looked over at me square in the face... then sauntered off, slowly too I might add, on its amble across the lawn towards the back gate.

Time passed astonishingly slowly, or perhaps it just stood stock still...

An age seemed to pass by. I was stood there, head bowed, staring through the plastic/glass stuff of this miniature door/window thing. I might not have moved a muscle, but my blood had certainly begun to boil. I don't mean a slightly raised temperature either, I mean a big fat thermometer up the bum exploding kinda boil. I was livid. That bloody moggy was dead meat, seriously dead. There was no question about it in my mind, then or now.

However, being still early days living at The Suit's, and having not yet mastered jumping up and turning the door key or pulling down on the door handle in order to let battle commence, I inevitably found myself simply staring with demonic eyes at the assailant.

Right, enough of this crap, I thought, I'm the dog, right? I'm the superior species. And it was my patch too, plus I was a proud Staffie. Mister Pussy-features, well, he had meowed his last! Famed for having skulls as tough as ebony. I mean, crack a Staffie with a knuckle punch and he'd more than likely just laugh back at ya. Sure, everyone has a weak spot, but my noggin ain't ever been close to being mine.

To be honest, it wasn't intentional, the act that followed I mean. I did try to explain that to both The Suit and to Ms Noodle in the days to come, but they seemed less than enamoured with my so-called 'excuse,' and ended up accusing me of all sorts of treacherous shit, when it was really very simple.

There I was, just watching 'Mister "I'm soon to be fucking mincemeat" Pussy Cat' saunter on by, and, ya know, doing my mad 'n' vicious barking routine, as was my dog-given right of course, when he passed beyond my initial line of sight. Of course, I shuffled a bit to the right in order to gain a somewhat better view, and even pressed my big black snotty old snout up against the door/window thing as I strained to see to my extreme left.

Four very slow seconds passed by as I followed 'it,' and then I found that I'd lost sight of it altogether. Fuck!

What the heck was I supposed to have done? I didn't rightly know. Frustration built, I was like the infamous Doctor Banner, about to transform into The Hulk after exposure to ultra-high levels of gamma radiation whilst working late that fateful night at the Culver University. Harder and harder I pushed, but still I couldn't see that damned cat! Moving towards almost blind panic at being faced with possible territorial forfeiture so early after having moved in. I saw no other alternative.

I reversed back towards the wall, and then, once my butt had made contact, accelerated in a forwards direction at a speed nearing 84 metres per second, and suddenly rammed my skull straight at the door/window thing.

Bang.

Crack.

Smash...

Cold air hit my nostrils like nitrous oxide entering a burn chamber.

Whilst unbeknown to me at that precise moment in time, the door/window thing had been obliterated into a pile of shattered PVC Plexiglas, moulded plastic framework and splintered wooden doorframe of unknown origin.

The feline invader froze at the sound, and also probably at the sudden appearance of my fat head and gob full of big shiny teeth. One thing was certain, my jaws of death were at last sharing the same air as pussy-features. I was outside.

'Ha pussycat, you're fuckin' well mine now,' I howled into the cold Yorkshire air.

The cat, of course, just stood its ground and looked over at me with a certain disdain and did nothing else whatsoever. Me, well I farted really loudly for starters, it was all the excitement you see, but also did nothing much else as my rage again started to build. Where was the cat's natural born fear of me? I mean, come on, I'm a big hairy-arsed angry mutt (not so hairy I might add in actuality; we Staffie's have a close coat, good for combat, and especially kind to asthmatic owners), so why wasn't it petrified at the peril it so obviously faced?

I learnt an important lesson that day; cats are brainy little fuckers. Dunno how that stupid little mouse-chaser knew, but he just seemed to sense that he was fundamentally safe. Yes I was outside. Yes I was barking and growling and snapping... But I was also well and truly stuck! My broad shoulders and muscular torso had become firmly jammed in the 'not quite so bloody big as I'd thought' hole I had sort of inadvertently created in the back door. Whilst making a shedload of noise was quite doable, moving more than one millimetre in any direction was absolutely not.

Oh crap!

Emergency rescue services soon arrived, in the shape of Ms Noodle and The Suit. Well, it would be safe to say that they were not best pleased at what they discovered, nor with me as it seemed I was being blamed rather than the cat, which really wasn't what I'd been hoping for on the support front.

The cat, of course, smirked, turned its puny head and pointy ears towards the back gate and slowly continued its amble across the garden. My garden. Bastard. Then, much to my surprise as I of course could not physically see behind me, being stuck half in, half out, The Suit, or perhaps it was Ms Noodle, promptly delivered an almighty right-footed butt kick that made direct contact with the gonads in a single swipe. Thankfully, whoever it was had been wearing poncey carpet slippers rather than steel-toed boots, but all the same I didn't half let out one hell of serious 'woof.' Albeit in truth it was more from sheer surprise and shock than actual physical pain, but still, I owed whoever it was a bag full of revenge somewhere down the line.

The Suit then spent ages trying to slowly extricate me from the now bust doorframe, and I continually verbally threatened him with various forms of retaliation that of course came to absolutely nothing. Apart from verbalising my disgruntlement, there was basically fuck all I could do but wait it out. Ms Noodle was also giving me a right old verbal dressing down. I was her literal captive audience of one, but at the same time I think she was attempting to calm me; explaining how the door/window thing that previously occupied the hole I was wedged into was in fact known as a 'cat flap.' These contraptions were deliberately installed, apparently, and all so that any resident moggy had some legitimate means of access into and out of the house, even when the bosses were out. To say I was less than enamoured with this informational update was an understatement.

'You mean they get their own fuckin' doors!?'

Vehicular Acclimatisation

What's with hoomans and their sodding love for motorised transport? Us woofers have the upper hand I guess. At least we use all our four legs rather than hobbling around on just two. Talking of hoomans, The Suit, he seemed a bit of a lazy shit; ya know, like saying we were going for a walk… then climbing into the car. Seriously? We lived in a country village surrounded by open fields on top of a hill in Yorkshire for fuck's sake, but nooooo, we'd all get in the car and drive somewhere miles away, go 'walkabouts' there... then all pile back in the car and drive back home again. I mean, doh!

In my former pre-cottage life, cars meant only crap rides where crap things happened, such as visiting The Oppressor, a.k.a. 'The Vet,' some balding, ruthless white-coated Dr Victor Frankenstein wannabe who just loved jabbing long metal needles into my butt cheeks. The other car trips I recall were heading off for 'inspections,' where my knackers somehow became the talk of the day. What held the hooman's fascination with my dangly baubles was beyond me, but there ya go, weird bunch. However, I must admit any return trips were more than passable, as it usually resulted in bagging a girlie woofer for half an hour, so no complaints there if I'm honest.

My initial vehicular transfer from Guy's dump to cosy cottage life was, well, satisfactory at best. The Suit had talked incessantly the whole way, whilst I stared out the window at passing car and street lights, and of course farted profusely as the old nerves kept pulling my chain. I was never really into those four-wheeled things, and had often ended up with either a bad case of the squits or upchuckery due most probably to a mixture of nerves and vehicular motion.

But as it happened, life with The Suit and Ms Noodle soon semi-forced me into enduring life on four wheels. That little pretend 4x4 Jeep-thing was okay, but to be honest there was naff-all room in the back for me, and notably within a few months of my joining Clan Suit, they'd done the decent thing and upgraded it for a Jeep proper, with wodges more room for me to shake my booty at passing traffic. However, the old bastard had immediately fitted a pretty solid, purpose-made 'dog guard' – a kinda thick metal grill that completely separated the open cargo area (my bit) from the comfy seating (their bit). I guess those first few outings in the little blue thing, having drool slobbered every 93 seconds onto their shoulders and my semi-deliberate dumping of snotty deposits into their ears had not been to their liking. Bloody southern wimps.

Anyway, this Jeep was more like a squat truck really, so bit like me really. It was wide-bodied, same; low-down, same; solid, same; and could handle most types of terrain. Yep, they'd only gone and splashed out on a Taz truck!

However, just the sight of the hoomans grabbing the car keys would still fill me with dread. Suddenly, I'd find that my legs wouldn't work that well, my ears would droop and my tail would almost disappear up my butt. Plus, rumblings inside would usually start up well before even getting to the front door, preparing for some inevitable bodily crisis once we hit the road.

'He just needs a spot of "acclimatisation," that's all,' I heard Ms Noodle say to The Suit.

What the hell did it mean, 'ack-lie-mer-tie' what? Climate is summat to do with weather, right, or was it mountain climbing? Dunno, but at that point I was more worried about Ms Noodle and her climate-wotsiting than the damned car, even if it was bigger and all that. What the chuff were they plotting? What weird relationship had they dreamed up between a Jeep, the weather, and me?

'Oi, Ms Noodle,' I asked as she grabbed the lead and clipped it to my collar, 'What you and the old sod going on about?'

Ms Noodle just looked down at me and smiled warmly. She then snatched up the car keys and with a happy-go-lucky, 'C'mon then Taz, you're coming with me today,' we headed out the front door towards the Jeep.

~ ~ ~ ~

Having a dog throw up all over one's car is not a pleasant experience in any way, shape or form, as any current or former self-respecting pet owner will attest. That stench alone can rip through one's memory for near-on a decade. In the past we'd been the not-so-proud owners of some rather 'ralphy' animals who'd self-evacuate within the confines of a vehicle, and usually on cold wintery days where the opening of the windows to let in badly needed fresh air was also a sure fire way of getting hypothermia before reaching home.

So, from the outset with Taz, I was determined to avoid a life of car squits and car barf. Within a few months we had upgraded the far too small for operational purposes little Japanese 4x4 for a sturdy old fifth-hand diesel Jeep proper, which was far better suited to our life, our location and our recent newbie in the family. I then set about the task of acclimatising Taz to a life in which cars would not instil instant panic or suicidal inclination – on his part or ours for that matter.

The day after we changed the vehicle, I tried a fresh start, determined to help Taz get over his fears, and thereby deliver some tangible improvement to all of our lives. Michael happily left this one up to me, admitting that my patience was better suited to the persuasive tactics required for such a task.

As 'Step One' of my plan, I took Taz out to 'see' the new Jeep – but with no intention of going anywhere at all. I think at least three times that first weekend I just opened up the large rear tailgate, which would rise up with a gentle yet reassuring 'whoosh' of the three centimetre supporting gas struts, and just sit there on the flatbed and proceed to chat to Taz, nothing more. He, on the other hand, opted to keep his butt firmly glued to the flagstone driveway in absolute defiance. There was no way he was going to voluntarily join me 'inside' the vehicle, door open or not, preferring to remain well and truly 'outside.' Considering his past life, and the negative connotations probably associated with car journeys, I could appreciate his reticence. However, in our life, vehicles were somewhat of a necessity. We lived in an area which wasn't exactly remote, per se, but a vehicle was certainly needed if we wanted to say purchase anything more than a litre of milk or an unhealthy deep-fried snack. Plus, nearly all our friends and both our families were some six or seven hours drive to the south, minimum.

After a couple of unsuccessful attempts to persuade Taz that sitting in the open back of the Jeep was not necessarily a precursor to a trip to the vet, his love for yummy little snacks proved too much and he eventually agreed that sitting there next to me was 'okay,' if not top of his list of favourite pastimes. Together, we must have spent some four or five hours sat there in the car over a period of a couple of weeks. Each time it became less of an ordeal for our belligerent mutt — familiarisation was key, and the perceived threat to life seemingly began to dissipate over time.

Next, I moved on to 'Step Two' of the plan, to see if the car could actually be started. Another week passed with Taz pretty contented, if not ecstatic, to go 'sit' in the car, engine running or not, and even us taking trips around the village together. Another week later again, and he had become so contented was he that he would happily chomp down a bowl of food whilst sat in the open back of the Jeep. The place had become like a second home to him; a safe haven, his new sanctuary.

~ ~ ~ ~

From what I could see, Penny had achieved miracles in helping Taz become comfortable with the car. They would nip out there together at all sorts of odd hours, she'd tell him stories out there like a mum with a kid, he'd have his dinner out there, and when we just needed something from the local shop just 200 metres away, they'd even started driving down there together, with perhaps a little detour or two thrown in for good measure.

One Saturday afternoon I was looking through the cottage window that overlooked the driveway. I noted that Taz, having not long scoffed his way through the contents of yet another bowl of grub, was just lying there flat out in the back of the Jeep. Penny, on the other hand seemed concerned, and the situation was causing her a fair spot of bother. Taz had indeed become so contented in the car, that he'd lain down and then simply nodded off, snoring like a worn-out Santa on Boxing Day. The problem was that all Penny's attempts to wake the beast failed miserably; he simply wasn't going anywhere. After what seemed like an age, Penny seemed to give up and headed back indoors, leaving Taz in doggie dreamland snoring away in the back of the car. The strong cage-like dog guard meant he was at least safe in terms of getting loose close to what was sometimes a busy nearby road, and she'd also left a couple of windows partially opened so he was in no danger from lack of air either.

She came in and explained the success or whatever you might call it, and went on to do some house chores as there was no point sat there watching what was ostensibly a comatose smelly old mutt.

And there Taz stayed, for two and a half bloody hours!

The primary aim of the operation was thereby deemed a notable and significant success. To all intents and purposes, Taz had officially become 'vehicularly acclimatised.' Finally, we were able to move on to a life without fear of the back seats or us being coated with unwanted smelly stuff, or having to deal with 'doggie presents,' deposited from either end, before we'd even left the driveway, or just a mile or two down the road.

PART II

The Rural Rascal

Apprenticeship News

Cottage life had come to suit me, well mostly at least, having survived the various initiation tests and rituals imposed by my new hoomans. Within a couple of months of my investiture I felt relatively settled as Apprentice Resident Rascal of Brack Cottage. I was certainly having lots of new adventures in life, but before getting into all that, here's a brief update on my so-called 'progress.'

Bath time, as it happened, turned out to be a scheduled monthly skirmish between me and The Suit. It was almost tolerable in terms of the 'poo of sham' being rubbed into my bits, but as for that bloody hosepipe... On at least two occasions I'd managed to sink my gnashers into the rubbery fucker, spraying water in all directions, except for where The Suit intended of course. I thought it was all quite comical, but said actions seemed to attract intense disapproval from The Suit; although I was sure I caught a slight smirk on Ms Noodle's face seeing the hubster getting a thorough soaking too.

One bone of contention did raise its ugly mug, and that was the 'monthly' ritual being immediately brought forward if I'd happened to have found a steaming pile of fox crap to roll about in when off on our walkies in the fields. Whilst considered fairly high up on my 'fun to do list,' I soon discovered that Ms Noodle held a completely opposing viewpoint. One sniff of Perfume Le Foxy triggered an impromptu episode with the hosepipe, no matter what the calendar happened to have read. It was one of those crossroads decisions... fox poo or butt wash, fox poo, or poo of sham. Bugger that for a game of soldiers; the bastards won that one. I opted instead to try and 'give up' the fox poo, although I did have a couple of relapses admittedly, just to show them I could.

As for the so-called cottage rules that Ms Noodle kept banging on about; well, they certainly got on my tits, big time. Attempts at renegotiation mostly delivered a win for the hoomans, that is, except for my scoring a significant escalation in the scoff stakes, with some hooman nosh such as pasta being added to my bowl once a week to lessen the tedium of the birdseed.

There were, of course, the inevitable rule infractions on my behalf, which brought about frequent staycations of yours truly in the virtual doghouse. Mostly it was castigation by way of having rights temporarily revoked, such as not being permitted to enter the lounge of an evening, or getting boring instead of meaty-tasting snacks after a long walk. But I put it all down to being part and parcel of the apprenticeship learning game, for all of us.

Now, as to me and cars, I'm proud to say that the words Taz, car and barf were no longer auto-associated. Can't say I was necessarily always 'Yay, let's go for a six hour drive Ms Noodle. Oh pleeease, lets, please!' but journeys here, there and everywhere no longer seemed a threat to my din-dins staying put in the old tum, so on that score one could say I was almost grateful for Ms Noodle's patient yet incessant 'training.' After all, these wheeled beasties certainly played a big part in both their lives, and therefore by extension, mine too, so I had to try at least to get past my issues.

I could even do the single leap up into the back of the Jeep unaided, and even once managed a clean jump from the bottom step outside the cottage straight into the open cargo area, although I had failed miserably on numerous occasions before that, and since I hasten to add, with bruises to show for it after going 'splat' into the rear bumper like an idiot.

Jeez, I'm almost sounding like some obedient and well-behaved house pooch aren't I? Never fear, it's a ruse at best. I still had a sack full of shit to throw and mischief to be had in the process. Well, fun for me that is, I don't think either of my hoomans would have agreed, certainly not based on the crap I got myself in to on an all too regular basis, and just for 'doin' my thing' too, mostly.

Zero Gravity

Us men do like our cars. On the whole that's a fairly true, if not somewhat generalised statement of fact. Personally, I've been a fan of cars and bikes since a young lad, with memories of my parents various cars throughout my childhood, as well as my elder brother's big, fast 50 cc 'motorbike,' well it seemed like some high-powered beast to me back then, being aged ten of so at the time.

Oh, and then there was our 'taxi,' in the back garden. In fact, I sincerely doubt it ever was a taxi. It was just an old black but rusting Series II Morris Minor that hailed from around 1953, that had somehow become a permanent fixture in the paddock where we kept sheep on our smallholding on England's central south coast. It had long been stripped of parts, but the engine block was there, so were the old hand-stitched horsehair stuffed leather seats, a mostly intact dashboard, and a solid old steering wheel. Therefore, through my child's eyes, that car was of course in 100% working order, just as if it had rolled off the factory line at Cowley near Oxford one month before. In reality it was of course totally rusty, full of spiders, and with a floor that had long since rotted through to the bare earth below. However, to a small boy there was no question that the car could go anywhere on the planet, subject to the odd bit of refuelling, and a packed lunch, a bottle of juice, plus of course some Digestive biscuits.

At the time, my maternal grandparents lived in an annexe to the farmhouse. My 'Gran' was a bag full of fun. If the weather was fine, and sometimes when not, she would let me take her 'for a ride' in the car after school. We'd go all over the place, London, Paris, and even New York once, as I recall. It was incredible how far that 30-horsepower 803 cc engine, with a good dash of imagination thrown in, could take one boy and his Gran.

~ ~ ~ ~

As teenage years moved into adulthood, the attraction moved more towards two wheels than four, with motorbikes of varying shape, size and noise level as my life's focus. It was only later in life that I discovered a shared passion for automobiles, again also of varying shape, size and noise level.

I went through a number of pretty 'normal' vehicles, including an off-white Volvo estate which, to be honest, was actually a really enjoyable car to drive as well as being highly practical. That said, it was also associated by almost everyone I knew to being some grandpa car, or that 'family station wagon' that appeared, usually in mustard-yellow guise, in almost all made-for-TV American movies of the early 80s, and which were usually driven by a busy stay-at-home mum with a Labradoodle and two point three perfectly white-smiling offspring.

Next on the memory list was a dirty old Datsun three-door 'sports hatch,' complete with lowered (or possibly just rundown/broken) suspension, faded, torn but functional racing-style bucket seats, and a 1200 cc engine that I was convinced had been made on the sly by Ferrari. In reality it was a far less spectacular ride, and one in which I ended up living in for much of one summer, but that's a whole other story.

One extreme and definitely notable ride had neither two wheels or four, but three…it was a turquoise-coloured Reliant Robin, as infamous a ride as they came. Sometimes affectionately known as a 'Resin Rocket,' with its 850 cc four-cylinder block tuned to the hilt, that little go-kart was one serious kickass big heap of fun, and absolutely ace at scaring the living shit out of unsuspecting fellow motorists. On a good day, and with a bit of downhill assistance and a decent tailwind, it was able to blast along at speeds in excess of 83 mph! Let's just say this, it brought a whole new meaning to flying by the seat of your pants! Cornering was dodgy as hell though, and navigating roundabouts was particularly fraught with danger at anything above a crawl. One of my biker mates back then, Rob, was a good six-foot tall, and thus made for excellent ballast – chucking his weight about from side to side on the tiny back bench seat in order to stop us from tipping right over on corners taken at some breakneck speed, all things being relative of course.

Decades passed, needs changed, and bravado waned. The wheel count settled at four and manufacturers become more distinguished as the pocket allowed, providing a corresponding increase in comfort. Upon migrating due north, from the sunny south coast up to the Pennines of Yorkshire, a new love was discovered, that of the 4x4. To clarify, that meant vehicles with the necessary clout and muscular tackle to handle a bit of off-road driving in relative comfort and to handle the more wintery conditions of the north. A few different 4x4 beasties subsequently came and went over a ten year period.

Second only to a 4,000 cc V6 thirsty lump of American machinery from Mr Ford, which was packed with bells and whistles way beyond that offered by its Japanese peers, the Jeep we had was probably the most favoured 4x4 by a long shot. Powered by a strong 2500 cc litre diesel lump with impressive torque, it tackled most challenges thrown its way. Also, the additional leaf sprung suspension and custom gas struts afforded the necessary ground clearance to make it one hell of a fun, go-anywhere beast indeed.

~ ~ ~ ~

Yowser, it was the weekend! The old man was home, and from what I gathered, he had no particular chores in plan except for taking yours truly out for a decent walk – my type of plan. The old fart took me out every morning, just like clockwork around five-thirty for a decent runabout in the fields before he then walked on to the office to do whatever bollocks he did there.

'Taz,' he shouted from his kitchen to mine, 'you ready for some fresh air matey?'

'Matey? Just who the fuck d'ya think I am? Matey…,' I grumbled as I lay there, refusing point-blank to move one muscle without at least receiving a verbal apology, or some nutritional bribe at least.

I'll admit, weekend walks were usually pretty nifty, venturing off to interesting places The Suit had no doubt discovered through chats with local geezers who knew the wider area far better than us newcomers. It did, however, usually entail a walk of maybe eight to ten miles, and as I was never that long in the leg, that was more than enough to knacker me out big time.

'Oi, Suit, we going "out" out or just walkin' from 'ere?' I hollered back.

It was an important detail. If we were walking from the cottage, well, I knew all the usual trails and fields he'd come up with, but 'out out' meant headed off in the Jeep… now that was a different bucket of spuds as who knew where the fuck we'd end up, and that made for truly Staffie-sized adventures being on the cards.

As usual, The Suit never answered. Ignorant twat.

Then we had some action. The Suit wandered in, car keys in hand. I jumped up from my pit, stretched my legs like some nimble yoga freak, farted twice for good measure, had a good old shake from my ears to my tail, then trotted over to let The Suit know that I too was ready for the off. His big old walking boots were laced up and the lead promptly clicked onto my collar. Finally, a Yorkshire flat cap was deposited upon his slightly balding nugget (yeah, I know, but the southern dick honestly believed that made him into a Yorkshireman – as if).

'Ms Noodle! I'll be seeing ya,' I barked, and quickly proceeded to drag The Suit down the cottage steps at a rather uncomfortable pace, for him. I was fine, well up for it in fact; whatever 'it' was. The tailgate was opened and in I piled. It'd taken me a few weeks to perfect my jump and barrel roll attack, but by then I could get in and out with some degree of style.

After a bit of an engine warm-up, off we roared. The Suit had selected some great backroads and farm tracks for our adventure which took us out on to the open moorland and eventually up to the highest point of the

Pennines, so most certainly not the usual roads around the village.

I guessed that The Suit had experienced a bit of a shitty week in the office as the upgraded suspension was being especially hammered that day. Being his wingman, albeit in the rear gunner's position, I offered the appropriate encouragement from the back, shouting 'C'mon then, let's give it some shit!'

Had, per chance, The Suit recently learnt some Dog? Dunno, but it certainly seemed so when his eyes met mine in the mirror, coz he semi-smiled and then floored it. The Jeep took off down this old quarry track, wallowing and bucking at the uneven ground as branches and brambles tore at the old bodywork. He didn't mind and neither did the car, having been used and abused for a number of years before our time.

Bloody brilliant it was – 'I'm loving this!' I howled, whenever I managed to maintain any sort of balance.

The track eventually opened out onto open moorland, with deep drainage ditches catering for the often severe and pissy weather conditions seen that high up. And then there was the occasional big concrete drainage pipe that went under the track, causing some not so insignificant bumps. Whump... whump... whump – we'd wallow over these every hundred metres or so, providing some bona fide testing of the new suspension at least, not to mention my own personal balancing skills that were somewhat akin to a surfin' dog.

'Hey, you okay back there Muttley?' The Suit hollered over the noise of the roaring diesel block.

'Absolutely fuckin' great!' were my only thoughts, but I never managed to get them out as I was too busy trying to stay upright; all the time peering out at the huge smog-like cloud of mud and spray the off-road tyres were churning up in our wake.

Screw the walk I thought, we should just do this all day and then head back appearing 'ever so tired,' hoping for some scrumptious delight

Ms Noodle would most likely knock up for us after our 'very long and tiring walk.'

But my thoughts were suddenly stopped dead; something happened that I hadn't seen coming…

The Suit had though, just, as all I heard was a loud 'Oh shiiiii…!' from him before the Jeep literally launched into thin air. We'd presumably hit a bump that was much larger than the others, more like a small humpbacked bridge, hence the 'Oh shiiiii…!' was deemed appropriately fitting to the circumstances.

All one point seven tonnes of the Jeep quit physical contact with Mother Earth as the tyres span in mid-air as the engine raced to drive four large wheels that had all simultaneously lost their traction. At the same time I too was robbed of all physical contact with Mother Jeep. It seemed we had jointly achieved 'zero gravity.' At one point The Suit glanced at me in the mirror, I was floating mid-air like some fat canine piñata at a kid's party, minus the stringy tether tied to my junk.

I was a flying Staffie. 'Woo hoo!'

~ ~ ~ ~

Later that evening, back safe and warm in the cottage, we were all sat there chillin' out watchin' some crap on telly. For a change, I was obviously not being held on any form of behavioural restraint for that week's misdemeanours as Ms Noodle was fussing around us both, me included. Our collective boy-thoughts from earlier proved correct, as Ms Noodle's presumption was that we'd been out there trekking for miles and miles considering the length of time we'd been away, and were being treated like conquering adventurers having returned safe from the wilderness.

Me and The Suit… well, whilst we didn't exactly discuss it, we did exchange sideways glances and smirks a few times. Let's just say a gentlemanly bond of secrecy had been formed.

From that moment on, The Suit was elevated in my eyes from the status of 'complete wanker' to just 'minor twat' – he was, on balance, actually fairly alright I thought.

But what was more important, I also realised that I had something to trade at long last, information of intrinsic value. It was something I could keep stuffed away, but had the potential to be shared with the authorities, Ms Noodle that is, should the need, or want, ever arise. I wouldn't call it blackmail exactly, but it did afford me a certain upgrade in the bloke-dog relationship. I knew it, The Suit knew it. Ms Noodle, of course, was left largely unawares of this relational development. She'd gathered something was up, but us boys had a bond, and a secret that could not and would not be divulged, not ever (well, until now).

A Spot of Cooking

As a former caged inmate over at Guy's place, it didn't take one heck of a lot to register as an improvement to my residential state of affairs. It had to be said that hanging out in the old kitchen of Ms Noodle's cottage was indeed pretty cool. Actually, it was pretty warm as the butt-heater hangin' on the wall by my blanket was bloody brilliant, and most welcomed during those first few days and weeks as I adjusted and settled in to my new home.

But all things change, develop. It's what they call progress, right? Even us dogs have needs and dreams, just like you hoomans... and my eye was firmly planted on a rather comfy-looking old armchair in the hooman's area of the cottage.

I mean, that armchair was just like, wow... or certainly looked that way. It was a large old thing, with a pretty naff floral pattern admittedly, but really, really deep cushions and big wide rounded armrests. On the occasions when I was allowed to walk through the lounge or sit in there with a chaperone, I would stare longingly at it, imagining resting my nuts on the soft cushioning, or just drooling on the armrests to dream of pink poodles. Of course, all the time I would also be farting away quietly into the back of the chair – aww, what bliss.

Ms Noodle caught me once just standing there with my head resting on the chair's seat cushion, half asleep. She wasn't upset particularly, just wasn't sure what to think, after all, she was one house-proud mama. Meanwhile, I was her dog and famed for not much beyond a dodgy bum and some pretty crass habits, so one held out little hope for the chair ever becoming really mine.

One particularly lousy week late that first winter and the weather had changed for the worse, just as we'd thought spring had sprung. Wrong. There was snow swirling around once again, driven by a bitterly cold northerly that would grab hold of all the fun in our morning proverbial and stamp on it till it was squashed beyond recognition, like a hedgehog who'd argued with a quarry truck. Daily walks had turned into the daily grind once more; battling headlong into the wind for about a mile from the cottage, and then being blown like ragdolls very quickly all the way back. Basically, it was so fuckin' cold that my dangly bits had almost retreated within for fear of becoming more akin to nothing less than frozen pre-cooked Chicken McNuggets. It was just foofin' cold.

Ms Noodle had felt particularly sorry for me when we returned back home one Tuesday morning, and had me wrapped up in an extra blanket for good measure. You really had to love hooman ways. Sometimes a dog could get quite used to it.

Not long after we'd arrived back, The Suit donned his office garb and set off to walk the 40 minutes for another day of whatever shit he got up to that paid for my now comfy lifestyle, amongst other things.

A little later that morning, Ms Noodle lit the wood burner to warm the place through as the day seemed set not to improve in meteorological terms. Whilst my room wasn't freezing, coz of the metal butt-heater thingy, it wasn't exactly toasty either.

Ms Noodle popped her head around the door to my gaff and politely asked, 'Hey Taz, you wanna come in here with me for a bit?'

'Too bloody right!' was my immediate reply.

In less than a second I'd shot straight past Ms Noodle and into the sublime comparative toastiness of the lounge. Yep, that was well-nice. Burning beach logs were rapidly heating up the thick cast iron casing, and the wood burner quickly started radiating some serious heat. Ms Noodle had placed a large old blanket down on the floor in front of the hearth and I headed straight for it, instantly collapsing in a dog-like pile; front and back legs outstretched, balls to the blanket and head facing the heat. Heaven.

Time passed slowly by as I lay there, half asleep, half awake, but very much contented with life. Ms Noodle faffed around in the kitchen with that night's dinner preparation, as well as baking another batch of her scrumptious rock cakes. Upon sniffing the air, I was praying to the big woofer in the sky she would drop one or two by accident or miracle so that they became instant Tazzy-snacks. Closer to reality, what I was hoping for was those few extra throwaway bits that she'd sometimes bake to then later chuck into my bowl.

But 'Wake me up when it's nosh time won't ya?' was all that came outta my sleepy old gob.

And with that, I fell into a blissful, warm, cosy long snooze by the fire…

~ ~ ~ ~

'Hi Penny, I'm home,' Michael called out as he opened the front door. He was back after putting in just a half-day, an arrangement that was not uncommon as he was on call for the following 24 hours.

I was on the way to meet him at the door when he followed up with, 'Penny, I hate to be blunt love, but what are you cooking in there, a dead rat or something?'

Perhaps appearing a bit sheepish, I calmly replied, 'Hello love. Yes, doing a bit of baking today whilst I'm off. It was so cold too, so thought I'd put the burner on and heat the place through.'

I paused. I could see that he knew there was more to be told. So, somewhat gingerly I continued, 'I have but one little teensy-weensy confession though… we have a sort of… err, guest,' I blurted out.

'Eh, who?' enquired Michael, 'I don't mind at all. I was just wanting to know what's making the cottage reek so much. Can't you smell it?'

With that, I made him promise not to say anything untoward, and then led him by the hand into the warm, but admittedly very smelly lounge.

He immediately sussed out the source of the mystery pong. Lying there sprawled out in front of the roaring wood burner was Taz. He was parked upside down, lying there on his back with his legs dangling mid-air, and of course, with all his worldly possessions on open display to all. He was also snoring like a freight train, as he had been for ages, and oblivious to Michael having arrived home or to one word of our discussion. He was tilted slightly towards the fire so that his belly was facing the heat at less than one metre away.

The source of the abominable smell was simple. It was half-baked Staffie. Probably not so severe for me, having been indoors all morning and therefore 'used to it,' but I don't think Michael had ever smelled anything quite like it till then, nor probably since.

Taz was an endearing creature at times, but others, like then, we both truly wondered what sort of ill-informed decision we had taken in inviting that 'thing' into our lives and into our home. What a stomach-churning memory that will forever be, especially for Michael.

Monday Could be a Strange Old Day

Ms Noodle was not often heard to swear out loud, but cuss me she would on a pretty regular basis. That's posh hoomans talk for referring to me as a complete arse, or similar, and the reason was usually down to something connected to my apparent inappropriate levels of personal hygiene. Mostly that meant my lack of bum wiping before entering the cottage, or general weakness for leaving crap all over the place. Oh, and by that I mean stuff like toys left wherever they happened to land, half-chewed bits of food found days later under the sofa, stuff of theirs I'd nicked but not hidden well enough, or on the odd rare occasion it may have had more to do with the literal meaning of the saying. Anyway, so what… they say 'shit happens,' right?

Ms Noodle was proud of her place. Fair enough. But me, I'd mostly register as a general fuck-up on the cleanliness scoreboard, and therefore in regular receipt of a verbal butt-booting for alleged partaking in ways deemed highly inappropriate, well, according to M'lady Noodle. But I decided early doors to just take whatever castigation was being doled out, and then just carry on doing well, whatever the heck I wanted.

Speaking of this house-proudness lark, one Saturday afternoon I overheard heard Ms Noodle talking at some length with The Suit.

'It's always such a mess these days, ever since we got him that is. So I know it's the best thing, but do you think they'll get along?' she said.

Hmm, intriguing. Something was up, and I instantly fell into nosey as hell mode. 'Who, what, where, when…?' I barked at neither of them in particular.

No answer of course, so I kicked it up a notch.

'Hey. What the fuck's goin' on?' I shouted with a touch of mild panic added to my woof.

The doorbell suddenly rang. Someone had arrived. They both went to greet the arrival, but the inner doors remained notably closed, leaving me stuck out back just guessing and unable to hear what was going down. Obviously it was someone they'd been expecting though. Lengthy discussions were held with said visitor in the other room. Of course, try as I may, buggered if I could make out what was being said, even with my best ear slapped flat against the glass door. Arse.

Another ten minutes passed by and then the door to my room suddenly opened. Almost comically the door banged my head, having been too close to escape its swing in time as it opened coz I had been straining to find out what was happening. Unexpectedly, it was 'the visitor' rather than one of my own hoomans who poked a head around the door.

'Hey there… so, you're Taz, am I right?' a short and smiley woman said. 'Now then sweetie, I'm Gina and you'll be seeing me every Monday from now on. How does that sound? D'ya think we can be friends?'

Well that was weird. Mrs Gina spoke to me with warm eyes and a rather kind voice; local dialect too, none of that southern softie shit. On that basis alone I reckoned me and Mrs Gina, or Aunt Gina as I decided she'd be named, would be all right… although I still hadn't a clue as to what was really going on.

It turned out that with both of the hoomans out at work, most days at least, earning the pennies needed to pay for stuff 'n' shit, Ms Noodle had decided it was high time that they had a bit of extra help around the place, although partly blaming me for said need seemed a bit rich. Anyway, Aunt Gina was gonna oblige by popping in every week to keep Ms Noodle happy on the tidy home side of life.

With both my hoomans out most days, it left me in peace to sleep and dream of getting my end away. But in truth, it also got a bit lonely, so yeah, sure, I reckoned was up for a bit of Monday company from this smiley Aunt Gina character.

True enough to her word, the next Monday she arrived around nine in the morning, letting herself in with her own key I noticed. No shit, her first action was to come straight through to see me, and then immediately gave me a crunchy biscuit shaped like a small bone – top points lady! Aunt Gina even promised that we would go out for a walk later too, but only if I was a good pooch while she did her work.

Having smiled my best doggie smile, I then returned with a, 'Me? Of course love. I'm an angel. Whatever ya say Aunt Gina.' I guess word had spread that walkies and biscuits were a sure fire way to this particular woofer's heart. And so I reckoned I'd stick to my very best behaviour, at least for a short time to see how it all worked out. It was of course quite a challenge and wholly unnatural for me, taking some degree of effort to behave all proper like, but those bone-shaped biscuits and possible extra walkies dangled before me like a lump of steak had me sold.

For the next few weeks, Ms Noodle was pretty much the happiest I'd seen her too – I guess no longer facing the Saturday morning battle with the vacuum thingy had something to do with it.

As for me, Monday's became something to look forward to, with a guaranteed cuddle and a yummy snack or two thrown in for starters, and then a good brisk field walk almost always seemed to be on the cards when Aunt Gina had finished cleaning the cottage. I found out too that she had three girlie dogs of her own over at her farm on the other side of the village, but as much as I tried to persuade her, she never seemed agreeable to the idea of letting me go over and meet them. Dunno why, coz I promised to behave.

~ ~ ~ ~

Renovations of the cottage took some five years in total, although we'd pushed to get much of the serious construction work out of the way in just the first nine months. After that, the most significant change was transforming the formal dining room into a large open kitchen/diner, which entailed some serious replastering of 250-year-old stone walls, adding water and natural gas connections from the complete opposite end of the cottage, constructing a fully-fitted kitchen with built-in appliances, lots of electrical rework, and we finished off with a half-tiled, half-carpeted floor. It was a superb room once finished, but it took some serious graft over a period of four months between myself and Parker, our next door first responder and talented weekend handyman.

The cottage was old, really old, originating from when London's famous Westminster Bridge was first officially opened. I might add that over the centuries, many alterations had taken place with the cottage, and almost every attempted change resulted in some strange find or weird happening, such as uncovering an old doorway under the plaster that connected ours to the neighbouring cottage, or when decorating discovering we had original stone mullions that had long ago been 'boxed in' with hardboard that had then just been painted. It took some effort to uncover and properly clean the stonework by hand, but the result was stunning, and a great if rather unexpected find.

The addition of a new two-stage wooden staircase probably not long before we took the place on saved one major headache at least. It was located in a corner of the main lounge, and led up to a narrow corridor-type landing and hallway, the two bedrooms, and the cottage bathroom and only loo. It gave an overall feeling of openness to the place, which was much needed with such low ceilings and not that many windows, unlike more modern constructions.

However, the staircase was 'open-styled,' with polished thick wooden treads and matching newels, handrails and facia boards. It was quite attractive, but had no risers – that's the vertical wooden planks that stop your feet poking over the edge as you walk up. It therefore made for serious fun and games with slippers falling through onto unsuspecting sofa dwellers beneath, as well as being problematic in terms of controlling the inevitable draughts in such an old place, or from stopping Taz's toys falling through the gaps it seemed.

~ ~ ~ ~

Based on Taz's somewhat improved behaviour indoors, Michael and I saw fit to allowing our four-legged friend into the lounge with us during the evenings and at weekends, subject to him being clean and dry of course. However, this change also brought about another stairs-related issue.

Taz was pretty adept at mastering the wooden stairs from Wednesdays through till Sundays, charging up and down for no reason, or playing tennis. By that I mean he would drop a tennis ball from the top stair and just watch it bounce all the way down. Then, he'd charge down, retrieve it and take it back up for a rematch. This could go on and on for a good hour sometimes. Like an only child, he proved quite adept at entertaining himself.

However, Mondays and Tuesdays became very different and far more disaster-prone when it came to Taz versus the stairs. Every Monday, without fail, the lovely Gina, and sometimes accompanied by Trisha, her daughter who often visited, would meticulously clean and polish all the wooden surfaces throughout the cottage, and that amounted to rather a lot I'll admit, hence I was extremely grateful for her help each week. However, we seemed unable to hold Gina back from cleaning the stairs to the same degree. Of course, Taz was equally reliable in failing to register Gina's legendary stair polishing and would more often than not land in a pile at the bottom of the stairs after slipping and tumbling all the way down each Monday evening. Stupid thing was, he'd just dust himself off, shake his head a bit… and then head right on back up and do it all over again, and again, and again, this time like some canine version of his tennis ball trick.

In the end we opted to change the staircase design, with Michael to the rescue. It wasn't just the Taz issue, but our own safety came into it, plus the incessant draughts down the back of the neck from 'my spot' on the big sofa had always made winter evenings less pleasant and cosy than they ought.

Thankfully, the overall structure hadn't needed alteration, so Michael just added wooden risers to effectively close off the open style into what then formed a more traditional staircase. It was all part of a larger plan too, as we were also renewing the carpeting for the lounge and upper hallway, and therefore included the now closed staircase too, top to bottom. It was much safer for all, definitely less draughty when sat downstairs, and much quieter too. However, the improvements did detract from a certain level of amusement when it came to our Monday evenings and Taz's antics.

But Taz being Taz, he of course continued to play tennis, albeit much more quietly, and whilst there were no longer slippy surfaces to expedite his personal descent, he did however find that carpeted stairs were great for something else; lifting his tail and wiping his rear end on each stair as he came down. I loved him, but oh God, he truly was a disgusting teenage creature at times!

Body Clock Wonders

Early days livin' with Ms Noodle and The Suit saw me mostly hangin' out in my own room at the back. Whilst it was always my daytime farting zone coz they were mostly out at work, some six months after my investiture I was promoted to nighttime lounge lizard based on my apparent good(ish) behaviour and coz it was heading into the colder months of winter.

According to the territorial rights appointed by Ms Noodle (guessing here The Suit had no say whatsoever), that bloody great and lovely looking comfy old armchair I'd had my eye on for absolutely ages was suddenly mine, all mine! Okay, so the narrow double doors to the posh big kitchen remained firmly shut and therefore continued as 'Don't even fuckin' think about it territory,' but at least I had been awarded nocturnal roaming rights for the open lounge as well as to my own room, should I feel the need.

If truth be known, I still spent a fair amount of time crashed out in my own pad, familiarity and all that jazz. But when it came to proper nighttime sleeps, I would mostly opt for a spot of armchair heaven to rest my weary butt. I had been right all along, the huge armchair was very comfy indeed, and Ms Noodle covered it with a large old blanket, which I also noted she would change every two or three days and then spray all over and around the chair every morning with some special fart-obliterating aerosol agent – clever shits these hoomans. Sometimes ya just gotta put up with whatever makes the hoomans happy, right? Well, that was my take on it coz I was the winner however you flipped it.

Every morning, me and The Suit would take in the sights and sounds of the countryside on our dawn walkabouts. Dunno if dawn's the right word, but sodding early, around five in the morning usually he'd appear downstairs looking for the lead, and me to clip to the end of it. He'd then be dragging out his wellies and his trusty old green jacket. At the weekends he'd be later by about an hour or so, but weekdays he left for the office around 6:30am, so we had to be up and out pretty damned early. Summertime it was great, sure, but wintertime when it was mostly pissing down and dark, it was a bit fucking much really, just all very yukky and horrible.

But then, when it snowed, now that was a whole different ballgame. Even though it'd be officially nighttime darkness hours, coz snow only happens in winter, right, it was always amazingly bright outside, as if the snow had lit everything up. First time I saw that I freaked out. I was a city pup, born and bred, so country life took a little adjustment at first, and so walking outside and seeing the brightness of the snow in what was normally the pitch-blackness of the open fields, and with our village lanes mostly having no street lighting was just, well, weird. However, snow could be really fun shit too, especially when it meant you could make steamy hot yellow patterns when having a wazz! Hmm, I always wondered, did that make me a 'piss artist'?

~ ~ ~ ~

As a teenage lad I would sleep all hours, which was probably attributable to those good old adolescent hormones. Although never quite convinced if any degree of actual physical tiredness was involved, most would probably agree that mental exhaustion certainly played no part (i.e., I was a lazy sod at school). Waking up early and chasing girls was about as taxing as life came, with schoolwork always seen as an 'optional extra,' as clearly confirmed by my school grades, or lack thereof. But apart from my early teen years, I've always been an early riser. With a country childhood upbringing on a smallholding surrounded by arable fields and grazing cattle or horses, I was always up and about with the larks, off seeking adventures untold, although not always to my parents liking, or even knowledge.

By aged 16, the legally required minimum for cessation of all things educational, my schooling days ended abruptly and work life begun in earnest, although I'd worked weekends and holidays ever since hitting double digits.

I moved all over from the get-go, often necessitating commutes of one to almost three hours each way, so again early rising was a necessity if not an obligatory part of my life for many years.

At the time of having Taz, and we are talking 20 years further down the line, life was still geared around the early start at around five o'clock on workdays, and never much past six when not. It was in my bones I guess, and there it had stayed. However, as much as Mother Nature did her bit, that old invention of the bedside alarm clock was always on hand to religiously kick the grey cells into action each day, should the need arise.

Morning exercise always featured, be that cycling three miles each way to primary school, walking 20 minutes to the train station and then traipsing a similar distance to school the other end, or as then, walking to the office which involved a steep hill climb of an evening. Therefore, a 45 minute dog walking session to start the day was never something I griped over. In fact, I would relish the cold, wet, and windy start, which could be as invigorating as any power-shower.

My morning proverbial with Taz was ritualistic, yet varied. Routes ranged from yomping across open fields that backed on to the cottage, to narrow walkways between oak trees that led to the hellishly windy crest of a hill overlooking three valleys, where an age-old beacon towered above that was still lit for ceremonial occasions such as the Millennium. Other routes included a rutted old track near a small open quarry, or the series of 95 steps created from centuries-old slabs of local rock that formed a pathway up and down the western slope of the hill. But one thing was for sure, whatever the route, the weather was always sure to awake man or beast alike.

Waking early was never a big issue for me, but of course our four-legged cottage dweller also had to adjust to said regime. Initially I was met by a stern-faced canine peeking over his paws harbouring deep-seated resentment when jangling his lead when still obviously completely dark outside. But, whilst initially unconvinced with the whole 'getting up at the crack of dawn lark,' it seemingly grew on him too. Taz soon came to adore his early walks, or so it appeared, and even more so once the trust between us reached the dizzy heights where he'd be released off the lead for a 20 minute tear around an open field like one of Gandalf's fireworks gone rogue.

As to all the early starts, eventually he'd learnt to pinpoint the moment the alarm clock would do its thing and would bark within seconds of the first chime. He'd then be sat eagerly awaiting my arrival at his door a couple of minutes later, all ready for the off.

~ ~ ~ ~

Marching on in time a few more months towards summer, and Taz was awarded the 'freedom of the lounge,' which meant he was allowed to sleep either in his own back room, or in the open lounge on what was by then his own blanket-covered comfy armchair. From there he graduated from barking on the sound of the alarm to running up the stairs in order to greet me each morning.

But it didn't stop there either...

With just the two of us in situ on a permanent basis, and Taz, there was really no point in locking the bedroom door, in fact the door had no lock fitted anyway, but that was fine as Taz never seemed that interested in coming up to disturb us. He valued his own privacy far too much, preferring to snuggle into his chair and traf the night away in blissful peace. But that all changed when it came to 'alarm time,' which of course directly correlated to 'walkies time.' His slow saunter upstairs then progressed to head-butting the bedroom door open, and greeting me as I began to get dressed. This was something that scared the crap out of me at first, and was much to Penny's annoyance as she was always one to choose her bed over an early rise any day.

The next level was when our Staffie started to tell the time!

Err, I know, that sounds weird, right? Initially it started happening about once a week, but escalated to a bizarre six or seven days a week ritual. Taz would creep up the stairs like an extra-large but silent mouse, carefully and almost inaudibly push open the bedroom door, and then sit there next to the bed and just stare... waiting for that moment I'd open my eyes – which was very disconcerting and scary on the first few occasions I can tell you. One time, Penny and I swapped sides just to wind him up, but still I was met by canine eyes boring into me, albeit on the other side of the bed. So that obviously hadn't fooled him.

And then the day came when the clocks changed to mark the end of British Summertime (BST or more commonly known as British Daylight Saving Time) back to Greenwich Mean Time (GMT). I was convinced that such a change would at least throw him off kilter for a few weeks. I couldn't have been more wrong.

So, in body clock terms, the Friday morning wake-up of five o'clock was effectively still four o'clock in new money when it came to the next day's Monday morning alarm.

Of course, up he came at four and I just said, 'Nope, sorry mate. Back to bed for an hour, the clocks have gone back for winter, so it's now only four o'clock actually, not five.'

He hadn't looked very impressed, or even that convinced, but he turned and disappeared back downstairs and waited until I went down an hour later. He seemed a little confused by it, but within two days, those eyes were back at my bedside at the now correct and new version of five o'clock. He'd somehow sussed out waiting that extra hour. How the hell he did that I never could fathom, but he did.

Six months later still, when the clocks changed back again the following spring, and back to BST, Taz was a face of total surprise that first morning when I went down what he perceived to be 'some very early hour.' But the next day, he'd readjusted his body clock once again, and was back at the bedside on time, the new time.

This went on for a few years, and each equinox Taz bizarrely adjusted himself within one or two days at most. Dogs can indeed be the most strange and curious creatures.

Snowdrifts

Summer was definitely my favourite season. It's that glorious time of year when daylight lasts like, forever, so ya get lotsa time outside sniffin' about as well as lots of pastimes that Ms Noodle really disapproved of, big time. Living high up in the Pennines, real sweaty armpit sort of summers never featured that much, although if and when it did 'turn out nice,' I reckon anyone, beast or hooman would find it hard not to be happy with life.

Summer would also mean The Suit staring longingly out the window, desperately hoping for a fine and dry day so he could disappear off, trying to assert his manhood on his noisy-as-fuck two-wheeled contraption – the bike. If it was just gonna be a solo ride, you'd more often than not find Ms Noodle dusting spiders off the sunbed, then slipping into a bikini that even made me take a second sideways glance. She'd then go stake claim to part of my/our lawn for an hour of sun worshipping, whilst I would either try my best to wreak havoc in some way or just lie there at her side just enjoying the moment.

Spring and autumn; yeah, they sorta happened, but were largely boring. It just went from winter into a quick summer, and then back to winter once again. Wind was the most common factor living there. Not the smelly butt kind, although traffing away on a windy old day was one of life's simple pleasures, no I mean that living there meant temps plummeted the moment the calendar flipped a page over from August to September. True to form, that big woofer in the sky would ramp up the fan and blow almighty fuck outta life for days on end as autumn came crashing into play. That change would signal to all creatures that summer was gone, finito, busted, outta here, ended… and autumn was happening whether we liked it or not, so it was time to batten down the hatches coz winter was definitely on the way.

Winter, yep, that was a different story altogether. Okay, we didn't go for Canadian freeze yer nuggets off, blast from the Ice Age kind of winters, but certainly we'd see six, seven or even eight months of nothing but cold, drizzly shit, earflap-freezing wind, ice, frost, snow, or just for fun, snow with ice underneath. Yep, it could be pretty crappy sometimes, but it was mostly my 'norm,' having lived all my days thereabouts. But of course, both The Suit and Ms Noodle were wimpy-arsed Southerners, so part of the delight of my winters was to watch those two prancing about as if overpaid Disney-On-Ice characters – lovable idiots, the pair of them. They really weren't cut out for anything less than room temperature if I'm honest.

Not that I knew much of my parents, but from what I gathered from my canine lineage, snow used be a big thing 'back in the day,' with most winters dumping enough snow that would have simply made me disappear like an ant falling into a bag of flour. The snow I saw throughout much of my lifetime was often 'in the wind,' so to speak, just white fluffy shite blowing in eight directions all at once so ya couldn't see for crap, but rarely would it settle more than paw deep.

But there were exceptions, and by fuck almighty was it impressive when it did happen. About two or three times each winter we'd see what was termed by local hoomans as 'proper snow.' In my years with The Suit and Ms Noodle, 'proper snow' was always a time of great excitement, with them dancing outside like a pair of kindergarteners. Either that or I'd witness inane hysterics as they'd start prepping for the next Ice Age, panic buying food and non-essential rubbish to 'last us through…' [the weekend], although rarely was the snow that bad it actually caused life to grind to a halt, or even slow it down much. Again, lovable idiots.

~ ~ ~ ~

Staffie's are stout, solid, hefty little beasts, and most are almost as wide as they are tall. However, their limited height is not something that even slightly bothers them. For example, are they intimidated by an approaching Great Dane, large Alsatian or an angry Rottweiler, nope, they'll take on anything beneath, at, or way above their own size if they perceive any threat to either themselves or their 'family.' They are dogs of immense power, tenacity, and determination, if not vertical stature (i.e., tough short-arses).

But, how do they cope in the snow? Like most dogs, Staffie's slip and slide like ungainly toddlers on ice, usually ending up in some tangled mess, but in the snow, yeah not bad. Taz had his daily walks whatever the weather, and that included snow days, even when deep too. Sure, it was rarely knee depth, but bearing in mind the cottage's hilltop position, there was always the chance of snowdrifts piled up against the drystone walls that crisscrossed the fields and moors, marking territorial and field boundaries, as well as providing efficient windbreaks for any arable crops being grown. Also, where there were bordering roads or pathways, they also helped shield pedestrian and road traffic from the elements.

Like many dogs, and similarly children, Taz would snap away at snowflakes floating down through the air, sneezing when they landed on his wet nose. But Taz's strangest antic related to his addiction to snowdrifts. With his stout muscular physique, and skull likened to a hardened, hairy old coconut, he loved nothing better than to run headfirst straight into snowdrifts, for he was clearly as nutty as a fruitcake. Unfortunately, some drifts were not really drifts, but snow blown up against drystone walls. Often I'd hear a muffled 'yelp' as the braindead mutt would dive into what he'd perceived as a 'tall snowdrift,' only to find that was actually less than half his length deep before unknowingly butting heads with a solid stone wall. Daft idiot. I say that as he'd just move along a couple of metres... and do the same bloody thing all over again! What do they say about 'no brain, no pain'?

However, on those rare occasions that saw 'proper snow' on a weekend, it was legendary. So long as the office didn't require my services, weekend snow meant time to try out the 4x4 on the hills and open moorland. Whilst our adventures may not have classed as real true-grit off-roading, it did mean that we could head way farther than most road traffic, and thereby get out for a decent walk in the pristine snow. However, with a relatively short but tenacious mutt, that always meant a great deal of fun could be had too.

When you head miles out of town up into the hills there are far fewer drystone walls compared to the more 'ordered' local farming areas. However, with moorland seriously exposed to the elements, it wasn't uncommon to come across huge areas of pristine white snow… that were in fact drifts formed between natural undulations of the land. What appeared as just flat snow was sometimes a significant dip such as a wide dyke, that had been snow-filled by the wind and was therefore an obstacle to anyone or anything that happened to stumble across its path. Of course, that would naturally include passing canines who'd suddenly disappear from view, completely. In our case, a second or so later, there'd be some excited but muffled noises as Taz would bounce up and down, coming in and out of view, ears flapping and jaws wide open for a split second before gravity would intervene and he'd again disappear from view.

Taz was like a kid in one of those indoor playpark ball pits, recalling here 'Bazinga' and Sheldon for any Big Bang Theory nuts out there. One very snowy February, Taz came across a few of these hidden drifts. He was belting across open moorland at the time in what seemed fairly shallow snow, just up to his belly, when suddenly, whump, he was gone in a puff of snowflakes. He let out some weird woof-yelp sort of noise and that was that… all I could see was a dark hole in the snow, but alas, no dog! I called out for him. Muted noises came back through what was otherwise silence. He didn't sound in distress or injured, he'd just physically 'vanished.' The snow was powdery, light and fresh, and I'd seen him on many occasions act as some sort of canine snowplough.

'C'mon boy, you can do it,' I called to him, 'just jump your way out. C'mon Taz, follow my voice!'

And jump he did, bouncing up and down like a demented kangaroo. Occasionally his ears would pop just above 'the surface,' as he started to make his way back across towards my voice. It must have taken some six or seven minutes, but eventually he reappeared, all snowy and super psyched-up.

He was like a kid at a fairground after that, diving back into the snow every minute or two, bouncing around and chomping up mouthfuls of the powdery white stuff. Thankfully, all ended well that day, and we both made it home safely to sooth next to a glowing warm fire and a hot drink, but boy did Taz sleep well that afternoon — he was one knackered snow-Staffie.

Springtime Bunnies!

Moving from the warm south coast up to some windswept northern hill was one heck of a change, but needs must, as they say. Michael had followed a career move that had looked more promising longer term, or so I kept telling myself on that long, slow full-day's drive up the motorway.

Nevertheless, hill life seemingly had its advantages as well as the more obvious challenges. There was always plenty of fresh air, true; but sometimes that came in the form of ruddy great gales that blew so hard it made walking anywhere close to upright darned near impossible! Not the largest woman on earth, structurally speaking, these gales were a nightmare for me when waiting at the village bus stop, sometimes sending me forcibly scampering down the street in the opposite direction to where the bus would be headed, and no doubt the cause of significant merriment to the hardy locals when this tall southern waif first arrived. Needless to say, my fashionable umbrella collection soon became a mix of tangled framework and manmade fibres headed for the rubbish tip, with a few favourites that I never even bothered trying to kill; opting instead for a brightly coloured insulated all-weather jacket with a secure integral hood.

Rain was another 'feature' of Yorkshire life, with deluges so torrential and persistent that even our cottage was threatened by flooding one year, and we were just two metres from the highest point. Go figure. That particular debacle came about when the arable field that backed on to the garden had become so waterlogged over the preceding weeks that the normally efficient drainage could no longer cope. I was at home, fortunately, when I suddenly noticed muddy water flooding 'through' the stone wall, across the lawn, down the steps and heading towards the back door! After a frantic telephone call, Michael managed to race home in less than 15 minutes in a colleague's borrowed car. Together we then started immediate sandbagging operations in order to avoid too much damage. Oh what fun that was.

The weather was pretty much the dominant characteristic of cottage life, with ample amounts of snow, rain, and wind, as well as the rare occasional blurts of warm sunshine added for good measure and some degree of sanity. But all in all, it made for decent living up there in or above the clouds. And that was no joke either… on quite a few occasions I remember leaving work in town on what were dull and very cloudy days, only to get home to find bright sunshine up there, whereas the valley had been concealed all day under a blanket of cloud and mist – looking back down over the town was weird too, as it would simply disappear from view… quite bizarre.

Weather apart, it was a great place to live and also to exercise one's four-legged friend. There were open fields as far as the eye could see, well almost, and also large areas of woodland that had probably changed very little in over a century or two. In addition, there were a couple of locally owned quarries and a few farms that left the whole area with a web of tracks and trails as well as open farmland for Taz to drag Michael around long before the rest of humanity was preparing to surface. But these varied routes were of particular benefit when it came to those longer weekend walks that would last perhaps all morning, or at least until a late brunch.

Taz too found that living there held certain attractions, as well as certain weather related trials, with occasional snow that tested those like him who sported relatively short legs. However, being of stocky build and vertically challenged were pretty useful attributes against the wind, but that was not always so. One morning it was blowing so particularly viscously that Michael described later how he'd struggled to walk headlong against the wind, bent over almost double. Taz, however, was generally oblivious to the wind, protected as he was from the elements by miles of hand built drystone walls that Yorkshire, Derbyshire and Lancashire claimed notoriety for. Of course, Mister Short-features just merrily wandered along, unaware of any perils that may lay ahead... until he walked past a farm gateway that led into one of the fields. Unbeknownst to him there was one heck of a gale blowing that day, and so much so that the second he moved from 'walled protection' to 'open gateway,' he was bowled over like a kids toy pram in a wind tunnel. Zonk, over he went, straight on to his back; four legs pointing up towards the clouds and his crown jewels suddenly exposed to the elements. Michael described Taz's look of astonishment, utter infuriation, as well as total embarrassment. It probably didn't help that Michael reportedly stood there and laughed like mad at the daft upside-down Staffie doing an impression of an upturned tortoise.

Whilst not one to partake in the boys' pre-dawn weekday walks, we would often take in longer walks together at the weekend as a 'family.' Some were ventures further afield in the Jeep, whereas at other times we'd opt for more local routes such as the steep hillside that overlooked the town. Just ten minutes' walk in the opposite direction from the usual walking routes, it was, however, not perhaps the easiest dog walking spot. For starters the field of view for dog walkers was limited, and that resulted in a worrying lack of situational control; ergo Taz could disappear from sight far too easily, and all too frequently of course did just that. Second, it was quite literally a narrow hillside animal track that we'd follow, with a very steep slope that dropped away. As well as the more than obvious perils, it did offer a few advantages too. Remember hill rolling as a kid, where you'd roll down some shallow grassy bank like a sausage roll? Well, this was the extreme version, to put it mildly. As a fairly experienced hill walker, Michael was particularly wary of this almost sheer incline. To me it was just dead scary, particularly when windy, but enjoyable too in a 'fresh air must be good' kind of way.

Taz, however, didn't give two poops either way. Call it bravado or just lack of adequate grey matter, who knows, but he'd happily meander or run along pathways more favoured by the local sheep than humankind. Then, all of a sudden, he'd do a disappearance act... and by that I mean he'd have missed his footing, slipped on some gravel or rocks, or just plain 'went the wrong bloody way,' and the next thing we'd see would be a 20 kilogramme short, stubby Swiss Roll go flying down the hillside, spinning over and over at a rate of knots. Usually some small bush or thicket would halt his descent into the abyss, but not always. Whilst it was riotously amusing to watch on the first few occasions, there was always this dread that some large protruding rock would bring about his sudden demise, requiring Michael, if not both of us, to perform some daring hillside rescue of one large injured mutt, or worse. Thankfully that never happened, but the extreme hill rolling certainly did and on numerous occasions too. But did he learn, Taz I mean... well, what do you think?

But the primary 'feature' of that hillside has yet to be mentioned, and that was the abundance of fluffy wild bunny rabbits, and a few gazillion of them too. Trouble was, at the slightest sign of even one of them, Taz would instantly transform into something resembling the doggie version of The Flash.

~ ~ ~ ~

There I was, ambling along a narrow pathway created by them large woolly baa-baa things, when fuck me... a bastard bunny shot right across the path less than three metres from my lil' black nose! The hillside we were on was not far from home, and somewhere we'd venture on a Saturday sometimes 'just for fun' (admittedly that being my take rather than the hoomans'). The path or track at that point was well steep, with a few bushes dotted around for good measure, but mostly it was a sheep-cropped, grass-covered and precipitously nasty old slope. But it was also bunny heaven around there too, which whilst perfectly fun for us canine's, was fuckin' hilarious when it came to watching hoomans struggle to even stand up on their two scrawny back legs without peeing themselves with fright.

Now, we all make plans, right? Well, mine that day were based on enjoying a gentle, no hassle morning stroll with The Suit and Ms Noodle. I seriously hadn't intended on exerting myself much, well, not up until Bugsy Fluffy-Butt broke into my world, and then promptly disappeared just as quick. Now, whether it was some split-second decision weighing up the pros and cons, pure animal instinct that had kicked in, or a forever lurking sense of 'Hey, why the fuck not?' but I immediately set off after him like a rat chasing a prized turd – Gone, whoosh, see ya!

When I say it was steep, that could be the understatement of the decade. The initial downward acceleration was exhilarating I'll admit, but then my soddin' brakes failed and within six short seconds I had piled headfirst into a large bush... and then straight out the other side like a '70s-style medicine ball flattening a bunch of preschoolers.

'Ow,' I shouted, then 'ouch,' 'ow, shit,' 'what the... ow,' 'dammit, ow,' 'fuck, ow'... That went on blah de blah, so on and so forth. But I'm sure you get the drift, right?

Passing 'through' the bush hurt like crazy, and not something I would have chosen to repeat. But of course four seconds later, oh 'yay me,' there was another bush that was just as prickly, just as butt-scratchy, and just as in the way. But, more to the point, where the fuck was that white 'n' fluffy-bummed little shit?

Down I went, bush after bush... Every now and then I'd catch a glimpse of bunny-features still ahead of me. I'm sure on at least two occasions the little bugger turned back to face me and gave me the finger! That, of course, only drove me on...

In the meantime, my subconscious picked up a familiar hoarse sound that had seemed dead loud at first, but soon receded as my hillside bunny chasing decent progressed. Ah yes, that would have been The Suit doing his 'yell like a lunatic' routine; like sure, I'm just gonna stop the chase, retrace my steps back up to the pathway and resume a gentle weekend walk. Ha, like fuck mate, the hunt was on!

Time passed slowly, the hillside did not. I reckon I must have covered some 90 metres and 16 or 18 bloody bushes before the land started to level out a bit. Bugs 'the total git' Bunny was of course nowhere to be seen. Bastard. I was pretty sure that he'd dove headfirst into a hole about half way down. The little shitters have these secret 'in' and 'out' holes all over the place, so it was no biggie that I never even saw it. Aww shit though, just my luck.

The levelled out section didn't last for long before I came across another steep drop, but with no bunny action in sight, I had the chance at least to catch a breath and to curse my bad luck at not being able to clutch fluffy-buns in my paws. Still managing to adequately 'not hear' The Suit's continued hollering, I opted instead to head off in search of other things to chase. That first race was just a warm-up I reckoned, or hoped at least. My blood, muscles and my every fibre was still in bite-a-bunny mode, and so off I went, bum up, sniffer down.

Less than a minute later, another white furry-arsed critter broke out of a burrow just before my hooter was to have rammed right into it. Part Two was obviously kicking off – the chase was back on once more. This one kept on the flat for a time at least, but darted left and right, right and left at one heck of a pace for a thing so small, and all the time his stupid bum-fluff was bouncing up and down – twat, I'd get 'im. But, try as I might, I barely managed to gain any ground. As soon as I made any discernible headway, he suddenly took a sharp right and plunged further down the hillside. You can guess what was next, yep, me.

Lady luck was on my side, as I managed to narrowly avoid colliding headfirst into not one, but three bushes in the first 30 metres alone. Heartbeat pounding away inside my ribcage, I ploughed on at breakneck speed – it was gonna be bunny pie for lunch, surely. The next bush, however, was just that bit too wide and I just slammed straight into, through it, and out the other side of it, but having only lost a couple of metres on my prey, it seemed the right course of action, at least in retrospect – as if I had any say in the matter whatsoever. On and on he darted, this way and that, and all the while I could smell what he'd had for brekky; I was that close.

Couldn't even call the next one a decent bush, just a straggly few branches, so I went into flying Staffie mode and leapt mid-air to go right over it and continue the chase.

'Fuck!'

For some peculiar reason I had stopped, physically at least. My brain was still in the chase, and so were my front legs, but somehow the rest of my body was no longer progressing down the hillside, and nor were my back legs. I was totally immobile.

'What the crap?' I hollered as my eye caught the bunny disappearing from view.

I was distraught. So close. So sodding close! I noted that my legs and upper body were somehow elevated above the ground. My front paws waving about like useless sock puppets as I squirmed about, trying desperately to work out what had happened.

'Oh crap. Really?'

The last excuse for a bush that I had attempted to leap over had obviously been much larger in days gone by, and had since been cut back or more probably had been just broken down by animals, so whilst there had seemed little substance to the small bush at first glance, it in fact was a few sturdy old branches, and one of these had caught me right under my bloody collar, half suspending me in mid-air like a piñata. I yelped, I cursed, I struggled, and even tried reverse mode, but nope, stuck like a pig.

It took a good five minutes of wriggling about to extricate myself. No more bastard bunnies in sight, but I bet they were watching, and pissing themselves laughing at my expense too.

'Your day will come fuckers, your day will come!' I shouted through clenched teeth, ya know, just in case one of them was still within hearing distance.

So, whilst going down was rather quick, heading back up was like 'not fuckin easy!' and really knackered me out, especially having overexerted myself, first from the two-part chase, and then from my piñata episode. Missing a simple paw-step saw me tumble halfway back down on a couple of occasions, which really hadn't helped either. Eventually I managed to retrace my way back up the original track, and reunite myself with a rather exasperated wreck of a hooman who was, by that point, sat there with his muddy boots pointing down the hill. And oh shit, Ms Noodle was not happy either. Personally I thought it was well-funny though, coz the old git had almost lost his voice through him incessant hollering, so perhaps she was just as mad at him than she was at me, well, just maybe.

I know one shouldn't have laughed... but it was really fuckin' funny, he was almost voiceless that whole weekend! Unfortunately, said walkies route was not then back on offer for a very long time. Them bunnies had won the battle, for then; but not the war. I'd be back.

Hedgehog Howls

All dogs can bark, whine, woof and growl, it's their thing and we all accept it as just a fact of nature. However, it's mostly only dog owners themselves that 'understand' the various noises their pets may be held accountable for. Okay, so I'm not purporting to possess Doolittle-type abilities, but most owners will claim that they comprehend one heck of a lot from even the slightest sound their pet may utter.

The cottage where we lived, and where all these adventures are based, was very much a country dwelling. Granted, the village was close to the outskirts of a town, and plenty of people lived nearby, but the garden did back on to open fields and there were plenty of wooded areas as well as natural open spaces, so wildlife was fairly abundant there compared perhaps to more urbanised parts of modern day Britain.

Foxes were a pretty common sight, particularly just after first light when they could be seen heading home in the early morning mist that drifted across the arable fields where we walked. Foxes were also often the cause behind my having hardly any voice left upon returning home some days, having attempted, usually in vain, to vocally restrain Taz from bolting off into the distance like a missile as he chased some bushy tail far off into the distance. Of course, he never came remotely close to catching one, but he tried his best, I'll give him that. As a consolation prize, however, he'd instead seek out and sample the delights of any mess the vixen had left behind, loving nothing more than a good roll around in what could only be described as the most foul-smelling crap on earth, literally. That in turn would cause me to almost run to work, having been made pretty late after needing to hose down and scrub Taz before either of us could even enter the cottage.

Squirrels were creatures rarely spotted there. I'm sure there were some around, but compared to the south coast where we were inundated by tall pine trees full of squirrels, there were very few to be found in Taz's Yorkshire-based life.

Birds were aplenty, as thankfully there were still numerous hedgerows and wooded areas to sustain an appreciable level of local birdlife. Also, the cottage was situated only a stone's throw from open moorland that supported its own varieties of birdlife and an abundance of nature in general.

Tortoises, nope. Lizards, no chance. Snakes, not that we ever saw. Hodgehegs, as I used to know them as a young country nipper, well yes, now that was one species of critter we would often come across. Hedgehogs were regular nighttime visitors to the cottage garden, both before and bizarrely since the days of Taz.

~ ~ ~ ~

I felt suddenly panicked. 'What the holy fuck's was that?' I quietly asked myself.

I was looking out the window late one Sunday night at the start of summer. Although the lights were on, I was balanced on the tall back of my new 'dog chair' with the thick, lined velour curtain draped over my back, so I was in virtual darkness and therefore able to spot outdoor goings on from within the relative seclusion of the deep window shelf.

What I had spotted out there was moving bloody slowly, like some lazy-arsed dark blob, heading right across the middle of the lawn having appeared out from under the fir trees by the old tool shed. I guessed it was aiming for the wood store. Whatever, he/she/it actually turned out to be was largely irrelevant, it was a bloody imposter, that's all I knew and all I cared about.

My first instinct was to howl and bark and do all sorts of bat-crazy shit, but then my training kicked in. My front paws were surrounded by photographs, ornaments and other fragile stuff that would likely scatter and smash into an untold number of pieces if I did anything remotely dramatic, so instead I retreated slowly back into the room from behind the curtain, back into the warm light of a nearby table lamp, and sort of slid back down into my personal armchair, but then kept on sliding down until all four paws touched the carpet.

Next, keeping remarkably calm, I stretched my legs, yawned, farted and walked over to the back room, my room. But the door was shut, so I retreated back to calmly inform The Suit about this fact. He may not have been that fluent in Dog, but even he was able to decipher my little dance – which kinda went like, 'Hey man, this 'ere dog needs a wee, chop chop!'

Ha, it worked. He was soon up and out of the chair, and went over to open the door for me. I then shot through beneath his legs and headed for the back door, the last hurdle that kept me from the garden, and from where I would hopefully be released to carry out the necessary investigations.

Thankfully, The Suit was tired and obviously held no interest in watching me cock my leg that night, so he just closed the door and fucked off back to his comfy chair. Result! I then turned and tore off up the wide flagstone steps. I slipped a bit as they were damp from the evening air and still a bit mossy as it was only just the start of summer, and landed in a pile on the lawn all ready for a scrap.

'Where are ya? Where have you gone, you little fucker?' I growled, but also more importantly I was thinking, 'What the fuck are ya?' too.

At that point I had no clue as to what the slow-moving lump could actually be.

Sniff, sniff, sniff I went.

I'd found his 'trail' sure enough, but the little bugger had gone and done a Lord Lucan on me. More sniffs. Move along a bit, then sniff, sniff yet again, and then, 'Ha ha, gotcha!' On the far side of the lawn was a narrow strip of 'border' where Ms Noodle had planted some pretty shit with all sorts of colours and weird smells – hoomans seemed to like doing stuff like that. Me? I preferred just to dump in there on a weekly basis, much to her obvious dismay and often confirmed by a swift kick up where the sun don't shine for me, if ya get my drift.

There, tucked under a short bush-like thing was 'the blob.'

'Oi, shithead,' I tried in my toughest, gruffest voice.

Nada. It remained stock still. Perhaps I'd scared it into having a spontaneous cardiac arrest.

'Now then knobhead, ya better shift your butt as this is my turf, err… literally. So, go on, you'd best fuck off in the next six and a half seconds or, or you'll be toast!' I woofed extra loudly, confident I was being sufficiently and adequately scary and intimidating.

Having duly laid down the law of the land, I was expecting of course that he, it, whatever, would then get up and haul arse as per my instruction.

Nuffink. It didn't move. Not one bit.

Hmm, fuck this, I thought, and without notice I gave it a hearty power swipe with my front-left paw.

'Jeeezuz H,' I let out, 'What the heck?'

The little turd was armed with flamin' sharp body spears! Ouch, that really soddin' hurt. I took a quick glance back at the cottage, but my hollering hadn't been heard or at least hadn't aroused any undue attention, enabling me to resume my interrogation of the little intruder.

I jumped across to where 'it' had ended up. It was like a round ball, but covered with little poisoned daggers. More cautiously this time I prodded it with my left front paw – yep, it was a prickly little shit for sure, but its smell was like that of a living creature; although perhaps not for long.

I thought to myself, 'What the fuck, let's have a go at getting into this thing.'

In retrospect, perhaps that wasn't the smartest move I'd ever dreamt up, but instinct just kicked in. It just had to be scoffed, right? Trespassing was trespassing. No trial, no jury necessary. End of.

Still it hadn't moved. Perhaps it was dead after all. Was it some freaky science fiction invader that hovered when moving, or was it something that could morph from a walking creature into a tight spiky ball at will?

Another check back at the cottage. Nope, all quiet of the western front.

'Right pal, let's get you sorted, ya little shit!' I growled angrily at the little dagger encrusted blob.

I then proceeded to lay down on my tum, nuts to the soil, front legs outstretched, ergo Staffie-style. Being of fine lineage, I had muscles that Uncle Arnie would have proudly displayed on stage, and so considered myself pretty well-suited to grabbing hold of any object with a vice-like grip that not many living creatures could readily escape.

'Yowwww!' I hollered, 'What sort of hairy-arsed, motherfuckin' little shit are you?'

My paws suddenly hurt like hell, again. The little critter had jabbed me with his spears, and I think 42 of them had just punctured my extra-thick paw pads. Jeez... it really was not my day.

So, did I give up at that point? Not on your bloody life.

Determinedly, I then painfully, but firmly, grabbed 'it' once more, and started to see how best to bite into it. Surely one or two decent bites from a pissed-off Staffie would be adequate to finish it off, enabling me to hang its remains on the garden fence for all its kinfolk to see; and dare them to try and follow suit and venture into 'my' garden.

My shoulders were in gear, my paws held it in what was a painful but firm grip, and my jaws were ready to clamp down once again. God it bloody hurt. I became acutely aware that I was emitting pretty strange sounds, so it was do or die time – the only given being that there was fat chance of me giving in, not then, not ever...

~ ~ ~ ~

At some quiet moment in the film we were watching, Penny looked across at me with a rather bewildered look. She pressed the little mute button on the television's remote control handset.

'Did you hear something?' she said, 'What was that? Sounded like something pretty weird is going on out there.'

We both sat still for a couple of seconds, just trying to get a handle on the sound, trying to work out in our own minds just what it could be.

'I think it's coming from out back. What's Taz up to do you think?' she asked, then adding, 'Do you think he's hurt himself?'

Penny was getting concerned. That 20 kilo lump had, in time, come to occupy a kid-like role in our lives.

'Go see what it is. Please Michael, go on, ' she asked of me.

I opened the curtains, but of course the lights were on indoors and it was fully dark outside, so that wasn't going to help much. I opened the window and the noise was certainly much clearer… It was indeed a distressed animal type of sound, but it was intermittent and distinctly strange. The yelps were indeed Taz-sourced, that much was certain.

'Not a clue love,' I said, 'Let me go and investigate. He's obviously up to no good, again!'

I headed out the room and marched purposefully out the back door, having quickly slipped on some shoes and a light jacket.

Taz did sound like he was in some pain, but it wasn't that timid whimper that dogs are prone to make post-injury, or that overly loud but short yelp when faced with sudden pain after having stepped on something sharp like a rose thorn or a discarded nail. Nope, this was a weird mix of a yelp and a howl, with a bit of growl added for good measure. Strange indeed.

I nipped back and grabbed the big rechargeable torch from its holder by the back door. Following the sounds, I came across Taz over at the far side of the lawn, desperately munching on something he had gotten a hold of, something that was obviously causing him some serious level of pain and distress too, by the sound of it.

I shone the torch directly at him. I noticed there was blood in and around his large wide mouth. It was then that I saw what he had evidently became so obsessed with that evening, and which finally explained the noises – it was a bloody hedgehog he was attempting to scoff.

It was clearly painful for him to hold, and even more painful to bite down onto. But for him it was still, of course, a food-based obsession, and knowing that I also knew he'd never give it up, not willingly at least, so I resolved there and then to take firm and decisive action.

Trying to remove the creature from the scene and away from Taz at that stage in the game would have been a futile attempt and only result in my being nipped, even if only by accident, not intention. I assumed straight away such a course of action wasn't on the cards. Trying to boot away the hedgehog would also likely have been an ill-advised move, as Taz would no doubt have bitten my foot in the process; he was that quick and focussed, plus the hedgehog was still probably within reach.

Suddenly I had a thought. I darted back across to the cottage and grabbed a small bucket. It was the type small kids use on the beach, except our bucket was a good ten years old and whatever Marvel comic-based scene originally depicted on its exterior had long since faded beyond recognition.

I approached Taz from behind and suddenly and firmly grabbed his thick leather collar at the back of his neck. Holding on to a rather manic dog that was writhing in a mix of pain and fixation to his task, I twisted the collar as hard as I could in an attempt to reduce his air supply. Now, before you start on about animal rights, cruelty and suchlike, I am guessing only owners of large dogs or Staffie's could even vaguely relate to the event that had unfolded. You simply will not get a Staffie to release its jaws through gentle coercion, pleading or even through light taps to his person (or should that be dog), and so I knew restricting his air supply to be about the only viable action worth pursuing if I was to stand a chance at saving the hedgehog's life, and also to prevent further damage to Taz in the process, so it was done with all good intentions.

After a long 30 seconds, his jaws popped open and the hedgehog hit the deck and rolled off to one side. With one hand I yanked Taz up and perhaps, rather skilfully I might add, unceremoniously toe-booted the hedgehog straight into the bucket. I then hoisted the bucket into mid-air as I let go of Taz's collar. He took in an immediate gulp of fresh air and then looked up at me with absolute disdain as I quickly chucked the bucket clean over the back wall – I'd go retrieve that another day, but at least the hedgehog was in relative safety. Meanwhile, Taz, realising his plaything and/or next meal had been withdrawn from play, slowly withdrew from kill mode and back into pet mode.

The hedgehog-induced Staffie yelp. A sound that I have never forgotten to this day and good job too, for a few times over the years I've had to go out at night, bucket in hand, to do battle yet again in order to save a life.

The Strawberry Patch

The cottage garden out back was not what one could've termed as being 'substantial,' but with both of us trying to hold down busy jobs, it was a decent enough weekend sanctuary into which we could escape. Starting from the top was a traditional hand constructed Yorkshire drystone wall, about one-point-two metres in height that probably dated back to the mid-19th century, based on maps and other information found lodged in with the property's ownership deeds. It separated our garden from large open arable fields to the rear. Almost at the summit, we were generally left open to all the abuse that the natural world managed to chuck in our direction, even though the garden officially faced south-southwest, and therefore the rear of the cottage was a bit more sheltered and warmer than the front could have ever have hoped to be.

Incidentally, that description was the wrong way around, as the back was the original 'front' of the cottages, having been reversed during the joining of the two properties some 15 years before our tenure. But at that time, the walled garden was the 'back,' whilst the open shrubbery and raised off-road two-vehicle driveway was the 'front,' and just used for parking and the official point of entrance to the enlarged cottage. Being almost north-facing, it often blew a gale with horizontal driving rain at the front, whereas the garden hideaway at the back was like a different world.

The top of the drystone wall was level with a point some two and a bit metres vertically up the back wall of the cottage. This in turn afforded a fair degree of shelter to the garden itself, particularly to the large open flagstoned area that lay between the cottage and the lawn, which was raised considerably above – an area that made a relaxing suntrap when mostly the wall did its thing in keeping the wind at bay.

There was one fairly well-established wild cherry tree providing a modicum of shade at the back of the lawn, with some tall, narrow fir trees off to one side, and a six-foot larch-lap panelled fence to the other. The lawn was cornered to one side by a moderate shrubbery, and a running border that followed the stone-edged contour of the sunken patio's retaining wall. Off-centre was a metre and a bit wide flagstone pathway and steps that led to and from the back door of the annexe, which is the room where Taz had set up camp. The path led to the back of the garden, then along the wall to the back gate, which in turn led behind the other cottages to what was a little used narrow local village road.

On the other side of that pathway was another area set to lawn, a medium-sized slightly dilapidated garden shed which housed all manner of largely inherited and since unused garden implements, a tall wooden bird table with moss growing around its slowly rotting legs, and a small area that had once been a vegetable patch but was rarely used. Other than that, the garden had a couple of raised shrubbery areas and perennial flowerbeds to add a touch of much-needed colour when spring was finally brave enough to show its face.

Not a great deal happened with the veg patch. My maternal grandfather had been the green-fingered one, but he'd passed on to tend the upstairs rosebeds many years before, so my inadequate attempts at self-sufficiency were somewhat lacking to say the least.

The singular success, well, relatively speaking at least, was the cultivation of a few strawberries each year. The Pennine weather was never a big help in terms of growing such a sun-loving crop, but we did have a few bowls each year to boast of. And rather tasty they were too, as is always the way for homegrown produce, irrespective of how small, spotty, or ridiculously looking they may have compared to shop-bought fruit.

Apart from the inclement weather and late frosts, the foremost strawberry-related hindrance we faced was of the four-legged variety, and of those, there were two. For our first couple of years it was the next-door neighbour's cat, who seemed to enjoy using our then strawberry patch as a public convenience, having been directed there by some innocuous 'Come bury your crap here!' signboard we'd yet to find. Naturally, all that stopped when Taz moved in; alas, our strawberry propagation had not improved much since.

~ ~ ~ ~

Spending my youthful days in a cage was not conducive to the development of strong bones or well-defined muscles; instead it rather favoured one's natural podgy bits. However, them podgy bits also kept me warm(ish) too, so I had good reason at the time to be proud of them. But then along came a whole new cottage life, a heated bedroom, a blanket to call my own, and a pair of hooman numpties to dote on my every whim. Well, maybe not quite, but for a couple of southern twats, they were pretty accommodating and down-to-earth folk, one might say.

It took me a good few months to lose the old tum-tum. It wasn't that I was particularly overfed or anything, far from it, the bitch back there would've let me starve if Guy hadn't thrown me scraps whenever she wasn't looking. But, practically a 100% block on physical exercise can play havoc with a young chap's physique! However, the new bloke, The Suit that is, now, he took care of all that, with dawn walkies every day of the year, come rain, snow, or shine. There were plenty of big fields to run around in, but he always made sure we were out and about loooong before anyone else – which I discovered was more about stopping me getting into a ruckus with the local lads. Shame. Having the odd scrap was also part of every dog's life, wasn't it? Bloody spoilsport.

Anyway, the fitness regime soon meant I was in trim, and could certainly outrun both of the hoomans – a fact that I thoroughly enjoyed proving on more than a few occasions. Although much to their extreme annoyance, the new-found speed was a bonus when Daphne, that young filly of a Cocker Spaniel from down Green Lane was about. Anything for a quick 'hey-ho' behind Farmer Stonehouse's hay barn whilst the hoomans took an age to catch up, calling my name over and over as I hid my actions from them and the world at large, then wandered slowly out as if nothing had happened.

Most of the time though, my life was spent indoors, cosied up in the warm, or sun-soaking in the back garden whenever the opportunity arose. Not that Ms Noodle was all that aware, but I always found one could get up to all sorts out there. She soon cottoned on to some of my outdoor antics though, but that didn't stop the fun one could have of inflicting minor-league distress and anguish on the hoomans —an honourable enough diversion to the eat, walk, sleep 'n' poo routine of daily life.

Games such as 'plant rearrangement' was a firm favourite. Although Ms Noodle and I did seem at odds as to the term 'amusing,' or even of 'mildly acceptable.' Other garden pastimes included the presenting of little gifts to Ms Noodle in the form of freshly dug up cat poo. That is, the leftovers after having already scoffed my fill.

Chemistry experiments were a fun pastime too, seeing exactly which of Ms Noodle's plants would die from a direct wazz by yours truly, and precisely how many squirts per day it took per species of flora before they shrivelled and gave up. It was all in the name of science, or that's what I kept on trying to tell Ms Noodle, but she and I weren't quite on the same page, more's the pity.

'You horrid little dog!' or similar were not uncommon words to be heard uttered rather too loudly in my direction, or 'Darling,' clearly aimed at The Suit, not me, 'Come and look at what your wretched hound has gone and done this time!' she'd say. Poor old girl – had to laugh though.

However, the real fun and games could begin when springtime arrived on the hill. In went the new plants (Ms Noodle), then out came the new plants (me).

'Oops, sorry Misses. Only trying to help,' I used to shout.

But then I'd scarper across the lawn sharpish, tail tucked well-under as she grabbed her spare arse-smackin' slipper that seemed to be forever within reach and would promptly chase me round 'n' round trying to make slipper-to-doggie-butt contact. As if.

The other cool thing about springtime was The Suit hilariously trying to 'grow' food. Twat, I ask ya. He was an office wimp, although he'd tell tales of growin' up on a small farm that never seemed quite believable. I'd agree he was an okay kinda fella, but 'Mister Garden Greenfingers' he bloody well wasn't. He'd spend hours out there farting around, digging here, digging there, planting this, planting that. What a plonker. We all knew fuck all ever grew, but alas, he tried; planting the same old shit over and over too. Not sure how much I influenced his gardening shenanigans, but thankfully he seemed blissfully unaware of much of what went down out there. Bless him, a lovable knob if nothing else!

However strange, The Suit did appear to find some modicum of success in the garden, for each year he was able to grow ten to 20 medium-sized tasty bright red strawberries, against all the odds of good old Yorkshire weather, and certain sordid canine activities.

Shop-bought strawberries have a really limited shelf life, and it's just as true when still attached to the plant. Mamma Nature gives a window of only 12-36 hours when the fruit is at its best and therefore at its most scrumptious. And with Pennine weather, that window was even shorter. Every time I ventured out there I'd nip over and check on their progress, suss out how near to yummylicious each berry was – and then start planning my attack. Unfortunately, Ms Noodle would follow my lead, coming out to inspect the strawberries she envisaged serving up with a dollop of freshly whipped double cream.

Bugger that lady. Those babies were mine!

Once my sniffer-mounted strawberry radar had targeted and achieved lock-on to a ripe berry or three, it was then just a matter of timing, agility and speed. The Suit, more often than not, would be the one to come down at first light each day, and open the back door enough for me to go out for my first wazz of the day. I'd bolt out like a fuckin' Scud missile, firing my way up the steps and along the path before veering right at the last moment to line up directly onto the strawberry patch. Having preselected the next most likely candidate for a quick scoff, I knew with military precision where to shove my snout, and where to target my gnashers. It'd go summat like this;

Door opens.

Fuckin' run.

Take a dive in head first.

Scoff, scoff, scoff.

Have a quick wee.

Retreat.

Door closes.

This soon became the daily ritual throughout summer. Unfortunately, the slipper-to-arse-slappin' moments equally formed part of Ms Noodle's summer morning ritual. Ahh, bollocks – it was still worth it.

Steak or Carrots?

Recollecting my earliest days at the cottage, I distinctly remember my first encounter with the birdseed shit.

'What the heck is that Mister?' I ruffed.

The Suit had just given me a round but trough-like metal bowl of what looked like birdseed. These southern-softie weirdo hoomans had somehow skipped the chapter from 'Doggie Do's & Don'ts' entitled 'How to Properly Feed Your Pooch.' I ask ya, birdseed? For fuck's sake.

'Oi Mister, where's the meat?' I cried out, 'Where's the steak?'

Being honest, looking back at my former life as a caged young stud-muffin, the food there was pretty dire. Mostly it was canned shit, never the decent stuff, just the cheapest crap from nondescript stores chosen based on whatever happened to be on offer that week. But it was always meaty looking, ish. Didn't taste very good though, and I was never convinced as to the meat to crap ratio, but... birdseed, seriously? What the fuck had happened to my life?

The metal bowl I had been presented with, now that was familiar. I used to have my canned shit dolloped into one of those at Guy's place, but coz I was so thoroughly bored there, I'd half-eaten the metal rim when The Suit first paid a visit. Interestingly at the time, he seemed pretty pissed off when he saw the raw metal edges of the bowl, and as we drove to the cottage that first night he muttered all sorts about animal neglect under his breath. I therefore took it as evidence The Suit was in fact a good bloke at heart. But then that didn't correspond with attempts to feed me birdseed all of a sudden.

Up until my so-called cottage life began, I'd only scoffed that processed tinned shit. It was all I knew and all I'd heard about, even from other chaps I'd chatted to through cage bars at nondescript warehouses on dark nights, having been dragged there to 'perform' with the ladies – in exchange for a wad of the folding stuff that would end up firmly rammed into Guy's pocket for my stud duties.

Changing over to birdseed took some getting used to, but get used to it I did. In fact, it became so much my 'norm' that I forgot, almost, about the canned substitute processed meaty stuff of old, and started to vaguely 'look forward' to scoffin' down a monster bowl of the seedy shit. Made my poo look very interesting though, I'd have to say. And yes, I did try it... It was pretty tasty second time around too. Yeah, it's a doggie thing, but oh, you should have seen Ms Noodle's face. She really wasn't impressed by my fact-finding poo-scoffin' mission. Bless... I remember her screaming out the window at me.

'Taz, don't! Don't eat that!' she shouted, 'Aww noooo, Taz, please!'

Immediately I noted that all cuddle-based activities had been abruptly suspended on account of said activity for about four or five days in apparent protest at my culinary choices. Seemed a bit harsh, but not a lot I could do about it anyways.

~ ~ ~ ~

So that was that. Life went on. I somehow managed to keep on livin' on birdseed. And then one day, something very, very weird happened to me. Late one summer's evening, I was sat outside on the lawn at the back of the cottage with Ms Noodle, having just wiped my butthole for a good five or six minutes up and down in stripes on the lawn. She then tried at length to explain the inappropriateness of my actions, but the words landed on my two very deaf ears. I never did understand the logic of her complaint.

Just then, she pulled out of her back pocket some bloody strange looking orange coloured object.

'Okay Taz, try this,' she said.

'Fuck off,' I replied in haste, being more to do with my natural dislike of any stuff 'new' than any logic-based reasoning.

'No, go on, they're really tasty. Go on,' she persisted.

'Nope, not gonna happen lady. It looks dangerous. It's totally the wrong colour for food. I'll die, or I'll turn into an orange cat or summat. Nope, ya can get stuffed with the orange turd,' I retorted.

She could say what she liked, but there was no way that orange 'thing' was gonna pass my lips.

On and on she went, chatting away like some loony-toon; telling me how yummy this 'kar-ott' thing was, that it was more than allegedly just food, that is really was something to eat, and how it would be really good for me, good for my diet, good for my teeth, and all sorts of dumbfounded and quite unbelievable shit like that.

It was good for one thing though I did admit, it was good for a game of fetch. Ms Noodle would hurl it across the lawn, probably expecting me to catch and chomp it up I suspect, but all I'd do was to launch into rocket mode and tear after it in the vain hope of catching it before it landed – just for the sheer hell of it. I reckoned that it was probably an okay and acceptable course of action with most things 'thrown,' even for the orange dick-like thing.

But then something rather unexpected happened.

After maybe 30 repetitions of throw, run, jump, miss, catch, retrieve etc. etc., I found myself in mid-flight when I made 'molar contact,' landing a tad awkwardly butt-first on the side of the little hill where the old cherry tree was.

Snap… the carrot thing had suddenly broken in two, both parts still in my mouth though.

Three drops of juice from the carrot had dripped down on to my tongue.

Ping.

'Whoa!' I cried out, 'What the fuck?'

That was unexpected to say the least. It was like liquid gold.

I had stopped dead still, frozen in an extraordinary mix of fear, delight and sheer embarrassment. Ms Noodle was laughing her lovely slim arse off at me from across the lawn, having guessed what had just gone down. Damn it, had that all been part of some cunning plan from the beginning?

'I told ya they were yummy, ya daft lump!' she blurted out with sheer glee at my obvious shock.

In a nutshell, that was how I met and fell in love with the world of carrots — my life having changed from that point on. As totally embarrassing as it was at having been proven so wrong, I was like a pooch reborn.

Then I remember thinking, 'Oh crap, does that mean I'd become… a fucking vegetarian?'

~ ~ ~ ~

We all love our kids; as a woman I was just the same whether talking about my human babies, or my pets. My own personal brood had long since flown the coup, and had each gone on to make what they would with each of their respective lives. Whilst not considered a replacement, I must admit that young Taz grew on me. Sure, he wasn't exactly a cuddly, fluffy little puppy, not by any stretch of the imagination. In fact, he was a thoroughly despicable mutt at times, but he was our mutt, and for that he gained my affection — far sooner than I had perhaps anticipated when thinking back to that first night he came storming into our cottage and into our lives, polluting the air every few seconds from the word go.

Taz was 100% dog, no question. Whether it was his nature or more to do with his former domestic circumstances I wasn't sure, but he ate, or rather consumed, his food as if his very existence that day depended upon it. So when people say that dogs are four-legged vacuum cleaners, I would have to agree. Canines are famed for being willing and able to consume all sorts of food, and all sorts of non-foodstuffs too, such as lumps of coal, dug up cat crap, lost wedding rings, bits of Lego, you name it. However, trying to get a dog to change its dietary habits was not as easy as one might imagine.

Take Taz for example. Introducing the muesli-type food took a fair while for him to accept. Mixed only with water, I'd have to agree that it wasn't perhaps the most attractive culinary delight to offer up, but it was stacked with nutrition and specifically created for the dietary requirements of the muscular dog, or so the advertisement and packaging had proclaimed. As his newly adopted 'mum,' I saw it as my duty to improve his nutritional welfare, not that he ever seemed in the slightest bit bothered either way, providing there was something served up to wrap his gnashers around on a regular basis. Fussy eater wasn't a term I would have ever associated with Taz.

The funny carrot chasing episode on the lawn was very much a turning point for our Taz. Carrots soon became part of his weekly diet and, somewhat surprisingly, he then ventured on to various other non-meat snacks such as chunks of cucumber, apples, lumps of cheese, biscuits and so on and so forth.

As with all pets, Taz firmly knew his own personal favourites and was of course equally happy to share these facts, just in case we, as mere humans, may have forgotten since the preceding day. Now, I wouldn't have particularly referred to the following as one of his 'party tricks,' but Taz did have a very keen ear when it came to the verbalisation of what food might or might not be on offer. He was a dog who knew 100% what he wanted.

Many will be familiar with the physical response of a dog should one happen to blurt out a single word of significance, such as 'walkies' in many dog-owning households. Usually it would involve some hairy-bummed little hound rocketing straight towards the front door, perhaps with his lead stuffed into his mouth, just itching to go off and enjoy said walkies. Taz was no different on the 'walkies' bit, but he also knew his foodstuffs too. As I mentioned, he knew what he liked, and just as most other dogs would only react to the announcement of an impending walk, Taz was equally responsive when it came to his favourites from the kitchen cupboard or the fridge.

'Okay Taz, now Daddy's at work, shall we see what goodies are in the fridge today?' I would ask.

As he wasn't normally allowed anywhere close to entering the kitchen, he had learnt to obediently plonk his bum down and sit right in the doorway, with his feet firmly planted right on the gold-coloured metal carpet gripper bar that delineated the clear boundary between the lounge (okay, permitted) and the kitchen (not okay, not permitted). Being a relaxed sort of chap, he often would lean up against the hardwood doorframe, but his gaze never wavered one centimetre from the fridge door across on the other side of the kitchen, deep in forbidden territory.

'Now, hmm, what do we have here Taz? Ooh look, it's a lovely apple,' I said in order to attract his attention.

Looking across at Taz, I was met with zero response having registered. His unchanged glare remained firmly in place.

'Okay, hmm, yes. Oh Taz, here's... (taking my time), an aubergine,' I laughed.

Still nothing came back.

'You'll love this, I'm sure... a really lovely juicy raw steak!' I announced, adding as much temptation to my voice as possible.

Nada. Now that was a surprise, admittedly.

'Or how about some biscuits?' thinking I'd go for the jugular.

There was, perhaps, some involuntary flickering of the muscles close to his left eye, but no more. It was clearly time to up my game.

'Hmm, now look at this. Leftover lasagne from last night,' I exclaimed, 'Hmm, wow. How yummy does that look? And it's one of your favourites too,' I even added.

A slight quiver of both eyelids that time, but all other muscles remained frozen as he sat there as if his tail were superglued to the carpet.

'Ah, I know just what you'd like…' I said, taunting him, speaking very slowly and ever so seductively, or that was the plan at least.

His back ever so slowly moved away from the doorframe until he resumed a fully upright sitting position. His bum then slowly raised a full centimetre from the carpet – he was a picture of unqualified canine focus.

'Here's something that's maybe, yes, a little orange it seems,' she whispered, 'It looks like...'

Taz was clearly starting to lose it at this point. He was salivating uncontrollably, and starting to shake with a slight whole body tremor as he anticipated the inevitable announcement.

'...a carrot!' I suddenly cried.

With that, Taz launched his 20 or so kilos vertically as if all four legs had little rockets strapped to them, their short fuses having been lit remotely in perfect unison. His muzzle then shot skywards and he let out a rip-roaring howl of delight.

It was... carrot time!

Maybe not absolutely, and certainly unintentionally, but I did wonder if we'd somehow pushed him unwittingly towards vegetarianism – oh, that poor dog, he must have been appalled and horrified at even the thought crossing his or anyone else's mind.

The Hotel

'Did you pack those two new sunscreens I picked up from the chemist yesterday?' Ms Noodle shouted from the bedroom to The Suit who was on 'packing duty' downstairs. Yep, it was their annual summer 'jollies' time once again, but where the heck they were off to I wasn't right able to fathom. It was supposedly some tiny Tunisian island — all sounded a bit bloody stoopid to me; I mean, seriously, just why the fuck would they go sit in the blazin' sun for hours on end, when they could brown their bits like I did under the old cherry tree? Hoomans can be just sooo weird.

'So, what the fuck is "sunscreen"?' I asked blankly at Ms Noodle one day, having just heard her shout downstairs to the old fella. She was still upstairs 'doing stuff,' organising clothes for some upcoming trip, or so it seemed.

Yes, jollies was that time when the hoomans would yet again fuck off and abandoned me for three or four weeks. This seemingly abhorrent failure in their duty of care was a regular occurrence, albeit sometimes just for two or three nights as well as these longer stints that happened but once or twice a year.

Yeah, so I like to whinge a bit, so what? But if I'm honest, it wasn't all bad, but not that I was ever gonna let on to the hoomans. You see, when they'd go away to visit Aunt Whoever-the-fuck, or sit on a beach and swear not to forget all about me, they'd always arrange in advance to pack me off to a hotel all of my own. It was known as a kennels, apparently, a sort of hotel for temporarily abandoned woofers. However, sadly I noted that they started letting sodding cats in there too, which in my book was wholly unacceptable. We didn't even get to chase and bite the smelly, meowing, scrawny little bastards either, which made the whole deal questionable at best, if not pretty crap really.

I kept on asking Aunt Gina, the cottage cleaner lady hooman and my once-a-week playmate, but she never did seem that keen on me going over to her place to stay whilst my hoomans were away. I'd heard that it had summat to do with my tendencies to sack anything breathing that sported some cute canine bum-fluff, and that said trait was apparently wholly inappropriate considering two of her own woofers happened to be cute girlies. Bit of a shame really, coz Aunt Gina also had a fab daughter called Misty. Her real name was Trisha, but Miss Trisha seemed a bit of a mouthful, so I had known her all along as just 'Misty.' She was real nice, a heap of fun it to be said, and she would come help Aunt Gina clean the cottage when she was back visiting her parent's farm. Shame she didn't live closer, but apparently it was somewhere a long way off, and too far for me to walk even in one whole day.

Anyways... I digress. The kennels weren't actually a bad hangout. Initially I worried it was gonna be like a temporary move back to Guy's cage, but couldn't have been more wrong. So, whilst the hoomans were off doing their 'thing,' whatever, wherever, and whenever that was, I was subjected to the hard life as a sort of hotel guest. Not too shabby a result.

A bit like Aunt Gina, Misses Mary and Mister Tom who ran the joint were pretty cool local types that I added to my list of 'okay hoomans.' They'd remember each of our names and had done the place up specifically with canine needs in mind; yep, screw the felines in their puny extension around the back. I got to take my own bed too, which was a nice touch, although that meant my blanket of course, not the whole armchair. They even washed it every week for me on longer stays. It was never that hot there, so overheating my dangly bits was not high up on my list of potential holiday ailments, but it did of course get pretty bloody cold. The kennels, however, were each heated individually. How's that for sweet as pie, eh?

Initially I was worried about the nosh. I mean, you hear nightmares about the crap served up at cheap motels, but I have to say, Misses Mary made a mean meal for us hungry dogs. It was a bit weird at first; like muesli with meat chunks, which might sound crap, but was actually rather yummy, and we got that slopped up twice a day, no less. So, I'd get to go home after my three weeks there as fat as a bulldog. Not unhealthy fat mind, they were careful on that score, but 'contented holiday podginess' would best describe it. Those morning walkies with The Suit and my weekly jaunts with Aunt Gina once back home were admittedly a bit of a struggle for a while, but much needed I guess.

Hmm, what else...? Oh yes, 'exercise time.' The place was situated right on top of the Pennines, and pretty much smack in the middle of nowhere. There were two bloody great fields to play in, not the usual rabbit hutch run setup most other 'hotels' for our kind had, that's for sure. My first two visits there saw me confined to solitary after trying to bite the arse off of some scrawny little turd of a Whippet they let out into MY field. I got my butt whooped for that episode admittedly, but hey, he made fun of my knackers being furry so he had it coming. Never saw him after that. Bloody wimp.

But I gradually became used to 'playing with others,' well, sort of, and twice a day we'd get to have a fab runabout together. One young hooman who helped out working there in the evenings and at weekends would come and kick a football with us for a bit, which was always fun, except for when I bit the fucker one year, killing it dead – the ball, not the kid.

Oh yes, food... apart from the meaty muesli sloppy shit, I got to have my own treats too when staying there... carrots and Granny Smith apples no less. It seemed that The Suit had some informal arrangement with Misses Mary and Mister Tom, as they'd supply these, my favourite two snacks, on a daily basis. I'll never forget the look plastered across that ugly mug of an Alsatian in the pen opposite mine one time.

He was like, 'What the fuck? You's a dawg, not a goat!'

Obviously his hoomans weren't quite like Ms Noodle and The Suit on that score, for I never saw him, or many others get special stuff quite like what I did, so he could take the piss all he sodding liked.

'See if I care matey. Better than your boring same old scoff, innit?' I used to bark across at him, knowing full well he never received treats outside of the prescribed and standard daily feedings.

~ ~ ~ ~

Many will relate to this I'm sure. No matter what plans we made, what time of year and whatever the weather, it was always a flaming race against the clock that last few hours before heading off on holiday. Always, and without fail.

Penny and I travelled a fair bit each year, usually sun-bound adventures to destinations in North Africa or elsewhere around the Mediterranean. Generally as far removed from Yorkshire as one could get, yet within just a few hours flight time in order to maximise the longevity of each and every holiday based on the available time off work. Some trips would involve long-haul flights, but those were 'special occasions' such as trips to China, Tanzania, India or suchlike. But in essence, any getaway was deemed a holiday, which I suppose is what it's all about; taking a break from the norm, irrespective of whatever that 'norm' happens to be.

Back home we didn't have goldfish in a bowl, or a cute little budgie in a cage, nor even a small reptile transportable in a mobile terrarium, but what we did have was a Taz. He was just a lump of a dog who was hardly a docile little Pekinese that we could proverbially dump into the hands of a neighbour or some unsuspecting 'good friend' or relative. Taz, therefore, would always head off to his own 'hotel' whenever we went away. Sometimes that would be for a three or four week overseas trip or one of our more regular weekend jaunts visiting relatives and/or friends in other parts of the country where taking him along was just asking for trouble considering his general tendency for boisterousness and sheer ineptitude for winning any 'Cute Pet of the Year' awards.

We had tried a few kennels during those first years in Yorkshire, but they were either ridiculously overpriced, overly crowded, or just plain dirty. Of course, we knew Taz was a fairly unfussy sort of chap, but after his near captive start to life, we also felt he equally deserved a reasonable level of comfort and care whilst we went off and did our thing. The place we eventually found, and used for quite a few years after, was indeed a marvellous find. Situated on the open moorland, the place occupied a fantastic position that afforded the 'guests,' as they were referred to, ample space to exercise, let off steam, socialise, and at the same time keep out of each other's respective spaces should the need exist.

The owners, Tom and Mary, offered a high level of creature comfort, with heated individual pens, low-level lighting at night, a 24-hour security system that any self-respecting hotel would be proud of, and a well-organised advanced booking register that allowed us to book in Taz many months ahead when arranging holiday flights and accommodation. They also offered personalised care like you wouldn't believe. Each dog, or cat I presume, had his or her own diet sheet, a choice of three basic supplied food types, or owners could provide food for their pet providing it was ready-prepared. But for our dear mutt, it was just a matter of shipping him off with his own bedding, a couple of toys, and a plentiful supply of his favourite snacks, those being carrots and apples, Granny Smiths of course.

As one might surmise, they also ran a tight ship as a business, and that included timekeeping to a military standard. Admittance, or 'check-in,' was strictly between 0930 and 1100 in the mornings, and 1600 and 1800 in the afternoons, but that was it. Turn up late and you'd find the hefty iron gate firmly shut, secured and padlocked. Try phoning up and saying you'd be late, and the answer was not quite as one might have hoped. But fair enough; their place, their business, their rules. They were also mostly fully booked all year round, so it obviously hadn't negatively affected their business.

Now, as with most busy people, our timing, in certain matters, was simply a matter of aim, fire, oh crap, try again. I myself had multiple responsibilities at the time in a busy head office, and therefore 'getting out' at a set time at the end of the working day was a challenge not even Sir Winston would readily have taken on. Organised I was, very; meticulously one might have said – 'painfully so' many even did. However, leaving work before a scheduled break involved the 'team handover'… and that meant contact with another human, a variable that often blew all the best laid plans right out of the water as we were talking someone more senior, and therefore unable to be controlled or even guided.

On one particular Friday afternoon in early August, we were set to take a late evening flight out of Manchester airport heading down to southern Turkey for one month's much-needed R&R. The aim was to leave work dead on four o'clock, drive home, take Taz to the kennels, drive back, have a leisurely cup of tea with Penny, grab the bags that were packed the night before, and await the shuttle car that always arrived promptly to ferry us to the airport. Yeah right, ha bloody ha. So much for those plans.

Four o'clock came around all too quick… and promptly disappeared in the same fashion. I was stuck in a meeting with the renowned pernickety boss of my boss who was 'filling in' and therefore responsible for reluctantly accepting the 'team handover' from me. But, what a prized tit that guy was. Every detailed line had to be gone over twice, at least, and question after unnecessary question was thrown up. I mean, as if the team hadn't been doing their jobs for years on nigh anyway. I truly believe to this day he was put on this fair earth just to test the sheer patience of lesser mortal beings. Times like that certainly made me wish I had coordinated my departure date to coincide when my own and much more amiable and pragmatic boss was around – who, by the way, had a completely different style, especially in the management of personnel. It was a skilled art that obviously not all senior management shared.

Anyhow, I made it out, eventually, and remarkably without any Crown Court criminal case having been levied upon my person, but all hope of a prejollies relaxed evening had long since been quashed. It was approaching ten-past-five before I even reached my car, which thankfully started up on the second attempt, not an absolute given based on its performance in the preceding few weeks, another reason I mostly walked to work.

With rubber burning I exited the works car park with some haste, weaved my way through town as fast as I safely could and blasted up the long hill towards the cottage. Penny, as one could imagine, wasn't sure whether to greet me or slap me as I slammed on the brakes, having hit the driveway at some speed, leapt out of the almost overheated old Jeep and charged up the flagstone steps two at a time — summer having made that a safe thing to do, but a potentially lethal action in winter. Thankfully she was not a bitter woman, but I think the fact that we were heading to the sun that very evening had more to do with saving my butt to be honest.

Taz was, of course, all ready and raring to go, with his bedding, toys and snack supply all packed into his usual bright green 'jollies holdall,' which even bore his own name having had it emblazoned on the side in bright red thick marker pen a year or two previous. He was certainly ready for the off, even if I was not. I charged upstairs, suit off, jeans on, and bounded back down, darted outside, threw in the holdall and opened up the back. Taz was next, he ruffed a quick 'bye bye' to Penny, ran down the steps and dived up into the back of the Jeep.

The time by then was just gone half-past five. Not overly late for our pre-booked airport shuttle, but bloody late indeed for the kennels, which we knew would go into military lockdown at bang on six o'clock. The car restarted okay, and that was it, off we roared with 21 long miles to go!

Apart from slowing to the sedentary legal speed set by law, and enforced by way of all too reliable digital technology at three well-known spots on certain roads, the engine raced like it had never done before. What speeds were hit I do not know to this day, but I do recall the engine temperature gauge doing a merry dance around the red zone for much of the journey.

Meanwhile, Penny had, in vain, attempted to phone ahead and announce our impending delayed check-in. However, even as a regular and with it being another one month stay pre-booked months in advance, they wouldn't budge. The call having resulted in a firm, 'We close the gates at six o'clock, prompt.'

I, of course, had no knowledge of the call nor its outcome, but knew all too well that these guys had people phoning every day looking for spaces for their beloved pets, so why should they relent? Reality meant only one thing, the race was well and truly on!

Once out of the built up area we tore the road up climbing up out of the valley. The Jeep was wallowing with speed and the odd bumps and rises took us close to take-off; and so much so, that Taz was bouncing around and levitating almost at will for much of the last ten to 15 minutes. Thankfully he was used to our road trips, especially off-roading – but this was a somewhat new experience again.

Four minutes to six and the kennels were in sight, albeit almost a mile away on the next rise. The car's lights were full on and its loud twin air horns were blaring over and over. Bizarrely, as of course they'd never hear, I was shouting too and Taz was joining in...

'Wait for us, we're almost there!' we hollered in unison.

Although what good that would do was plainly obvious. Nothing, nowt, zilch.

One minute to six and we screeched to a halt in a plume of dust as the duty kennel manager held the big padlock in his hand, and I swear he was looking down at his watch, counting down the seconds. We'd made it, but only just and with merely seconds to spare. One traffic light against us and that would have been it. Lady luck was on our side I guess, just.

My drive back home was quick but definitely much less fraught, and our own travel arrangements after that point worked true to schedule. Thankfully it was just my nerves that were partially shot during the experience. Like most, we loved our various pets, but sometimes, just sometimes the whole experience was beyond trying...

Hide & Seek

Shit, I just knew I was gonna have to just go ahead do it. Diving headfirst into a pile of dirty hooman knickers 'n' smelly old socks wasn't exactly high up my list of favourite pastimes, but what the heck. But anyhow, I was sure, I was absolutely bloody sure The Suit was in there.

The daft games we house dogs had to play in order to entertain the hoomans. I was fine with the 'Oh look, here's a lovely ball. Go fetch it, there's a good boy,' and all that crap. I'd pretty much perfected my fake cheesy grin when playing ball, tugging on that damned rope ragger, doing the 'sit' or 'laydown' thing in order to be fed a biscuit or two as a treat… Aargh, but enough with the silly games, per-leese! But no, I'd gone and got myself roped into yet another Sunday afternoon of 'yay, let's have some family fun together' type of entertainment coz, surprise surprise, it was pissing down yet again outside. Ya had to love good old Yorkshire weather.

So, for the game in question my job was, put simply, to 'try and find them' – yay, go me… First off, I'd be forced to wait for a full minute in my room, in the annex at the back. Actually, in truth, that wasn't so bad really. I'd just sit, eat, fart, scratch 'n' sniff, ya know, it wasn't much of a chore to just pass away a bit of time whilst they did the counting bit on my behalf. After one of them 'called out,' my task was to then race about the cottage in order to find where each of them had hidden their skinny asses. Bit bizarre, but it seemed to amuse them no end at least, and happy hoomans meant more doggie treats being doled out, so what the heck, right?

On this occasion I thought I'd heard both of them scamper up the stairs when the count started, so that was 50% of my job done right there and then. Next, I heard Ms Noodle still giggling, so I knew the daft bat really couldn't have been too far away in what was just a cottage after all – it wasn't some flippin' great palace or anyfink. Of course, being a canine of impeccable breeding, from that moment when the kennel hand left the gate ajar, I had all my senses working like a good'un, so in truth I could sniff them out in a few seconds, but of course would play along so as to heighten their sense of excitement and thereby earn a sufficient level of reward in the shape of a few extra-yummy biscuits, or maybe an apple or carrot, now that they had been officially added them to my list of good 'n' proper fart-inducing nosh.

Now, this so-called 'game' was simple enough, and any dog with a half bag of grey cells strapped to his shoulders could soon get to know all the daft places the hoomans would head to in their mission to hide themselves away from me. Oh, the excitement... yawn.

Anyway, kicking off downstairs. We always did the 'starting bit' and thereby the 'waiting bit' from my room, coz it was at the back of the cottage and sort of neutral territory, the 'end (or beginning) of the line,' so to speak. From there, the closest realistic hiding place for a hooman was in the large kitchen-diner. Whilst under normal circumstances that room was absolutely kick-up-the-arse out of bounds to me, during this particular game it was accordingly reclassified as 'temporary permitted territory.' In the kitchen there were very long curtains, or drapes. They were thick, heavy and lined, and whilst the small window looking out over the driveway had shorter curtains, the rear two-part stable door that led out to the garden, but was hardly ever used, except in mid-summer, had a full-length curtain that even touched the carpet, as did the two side-by-side double stone mullioned windows. That meant the hoomans could stand there all-quiet like behind drawn curtains and effectively be hidden from view, apart from stubby toes or slippers that often accidentally poked out from beneath the curtain. Doh, sometimes they were such Muppets!

Talking of windows, the ledges were bloody huge. With 50 centimetre thick stone walls, the window ledges too were naturally of a considerable depth. So, with a curtain drawn or even just half drawn, I would sometimes find one of my hoomans curled up on a window shelf like some sad elf waiting impatiently for Christmas Day to come around. Oh, and also in the kitchen was a large under-sink cupboard. But for that to be used, they'd have to kick out the kitchen bin to fit themselves in there, so that was a bloody easy spot. Should the bin be out, then I knew I had one of the bastards.

In the main lounge there were again more windows ledges and curtains arranged as per the kitchen-diner, plus two extra-long curtains hanging right down to the carpet (and with a bit to spare too) that were used midwinter to cut a third of the room off so as to keep the warmth within a single smaller area. I didn't give about a crap about intended usage or the economics of it, but it did add two more places to check for hiding hoomans.

Heading up the stairs, and there was again a similar array of deep window shelves and similar long curtains to be checked, but also it should be noted that all of the doors upstairs were solid, so, unlike the semi-glass panelled doors downstairs that couldn't hide a cat, let alone the odd hooman, I would have to poke my head behind each door as an initial check when entering the upstairs rooms. Plus, there was the bathroom up there. Yes, it was one place I'd been caught out a couple of times – one of them having been found lying down hiding *in* the bathtub! And on that note, today was Ms Noodle's not so lucky day, for there she was, all curled up in a ball lying in the tub with two small yellow rubber ducks for company.

Once spotted, she let out a dejected groan, 'Aww Taz, you're getting too bloody good at this game now.'

One down, one to go. The Suit.

Each bedroom had handmade wooden posted beds that were raised quite a bit from the carpeted wooden floors, so a quick head poked underneath each bed was always advisable as they were perfectly capable of hiding one or maybe even two hoomans. Beds, beds, yes, not just underneath, noooo, there was also a thick, or thin, duvet on each, depending on the season, so I'd shove my snout under the covers and take a good sniff for evidence of any stowaway, such as mister or misses flavoured farts, or just smell feet occupying socks.

Depending on how early in the mooring the game was played dictated the necessity for that particular check, mostly for fear of hooman fart-induced canine respiratory distress, not something to be risked for the sake of a silly game.

Where else? Hmm, oh yes, wardrobes… found both of them stuffed in one once too. But especially easy was the one in the guest bedroom, with its louvre-styled slatted door panels – dead simple and very much suited to my sniffer. So that left just three more places upstairs. One was the wooden coat stand out on the hallway. There was a circular ring a third of the way up, for holding umbrellas apparently, but therefore allowing enough room for a hooman to sort of hang there like a bat, with his/her feet on the wooden ring. The carpet was thick, and quite squishy so I was just praying that one day the coat stand would just topple over and go splat, dishing out its hooman cargo. Alas, I waited forever in vain for that to happen. The second other place was the blanket box, a big fat tomb-like thing made of polished wood that was stuffed to the brim with blankets… but sometimes a clever shit like Ms Noodle would dump out half of them on the floor and climb inside to hide.

And finally, back to where we started this story, knickers and dirty socks. What the fuck were they thinking, let alone me? The dirty laundry, that's the term applied apparently to their arse-wiped smelly old clothes they'd worn around for a day or three, and had been collected up in one place, the basket, until 'washing day' next came around, that usually being a Saturday. And the basket was no ordinary little thing either. Nope, it was a huge big snake charmer's basket, and as big as a soddin' upright coffin. With the inevitable mix of toxic smells that would instantly attack every blood vessel and nerve in my snout, I mostly left that hiding spot till last, on account of my lack of bravery, or as I preferred, just pure common sense. Sometimes I'd just bash my head against the side of the basket early on, coz Ms Noodle would invariably squeal if found to be inside. But nope, not this time. This time I had to tip the lid right off, hold by breath and jump/dive headfirst into God-knows what. Ah, the lengths I'd go to entertain those two, I ask ya.

~ ~ ~ ~

Playing games with your pet should be fun, right?

When Taz stormed into our lives, Penny and I became sort of instant parents to a stubborn, chest-pumped canine teenage rebel who possessed some seriously disgusting habits well-befitting said age group. However, once you got to know him, there was also quite a lovable streak there too. In time, we taught him all about toys, about playing, and about the concept and rules of human-pet socialisation. Admittedly, it was an uphill battle at times. That was hardly surprising though, since he came to us from a life confined mostly to a wire cage outdoors, with practically zero human or animal contact outside of the backstreet 'muscle shows' as a stud dog. His life had never, to our knowledge, involved even the notion of what toys were, hence the whole idea of 'play' was particularly alien to him.

But we persevered. He learnt to play with a rope ragger as a starter. In fact, he ended up with numerous raggers which he'd take to bed as his most prized belongings, and would guard them as if made of some exorbitantly priced precious exotic silk. After a few months, he even had his own teddy bear, but I'll add that such a fact was never shared beyond the cottage walls on the basis of reputational preservation. Taz loved Ted, but notably hid him away as soon as anyone 'not family' would turn up – he was as proud and image conscious as any teenager.

Outdoors, he had soon learnt to play fetch with a ball, a concept he was initially unfamiliar with, and obviously thought we were completely nuts, having seen the look he gave us when we first tried. One of us would throw the ball while he just watched. We'd shout encouragement, and he'd return a look that was totally blank. Now, chasing cats, that was his idea of a good sport, or come to think of it squirrels, or rabbits, or of course other dogs who he'd judged unworthy to be within 500 metres. All of those were fair game, but chasing a ball… nope. He'd just stop, stand or sit and look back at us with a 'What the heck do you want me to do now then?' look slapped across his chops.

With inclement weather often a 'feature' of life up in the Pennines, we spent a fair amount of time indoors, and so Taz had also learnt about indoor life too. In addition to just eating and sleeping, which were his favourite two means of passing time, we had other interests to add such as watching television, listening to music, reading books and magazines as well as the playing of games that were all 'new' to a dog such as Taz.

Hide and Seek was one such game that we mostly played indoors. In our version of the game, Penny and I were the 'hiders' and Taz naturally was the 'seeker.' Whilst he wasn't perhaps the best choice to be relied upon to legitimately count out loud to 100 with his paws covering his eyes, he would, however, obediently sit there facing a wall if one of us shouted 'stay' every ten seconds or so, and that modus operandi seemed to work fairly well in practice.

At the end of the count, one of us would shout playfully, 'Come on then Taz, come and find us!'

We were never quite sure of course, but he seemed to enjoy if not love playing the game – and he was pretty good at it too after a while. Each time he almost always remembered hiding places we'd previously used, and would cleverly rush off and check them first, one by one, upstairs and down. Watching him run about the cottage was hilarious in itself, especially when you'd see this big dog bash his head against the bathroom door so as to open it, run in as it opened and immediately check first behind the door, then shove his head over the edge of the bath as he mentally ticked through the list of possible hiding places we might have elected in any particular round of the game.

You could almost hear him mutter 'Bugger, not here… Bugger, not here… Bugger, not here…' at each point he didn't find us.

On one rather memorable game that took place on a rainy autumnal Sunday afternoon, I had chosen to hide upstairs, squashed onto the landing window ledge curled up in a ball and overlooking the driveway below. The curtain was drawn, so I was hidden from plain sight…

At that point I was wondering if I was to have been the winner. Meanwhile, Penny had chosen to hide herself downstairs in the lounge. That was generally a rarity in itself, considering how close it was to where Taz semi-patiently awaited the signal to 'do his bit,' and on that basis, she'd thought it would be largely unexpected by him so worth a try at least. She had been the first found in the previous two games and was feeling a bit miffed at her performance rating to be honest. While I sat upstairs hidden away on the window shelf, gazing out of the window across the valley below, Penny had found her spot, hunched down on all fours behind the sofa, which would have been in line of sight to anyone going up or down the stairs, but of course only if you were looking there, which of course you would be unlikely to do when traversing up or down the stairs.

'C'mon then Taz. Come and find us!' I hollered from my perch after the allotted one minute wait time had passed.

Suddenly I heard somewhere close to 20 kilogrammes of Staffie hit the bottom few stairs, but then he stopped dead. Five long seconds passed. Then, he continued bounding on up the stairs, so my guess was that he'd sussed out something wasn't quite as expected when reaching the stairs, but that he hadn't actually spotted Penny in her special hiding-in-plain-sight place. Cautiously, I peeked out from behind the curtain to see Taz suddenly dart past and head straight into the bathroom. He checked behind the door, and then checked the bathtub, both negative. Next he went into our bedroom and no doubt checked under the duvet, under the bed, behind the curtains and the door, and even probably sniffed next to the wardrobe doors… He then came pounding out of there and scampered along to the guest bedroom where a similar ritual would likely have ensued.

Still no luck for Taz. Out he came and checked the coat stand, and then backtracked to the laundry basket. He nudged it softly and listened, then gave it a fair old head-butt – still nothing. Lastly he ran over and I heard his paws hit the bottom of the window shelf upon which I was still hidden... Bugger, he'd found me. The fact was confirmed by a strange howl/bark mix of one pumped-up pooch. So of course at that point I gave in and congratulated him on a well-deserved win.

'So, where's Penny? Go find Penny now then,' I challenged him.

He turned heel and sped off back into the bedrooms and bathroom, 'just in case.' Then he shot past me and ran/tumbled down the stairs. I followed, pissing myself laughing, watching this funny lump of a dog check all the known hidey-holes downstairs at hyper speed. At one point he stopped dead still, standing there balancing on three paws listening... just listening... Nope, he obviously still couldn't determine her whereabouts, and so he started darting around like a lunatic, back upstairs, back down again, back upstairs, back down again..., with each round more frantic than the last.

Meanwhile, Penny was still crouched behind the sofa, quietly chuckling to herself, having seen Taz run up and down the stairs just above her, and witnessing seeing him do his level best at trying to find her.

Taz had stopped again, this time halfway up the stairs... He knew she was close by. He could smell her scent and maybe even hear her breathing.

Suddenly he turned about-face and ran back down. The sofa, it had to be the bloody sofa... He jumped on to the sofa, an action that was totally banned, and he knew it, but he was in full-on seeker mode by now and thereby gave not one shit about any of the cottage 'rules.' He then peered over the top, spotted Penny below and let out a series of mad triumphant howls. Next, he jumped back off the sofa and tried to run around behind it from the right-hand side, but that route was blocked by a small coffee table.

Bugger.

He then did a 180 and sped off around the left-hand side instead, and Bang. He ran straight *into* Penny.

I saw it all happen in terrible slow motion. There was a shocked scream, followed by prolonged whimpering.

One second later and Taz was sat there licking Penny's ears. She, on the other hand, was the one doing the whimpering.

'Oww, my sodding neck! Taz, what have you done you daft ape?' she screeched.

The next morning she was still in agony, her neck was continuing to hurt like mad, and so, carefully, I helped her outside and into the car. We drove slowly and carefully down to the local doctor's surgery. After just a relatively short wait, we were shown in. Of course, assumptions were immediately drawn.

'Oh hello Penny, not seen you in ages,' the doctor started off with, 'Looks like you've had a small car accident I presume?'

'Err, nope,' she retorted indignantly, whilst of course fully understanding his obvious jump to the most plausible of conclusions.

'Oh dear, I just assumed,' the doctor responded, 'Okay, so tell me then, what happened?'

'It was our dog,' she replied with a sheepish smile.

At that moment, the practice nurse burst out laughing.

'How bloody big is your dog?' she asked.

A little later, Penny left the surgery sporting a white neck brace, having been diagnosed with acute canine-induced whiplash, and given a one-week's medical report from work. She, in turn received plenty of crap from her workmates for some considerable time after.

Playing Hide and Seek still happened in the cottage, but after that episode it was never quite the same, and the sofa hiding spot was notably never used again. However, Taz had seemingly added it to his list of predefined auto-checkpoints.

Weaponised Farting

Dietary changes always play havoc with the inner goings-on of my butt. And when I moved go live in the cottage with Ms Noodle and The Suit, by crikey you should've been there to witness said goings-on; or perhaps best you didn't. My rear end became rather verbal to say the least. I could have farted for the nation, maybe even to an Olympic standard and, if luck held out, gained a medal or two, complete with corresponding photos of me and my butt occupying a podium position too.

As I awoke each morning, I'd start off by letting rip with a real good-un, just to blow the cobwebs away. In actuality, I probably did shake a few spiders in their webs, perhaps causing brain damage in a few, and maybe even killed off the odd fucker over those first few days and weeks after arriving at the cottage.

The smells. They say you get used to it... bollocks do ya. Many a time I prayed for the hoomans to return from their work just to open the back door and thereby letting me grab a gob-full of wholesome, natural fresh country air.

Sometimes I would even wake myself up as they were that loud, Jeez... and at other times it was just plain embarrassing (for the hoomans I might add, not really for me), when I'd start my famous 'trot-traffing,' whereby we'd be walking down the street and I'd be doing a steady 'parp, parp, parp...' in perfect timing to the footfalls of whichever hooman had the pleasure of my company, tail-end cheeks and all. I used to think it was sodding hilarious, but Ms Noodle usually appeared quite distraught, bless her, especially if visitors were out and about with us too, or we were just walking past someone's garden gate. Greeting her friends, say outside the hairdresser, was a great opportunity to dig deep and let rip a long and loud one. The smell was generally immaterial outdoors of course. Our hill village was mostly a windy old place, so it really was all down to the noise-based impact factor, but that was sometimes enough to trigger a decent response. Tough northern lasses her friends may have been, but they were still dead easy to shock, and that was something which very much appealed to my inner mischievous git.

Travelling in the car was always an occasion in which to fire off a few small 'n' juicy ones. Lost count of the times that all four car windows were suddenly dropped in order to permit life to continue for at least one more day. Didn't always work out that well though. Sometimes, like in the big old Jeep, the front and backseat windows being dropped would soon alleviate the hooman's discomfort, but the whole back luggage area where I resided didn't necessarily have adequate air replenishment in that short process, and they'd put the windows back up not knowing I could still hardly breathe. I guess it was what you might term self-inflicted divine justice, so doubt if they gave a crap anyway. But still – the power it ultimately afforded me over them was worth any slight personal discomfort.

Traffin' inside the cottage was good for a laugh too, but my personal favourite was dropping one inside the local village shop. Now the owner, Cyril, was an old git of maybe about 120 years, give or take. Whatever, he was a wrinkled old dinosaur, and crotchety as hell whatever time of day it happened to be. He was just a mean old twat if ya asked me. He never was keen on letting dogs enter the shop either, but the pavement outside his crappy little shop was really narrow so most folks just weren't prepared to tie up their precious pooches outside on the black and rusting iron fence for fear of returning to find some small fireside rug in the rough shape of their (very flat) dog, having been splattered to a pancake by some large quarry truck that rumbled past just a bit too close. We'd go down there on a fairly regular basis, mostly with The Suit rather than Ms Noodle – coz she'd apparently said I wasn't trustworthy in the company of other people – huh, as if?

Inside the shop you'd almost always find some bloke dragging his poor mutt around in there too. I didn't give a shit about them though, to me they were just unwitting collaborators in another of my dastardly plans. Basically, I'd wander about and get close enough to John or Jane Doe Dog and then silently let out one hell of a noxious beaut with a slow-burning fuse. Then I'd make some rapid 'I need to pee' type of noises aimed at The Suit in order to ensure we quickly exited the store rather sharpish… Then, minutes later you'd hear old Cyril giving it some verbal, and suddenly the victim dog and his owner would beat a hasty retreat from the store, having just been chucked out on their ears by the old fossil. I just loved those simple games. Happy memories of a youthful butt in action!

~ ~ ~ ~

Do dogs fart? Oh my word, yes they most definitely do!

Like all living creatures, intestinal gases have to be extricated somehow, lest we'd all inflate like balloons and simply explode. Not a pretty sight I'm sure. So yes, as unwanted and embarrassing as it might seem at times, our bodies emit gas up to 20 times per day, or per hour for some people I've known.

Of course, humans and dogs are no different, not on that score at least. Okay, so they may not be quite like humans in their ability to control their bodily functions to quite the same degree that we might 'politely hold one in till we nipped outside,' but I can assure you, they can fart with just as must skill, stealth, and copiosity as any school-aged rascal. Now, whilst I'm admittedly not aware of any published numbers, I do know it's a 'thing' for sure. I mean, there's even a Dog Farting Awareness Day, serious, it's on the eighth of April each year according to Scientific American, so I'm obviously not alone when it comes to having been an owner of a gas-emitting canine.

Taz had a rather extensive array of gas-based weaponry at his disposal. Was he some ex-military dog? Maybe he was classified as a mobile WMD, after all, some of his silent arsenal (pun here wasn't actually intended by the way) were certainly pretty bloody deadly.

On days when we were both out at work, Taz would be shut in his room at the back of the cottage. Upon arriving home, whoever was first would cautiously enter said room and then head immediately for the back door, having taken a lungful of clean air to ensure their own personal safety whilst getting the job done. Why? Simple; the room was usually so full of noxious canine gas that one sniff might have induced instant collapse or death by asphyxiation. I even used to avoid flicking the light switch on a dark winter's evening for fear of combustible gas igniting in a big whump – ending all life as we knew it in the village, dog, me and all.

Winter weekends were the worst, with doors and windows almost always shut tight 24x7, such was necessary on a cold and windy Yorkshire hilltop. When the big iron wood-burning stove was alight, as it was for at least six or seven months a year, the whole cottage became pretty toasty. Being a 'dual fuel,' we were also able to chuck in some large fist-sized lumps of hard anthracite, which burned very slowly and enabled the burner to be kept alight overnight or right through the day when we went out, thereby keeping the rooms at an ambient and more welcoming temperature to return home to. As you can imagine, insulation in the 1700s wasn't all that good compared to modern day standards of house construction, and keeping such an old building warm was always fairly challenging.

Taz would quite often meander over to crash out in front of the burning stove, doing that Staffie thing; lying flat out, with front and back legs extended fore and aft on the carpet. Other times he would be upside down on his back, right by the fire still, but belly-up, all four legs just hanging loosely in mid-air, knackers getting a good toasting, and his tail just redundantly flopped on the carpet. Of course, that meant his rear-end was free to emit at will, which of course he did almost routinely. When the telly was switched off, you could hear a regular 'pfffffft' every four to seven minutes, a bit like one of those automated air freshener contraptions found in posh hotel bathrooms. Emitting that volume of gas in a building with windows and doors closed during winter was one thing, but to do it next to a hot stove with a naked flame scared the crap out of me. In my mind I would run through some 'what if?' scenarios. Can you imagine completing a detailed drawing for some household or building insurance claim should ignition have occurred?

But it wasn't just me who found Taz's 'special feature' rather repulsive, if not downright disgusting. Nope, his butt had achieved notoriety far and wide, and was certainly known all too well to those who dared visit the cottage for a few hours or days.

It also led to some rather sneaky behavioural traits on the part of our canine friend. On a number of occasions you'd see him literally slide off the old armchair, dead slow, slithering off like a short, fat snake, except front feet first. Once all four legs were firmly on carpeted terra firma, he'd meander seemingly aimlessly across to the other side of the room, often to where Penny would be sitting with her magazines or cross-stitch. He would lay down at her feet or nearby for a minute or two... Then he'd slowly get back up and walk slightly faster back across and then jump back up into the armchair to resume his snoring.

Around a minute or so after he'd have completed said manoeuvre...

'Oh God, you filthy, stinky animal!' Penny would cry out, 'You did it again, didn't you Taz? You came all the way over here just to emit your killer gas, and then vamoose back to your own spot where the air was still clear, eh?' she'd continue. And finally she'd exclaim something like, 'You really are a horrid little beast at times!'

Yep, Taz was well-known for his antics of traffing anywhere he didn't have to breathe it in — the cheeky, but cunning little git that he was.

Biker Suit

'No fucking way mate... I'm not going out there,' I hollered. 'I'm staying right here, thank you very much!' Sat safe in the doorway looking out I may have been, but there was no soddin' way I was gonna go outside proper.

After numerous years, apparently, Ms Noodle had relented; agreeing to, or tolerating at least, the idea of The Suit getting himself 'another bloody motorbike.'

'C'mon – Wimp,' Ms Noodle teased.

She stood there tentatively eyeing up the old black bike that was warming up, rather too noisily for both my taste and hers, on the flagstone path in the back garden.

'Yeah, call me whatever lady. I'm staying put!' and indeed put was how I stayed, with extra glue keeping my butt fixed in position.

Now, the bike could by no stretch of anyone's imagination have been considered 'new,' but all the same, the old git seemed smitten by its arrival as it was new to him; Ms Noodle was plainly not so enamoured. However, in time it proved not to be a great waker-upper, with starting and reliability issues that meant it suffered more in winter than my old grandpa, having been left outside under a waterproof cover with all the damp and the snow and the rain – the bike, not my grandpa. There was talk of a garage being built at one point, but they just turned out to be just empty words once the building regs. had been inspected and the costs formally estimated as being 27-times the bike's resale value.

Some six months passed by, and after a run-in's with the bike vet, or whatever they called that greasy git from down the road who'd regularly end up being called upon to sort it out, the old black monster seemed happier, with the regular pissing of black gooey liquid having been fixed – good job too, coz that stuff was pretty slippy on the flagstones even for my pooch paws, let alone bike tyres. Ms Noodle too seemed more content with the idea of its being there, for they would sometimes leave me at home on a Sunday and fuck off for hours with that thing. What they did, where they went, I never had a soddin' clue, but they seemed to enjoy it nonetheless.

The Suit would spend many hours generally tinkering with the rusty old thing. Sharing my domain with the metal monster, however, really was not on in my book, hence perhaps a good job that he never cottoned on to me cocking me old back leg and pissing on the wheels most nights when out there for my late night proverbial. Admittedly, The Suit did shout at me a couple of times after finding greasy turds strategically placed just by the front tyre, which resulted in all wonder of unfounded accusations about my character. But bloody good fun all the same!

Try as I might, I never really became used to the two-wheeled interloper. Whilst somewhat bewildered when I first heard chatter between the hoomans about placing an advertisement and that 'a certain price may be attainable,' I was relieved upon hearing it was 'a good time to let *her* go.' The application of the feminine subject confirmed it was not a threat to my person, but a sales advertisement for the bike.

The next weekend a local couple were due to come and see the bike and to 'give her the once over,' whatever that meant. I did, however, soon discover that they didn't mean anywhere close to what I generally associated with 'giving any "her" a once over.' But good news though, coz the couple turned out to be Aunt Gina, my Monday hooman, with her pockets full of treats, large can of spray polish, and a keenness for taking me on additional, unscheduled long walkies on a Monday after her cleaning chores were done. Top lady in my opinion. Her bloke seemed like a real decent fella too, Mister George he was. He was a farmer and a tough Yorkshire geezer who spoke all proper when compared to my nancy-like hoomans from the South. He too, it turned out, had been granted the necessary wifely permission to resume a past love affair with these two-wheeled noise machines. But, he was also handy with a toolbox, unlike The Suit who didn't really know one end of a wrench from the other.

Anyway, Mister George seemed appropriately happy with the prospect of taking on the old black bike. Its mechanical glitches didn't faze him either, and so after some beard scratching, an appropriate sucking in of breath, and lifting his peaked cap to scratch his half-balding nugget, a handshake notably took place, and that was that.

Me, well I just thanked the doggie Lordie himself for ending tenure of the contraption that had invaded my world. With a celebratory parp of rear-ended delight, it was with great relief to hear they'd indeed sold the heap of junk!

Result.

'So, does that mean I'm gonna be getting my own garden back?' I asked Aunt Gina. She sort of smiled down at me, perhaps her way of saying 'yes dear,' whilst realising that the oil splattered old wreck was about to take up a good chunk of space in their own farm's workshop. On the other hand, Mister George looked chuffed with the negotiation as he proudly threw his leg over the old bike, started her up, after a few attempts, and promptly rode that heap outta my yard for good.

However, my celebrations hadn't lasted long. Just a few days later, The Suit was out there measuring up, making calculations, and making rough sketched plans for some type of construction. He was also talking lots of bike-related stuff to himself, and then later with Ms Noodle, and then with another chap who came armed with his own tape measure, clipboard, and a large all-business looking calculator. At that point, I really hadn't a clue what was goin' on. But a week or so later, all sorts of crap started to happen out there.

~ ~ ~ ~

There comes a time in the life of every busy working professional when one needs to do something just for oneself. For me it was the acquisition of a decent, reliable, new set of wheels. I'd always had pre-owned crappy old motorbikes ever since my first Suzuki single-cylinder two-stroke 'B-120' that was dated to 1977. Whilst each machine was a perceivable upgrade on the last, most sported mechanical issues such as starting problems, oil leaks, electrical malfunctions and the like. But, finally, my time had come… a new set of wheels were to be on the horizon.

However, first, some bigtime changes had to be undertaken in the backyard. Between the fence and the raised main part of the garden was a very wide flagged old pathway that sloped down from the back gate to the large flat open flagged area by the rear, or what was, of course, originally the front, of the cottages. First off, the wood store and coal shed I'd previously constructed out of pallets was brutally halved in size with a chainsaw in order to free up some badly needed space. Then I removed an area of thick century-old paving slabs and dug down about a spade's depth, before adding a load of rubble.

The next weekend saw delivery of a cubic metre and a half of building grade concrete that arrived in one of those big ready-mix trucks. After persuading the driver to hang around for almost an hour, together with a semi-willing work colleague who came over, we managed to wheelbarrow the concrete direct from the truck's delivery chute, as it was parked on the back lane, up the path behind the other cottages, and through the garden gate to our place. Then it was a precarious 'hold on tight' roll down the slope before being unceremoniously unloaded and then hastily rearranged and smoothed over. Exhausting work, said venture was probably equivalent to my weekend exercise for one month, but in just about one hour we had a very solid and secure base for a new custom-made bike shed. That was something special too, with its design including an extra-strong reinforced floor, various security considerations such as a wide yet shallow secure window that permitted a minimal but useful level of daylight to enter, steel bars on the inside of the door, and a steel anchor point sunk into the concrete which was subsequently used to chain up the bike. All in all, it was certainly fit for purpose and pretty much ready for its new occupant some four weeks after the initial clearing works had commenced.

Penny and I had been on the lookout for a genuine used American thoroughbred, but at the time, and probably always has been and always will be, we found the prices to be pretty astronomical, even second-hand, especially as we were after a full-sized model – we really didn't fancy touring around two-up on the much smaller range, genuine or otherwise. The other issue was that the older models were prone to needing a fair amount of mechanical TLC, and whilst keen on the polishing bit, I have always been pretty lacking on what you might term 'real mechanics,' if truth be told.

However, numerous Japanese offerings were by then flooding the 'cruiser' bike market, and so it seemed the sensible option all round given our somewhat limited pocket and my lack of mechanical prowess. We were then on the lookout for a modern-day cruiser that possessed much of the style and comfort we sought in the American original, yet combined with proven Japanese mechanical reliability, high performance brakes fitted as standard, and all at a price that our wallet could withstand without going down the road of additional indebtedness.

So, a few weeks later, we ended up, for the first time in my life, with an order having been placed for a brand new vehicle, complete with a few additional security features – yikes. However, one issue was that it came with a rather boring lack of rumble from its factory-fitted EU-compliant pipes which made the big V-Twin power plant sound more like a small nondescript car driving around a Tesco's car park than the brute of a machine it was born to be. Hmm, time for some aftermarket upgrades even before it left the shop.

The hard factory-fitted saddles were soon exchanged for a large, tractor-style very comfy handmade front and rear saddle set imported from the States, adorned with rather fetching studs and leather tassels. Other additions were twin spots and day-running lamps, a chrome registration plate holder, large rear footplates to replace the standard factory-fitted foot pegs for Penny's additional comfort, discreet but effective engine crash bars which I hoped would never be tested, a fancy padded leather and chrome sissy bar, a decent set of horns, and even a small cruiser-style fly screen that enabled riding at respectable speeds on the open road without fear of being unseated due to sheer wind resistance, considering the riding posture of the cruiser-styled machine.

The pièce de résistance, however, were the replacement pipes. Whilst there was no need to replace the factory-fitted downpipes, manifold or collector box, the boringly tame, noise-compressing big fat twin silencers were replaced by short turnout pipes that were miniscule in comparison to the originals. Almost totally devoid of the usual internal baffling, the 30 centimetre little pipes really did the job in terms of decibel increase and a tone more befitting the machine. Seemed pretty good to me, even if not in the eyes of the Law. The bike had instantly been transformed to sound like a bloody drag racer! It was Loud, and yes, the capitalised 'L' was completely intentional and warranted. With fuel jets adjusted accordingly, the total package was a noisy, fat beastie that was as road-ready as could be.

The final touch... a lasting and befitting moniker. Penny decided that bit. As always, the feminine touch added a bit of class to proceedings. She, the bike, for they are always she in my experience, was subsequently named Norma-Jean, after the infamous Marilyn. Innocently, I asked Penny for her reasoning... 'Pretty obvious... She's a curvy hot babe with two large bits up front,' although I was never quite sure if that referred to the twin spotlights or the V-twin cylinders.

Riding 'Norma-Jean' slowly and cautiously that first time around the back of the cottages was quite a challenge. My God those tiny pipes packed some punch, reverberating through the ground, walls and right into the soul. Loved it!

Somewhat bizarrely, Taz showed an immediate and positive towards Norma-Jean. The half-glassed stable-style back door of the annexe afforded him a basic view of proceedings when stood upon his hind legs, plus a little stretch up. Once the back gate was securely shut, I left Norma-Jean ticking over at a very slow rumble, and opened the back door... Taz slowly ventured out – distinct progress after his naked hatred of the old black bike; which, by the way, was going great guns after George had taken it on and put in the much-needed mechanical hours to make the old beast fly once again. Taz walked slowly up to and then circled the new machine, doing his canine black panther bit. Gone were his usual signals of distrust and guardedness. His ears and tail remained in their usual places. He appeared quite interested, even seemingly accepting her on an equal footing as a welcome addition to the family. However, we could not come up with any plausible explanation for this strange and unexpected behaviour. Was it the sheer size, the two-tone olive green of the large fuel tank she sported, the copious amounts of chrome, or just the noise?

As the days went into weeks, and the weeks became months, Taz and Norma-Jean seemingly formed a strange kind of kindred bond. Sometimes he would dash out there to just sit by the shed door, waiting or barking for a response.

'Hey, Norma-Jean, you coming out to play then girl?' he would seemingly call out.

On dry days when she would be brought out for a full clean down and polish session, Taz would just sit there happily and gaze up at her shiny bright pipes, bells and whistles like some lovesick puppy, which in a way I suppose he was.

Taz was understandably wary at the bike's initial engine start-up, which was pretty thunderous by any definition, and particularly the required minute or so of increased engine revs needed in order to move her up the incline from the shed's doorway to the main path at the back of the garden, and thereby in line with the back gate and pathway leading through to the road. However, beyond that, he would persist in a very strange habit of walking up to one of the almost baffle-free chromed turnout exhaust pipes and take a few blasts of hot exhaust in the face as it emanated at a steady and loud 'thwump,' 'thwump,' 'thwump.' One time he undertook an examination a little too closely after the engine having just been turned off by way of flicking the red kill switch on the handlebars, only to then hear a short sizzle as his soggy snout made skin to hot metal contact for a brief, if memorable, moment.

Busy with a career that necessitated long hours away from home, and the general inclemency of the Yorkshire weather, opportunities for a ride out were never as regular as desired. Often the only opening came early on a Sunday evening, affording Norma-Jean, and me, the chance to clear some weekend cobwebs on a one or two hour leisurely Pennine back road gadabout. As a very much laid-back kinda ride, complete with matt black open-face lid and shades, it wasn't a machine fit for riding at full-pelt like some young racetrack nut anyway. Nope, riding Norma-Jean was more about having a moment of soul connection, with relaxation, and of course perhaps a smidgen of self-indulgent 'me time' thrown in for good measure.

Dogs are famed for their acute sense of hearing, particularly in the upper-range auditory spectrum. For example, we all know of those dog-whistles; small metal pipes that sound like you are just blowing air, yet they emit a high frequency sound audible only to canines, and perhaps a few other species, yet cannot be registered by the human ear. I used one with Taz, or rather attempted to, but he elected either to completely ignore the sound or its significance, or had 'selective canine deafness.' That was something I had experienced long before as a child with 'Homer,' one of a pair of twin Norfolk Terriers that belonged to the family from when I was just nine or 10 months old. Homer was famed for never having heard a single human command in his life, yet heard his food bowl move one centimetre in the kitchen cupboard from a distance of 65 metres with the wind blowing in the opposite direction.

Cruising on Norma-Jean was not exactly a quiet affair, with V-configured twin large-bore cylinders pumping away at a rich, slow pace. The sound emanating from those pipes was as distinctive as it was resonating. Once I had the opportunity and pleasure to see and hear her in action myself, when a good friend took her for a spin as I stood on the pavement to watch her go by. Only then did I truly appreciate the impressiveness of the beast that she was. Taz too seemed to appreciate her vocal grandeur, and soon came to recognise her distinctive tone, and so much so that he'd sit and wait patiently for our return; listening into the wind with his very keen canine ears.

About three miles by road from the cottage, although perhaps half a mile less as a crow would fly, was a steep hill that climbed some 150 metres straight up. Even with its significant torque, a fair amount of power was required which meant significant decibels being registered in order to facilitate a climb. Whilst unbeknown to Penny, for it was not obvious to mere humans, Taz was readily able to pick up the bike's distinctive sound. Some five or even ten minutes before I'd appear back home on Norma-Jean, Penny always swore blind Taz would spend that time upended by the gate. By that I mean he'd be snout-first under the small gap at the base of the back gate, with his hindquarters still raised, and tail beating the air in anticipation of our arrival.

He always knew, always heard or sensed it, and was always there to greet us safely back home after every ride out. Rarely was he so obvious in his friendliness towards us than after a bike ride. And as Norma-Jean's engine and metalwork would click and ting as she cooled off, he would stay resolutely by her side as she rested and recovered from her workout, such was the indescribable and somewhat strange bond that had been forged between them.

Bananas & Bath Bubbles

Back in the late seventies, I'd spend my whole weekends washing cars, cutting lawns and working in the kitchens at a private residential school in order to save up for some respectable high-fidelity equipment. Basically, I wanted to upgrade my old ITT radio cassette player that I'd previously saved for and bought for the grand sum of 43 pounds sterling when I was maybe 11, to something far more professional, a hi-fi system comprised of 'separates' with an amplifier, tuner, cassette deck, turntable, and some impressive KEF speakers that I still have to this day. I saved for almost three years to get that lot, a spotty yet proud teenage nerd.

My, haven't times changed; I remember well spending hours drooling over the latest 'What Hi-Fi' and 'Hi-Fi Choice' magazines, studying and comparing all the various technical specifications of each component item. Of course, back then we had no Internet, no computers, tablets or smartphones, it was good old-fashioned page-turning shiny printed stuff, mostly nabbed a couple of months late from the local dental surgery waiting room so as not to waste my own hard earned cash.

One particular specification that mattered pretty much above all others was each component's output sound frequency range, the most commonly used indicator in its quality assessment. The audible hearing range of the human being is said to be from about 20 Hz up to 20 kHz, although in truth that is for someone in their prime at about 18 years of age. I was a nerd back then, so such things mattered. However, I'm pretty sure that the range of my own hearing decreased significantly as a direct result of the equipment's purchase, and in particular down to a second-hand set of large powerful Bose headphones, through which I would attempt eardrum meltdown listening to Black Sabbath, Motorhead, Twisted Sister, or Deep Purple blasting out every waking moment. Of course, by the time of Taz I was well into my thirties, and so my hearing was probably pretty much shot by then – yet another sign of a misspent youth to add to the list I guess.

But when it comes to animals and dogs in particular, you have to marvel at their natural hearing abilities. From what I have read, the average pooch can only hear as low as 67 Hz (against the estimated human 20 Hz minimal level), whereas mine is now somewhere in the region of 150 Hz. As for the upper hearing register, dogs can reach a staggering 67 kHz, over three times that of human's 20 kHz maximum, and my current 13 kHz (assessed by way of the modern marvels of Internet-based audibility testing). You can therefore see why those infamous 'dog whistles' sound like you are just blowing fresh air, whilst all the dogs in the neighbourhood go absolutely nuts, except for your own dog of course, who probably totally ignores it, relegating the newly purchased whistle to that kitchen drawer where all the 'junk' accumulates.

Anyway, yes, dogs can hear amazingly well, particularly in the upper registers compared to us as mere humans. And of course our dearly beloved lump of mischievousness, known as Taz, was no exception. Unless, that is, when he heard just fine, but had simply elected to 'not hear,' having been instantly struck down with 'selective deafness.' This near fatal disease was not something that only Taz suffered from sporadically, but seemingly afflicts approximately 60% of all canines, 98% of human teenagers, and 100% of bloody cats. Felines will happily ignore every single command uttered by their respective 'master'; listening just as and when, or if, they choose to do so.

~ ~ ~ ~

Taz always amazed me how he would hear Norma-Jean, that was the name given to my dear husband's big, fat, and very loud Yamaha, even at a distance of well over a couple of miles. Additionally, his upper and mid-range hearing was pretty impressive too, if not mildly annoying. It was like having our very own 'Bat Dog,' hearing anything and everything, and so much so that it was very hard to keep anything a secret in our cottage.

Certain audible happenings were simply ignored, such as when I'd say, 'Come on then Taz, time to go back to your room now as I have to leave soon for work.'

Yeah right, as if he was gonna drag his hairy butt from his armchair without being prised off by a full-length industrial steel crowbar. Nope, such requests or instructions would remain distinctly 'unheard,' without a drop of guilt, remorse or anything even reminiscent of self-reproach on behalf of Bat Dog.

The next bracket up from the simply 'unheard' would be the 'single eyelid twitch,' whereby one eyelid would raise momentarily and ever-so slightly. This barely recognisable action indicated that a decision had been reached as to whether or not Taz would completely ignore whatever was being said to him, such as telling him he could have five more minutes outside before he had to come on in. On occasions there would be some mediocre bodily response triggered such as affecting a slow slide down from the armchair prior to meandering over to the front door upon hearing the term 'walkies.' Whilst Taz truly loved his walks, the initial response was often that of just doing us a favour, or so it seemed and had little to do with the exercise and/or fun that going for a walk with Michael actually represented.

The mid-level hearing reaction was an involuntary triggering of the 18 muscles involved in a dog's ear, causing one or both to move about like furry little antennae protruding from his head, seeking out noise sources so as to reach a 'pounce – no-pounce' decision. An example of this would be the chiming of the front doorbell. At times Taz would race across to the door, driven merely by sheer bloody nosiness to be honest, or perhaps to try and scare off potential intruders just for the absolute fun of it. Other times, the Staffie ear-mounted radar system could detect 'who' it actually was. Most often it was Parker, the policemen from next door and a regular visitor for Michael, in which case Taz would promptly return to his snoring within eight to ten seconds and ignore all subsequent going's on.

Then, of course, there was the top bracket reaction, whereby a single sound would trigger an almighty burst into action, launching said beastie into mid-air within seven nanoseconds of the sound being registered. One hears of the 'fight or flight' concept, but I have always been astonished at the sheer speed that a dog can go from apparent deep sleep to something resembling a surface-to-surface missile in less than an instant.

~ ~ ~ ~

When hoomans say that I can hear a gnat fart at 600 metres they are probably pushing it a bit I'll admit, but fuck me is my hearing good or what? I lost track of how many times I said to Ms Noodle or The Suit that so-and-so was coming to the door at least one full minute before the doorbell even rang; but, did they ever listen to me, did they ever believe me? Did they bollocks! I soon gave up that lark. Didn't seem much point in acting as their 'neighbour about to visit' advanced early warning system if they subsequently chose to ignore me and go and answer the bloody door anyway. Numpties!

But some things, well some things really are worth having super-duper hearing compared to the hoomans, such as when a mozzie is hovering around yer knackers… no way I want one of those suckers jabbing his arse-mounted stinger into my crown jewels, not if I have any say in the matter! That's where doggie hearing really does come in handy. I would watch the little fucker upon his initial approach run, then snap my jaws and chew him right up, although they did taste pretty shit to be honest. Worst case, he'd get a serious migraine after a very narrow miss from 42 slightly yellowing but rather sharp and angry teeth. Next time matey, next time, I would say.

Other things I could hear included the slightest creak of the hoomans bed at five in the morning, which was when The Suit mostly got his arse up. That was my signal to get my own butt in gear and go grab the lead for the morning walkies that started the agenda each day.

The fridge door was another good example, especially as such an action was always connected with food, and thereby highly significant to the life of any dog. So, even if the fridge opener had no intention of feeding me, I would still go over to the kitchen doorway pretty sharpish and do one of my 'I'm ever so sad,' 'desperately underfed,' and 'abandoned in the gutter lost puppy' looks in the vain hope of charming my way into procuring that extra bit of scoff.

Oh, and then there was the bath being ran. Mostly an evening occurrence, but also sometimes on a cold winter's Sunday afternoon, Ms Noodle would jump into a hot bath upstairs and relax in a pile of foamy shit for a good hour, or more, with music and smelly candles added for good measure. For me, the call to action occurred the moment the taps were turned off — coz that meant Ms Noodle was then 'in the bath,' the temperature was near enough spot-on and therefore it was time for my grand entrance. I'd belt up the stairs two at a time and run straight down the narrow hallway and head-butt the bathroom door wide open. There she'd be, having already half disappeared in the fluff… Ms Noodle would then say words like, 'C'mon then, bite the bubbles,' or something similar, which is precisely what I would do, chomp, chomp, bloody chomp. Okay, so they tasted a bit weird, but they registered well up there on my 'having fun scale.' I'd hang my front paws over the side of the bath and just go for it. Occasionally there'd be an 'Ouch, ya daft bugger!' if I accidentally latched on to one of Ms Noodle's bare knees if not fully submerged in the hot soapy water. But other than that, a fun time was had by all — well, by me at least. And 100% worth dragging my butt off the armchair for a bit.

But if it ever came to a hearing contest, then I'd wager The Suit's monthly earnings any day on my winning it hands down. My bed, situated as it was then by the wall heater thingy in the annex, must have been some 12 metres from the fridge, based on an estimated walking distance from my pit through the lounge and into the kitchen-diner and then all the way across to the fridge. However, above the fridge was a virtual pot of gold… a china bowl that was nearly always full of yummy fruit. Now, although partial to a spot of veggies, the same could also be said for fruit, and one in particular... bananas!

When Ms Noodle and The Suit had social visitations that were struggling, they used to consider dragging this one out as a party trick to liven things up. First, they'd make sure I was in my old room, lying there asleep on the mattressy thing; usually upside down, legs akimbo, and dreaming of stuff perhaps best not shared. Next, they would each place small bets as to the number of seconds between the 'act' and my 'appearance' in the kitchen doorway. One Sunday in mid-December, some weird visitors turned up at the cottage, named Bryony and Derek, apparently. They were husband and wife workmates of Ms Noodle, and had come to visit 'for a coffee.' They must have kept running out at their house as, although they lived close to a few shops, they seemed to run out pretty regularly and then come and drink ours instead. Hoomans.

So, unbeknown to me, bets had been placed. Unbeknown indeed, for at the time I was on my back snoring like a freight train and dreaming of getting off with a certain fluffy poodle. But I digress... The Suit had selected a particular banana to which they'd all agreed upon. The stopwatch function on Ms Noodle's laptop thingy was open and ready, finger poised. Now, I had heard you should in fact peel bananas from the base, not the stem, and that way you don't have to deal with those stingy bits. However, for this lark they'd always start by 'snapping' the stem as it made significantly more noise and was also instantly recognisable. And that they did, and simultaneously the stopwatch was started.

'Snap,' would go the banana stem.

Mid-dream my ears immediately pricked up at the sound.

'Yes, that's... a banana stem snap!' I'd shout within my head.

Alert. Alert. Alert!

Action stations. Action stations!

My body went into emergency 'flight or scoff' mode, and my legs launched my still half-sleepy arse out of bed at an off-the-blocks pace that would be the pride of any Olympic sprint athlete. Across the carpeted floor of the lounge I would shoot, doing a kind of twist of the neck, shoulders and hip in order to ensure I didn't wipe out totally against the sofa or the armchair as I charged on by. And bang, there I would be, brakes jammed full on as I skidded to a semi-controlled halt right in the kitchen doorway, drooling like a schoolboy hanging over the girls changing room wall... Oh, and all in a rather impressive three point four seconds too by the way. Speed mattered, and Derek had suddenly become that little bit richer as he scooped up his winnings. As for me, well for my part in their 'game,' I was allowed to scoff half of that lovely banana as my prize.

Food and the entertainment of my hoomans were the endless spice of cottage life.

~ ~ ~ ~ ~ ~ ~ ~ ~

PART III

Livin' the Life of an Adolescent

Timmy the Todger

'It's gonna be another good'un I reckon,' I whispered to myself.

I had my soggy little hooter pressed up against the glass, balancing precariously with front paws on the polished hardwood window shelf, nicely dodging the array of stupid 'ornament things,' of course, and my rear paw set firmly planted on the tall back of my comfy old armchair.

Summer sun was a good thing, I had always known that, but since movin' into the cottage with The Suit and Ms Noodle, it had brought on a whole new meaning to my life. Back in my 'adolescent days,' which Ms Noodle said probably stretched back to just after my puphood, although not sure what she meant by that, I was just a caged mutt who got paid cash for the occasional shag. But, I never saw any of the dough, coz it was unjustly stuffed into Guy's back pocket, and then immediately squandered by his rather gross old misses.

It wasn't a nine-to-five kinda job either, nor was it as regular as I would perhaps have liked, but a job of sorts it was. About every six weeks or so Guy would arrange a 'meet,' having been contacted by the owners of some girlie Staffie for a discreet ten-minute hook-up, for us dogs, not the hoomans I should add. For some reason, my lineage, my bloodline, had become something others wanted a bit of – fine by me I reckoned, bring it on. Still, it seemed an odd arrangement, and whilst I saw fuck all in the way of financial benefit, the job did have its obvious perks for Timmy the Todger, as I liked to refer to my playful pecker.

I generally knew when a 'date' was coming up as I was fed shitloads of halfway decent grub for four or five days beforehand, and then hosed down and sprayed with some pongy shit that was obviously meant to make me as irresistible as a cash-rich Premier League footballer out on the razzle in Ibiza Town. Basically, I think the idea was to make whatever honey they'd lined up for me swoon at the britches within four seconds of spottin' my chunky lumps. Whatever, it wasn't so bad for me and Timmy at least, and way better than the early days when it was more of a meat factory, with larger-scaled 'events' taking place down dimly lit country lanes in what were normally disused barns. There you'd find 20-plus beefy blokes gather to show off their respective canines to what turned out to be a steady line of pimps, I'd guess you'd call them, who'd just come looking for some suitable 'mate' for whoever they were representing. Dodgy days indeed, and real glad it was in the past.

But, for those one-on-one meetings, if you'll excuse the pun, things were much more civilised. Never one for the small talk with the girlies, upon arrival I'd usually walk over, all nonchalant like, take in a casual sniff, as one does, and then with a sigh, get straight down to business and do my doggie deed. Now, whilst I'd heard hoomans might consider 'doggie style' to be something rather risqué, for me it was of course just as Mamma Nature intended. Guy always seemed pleased with me at first, but that was generally short-lived as he was a grumpy old fart, although probably understandable considering the domineering old hag he'd shacked up with. She hated my guts, and I hers, no argument there... and there was physically plenty of her to dislike too. Urgghh, the thought of her still makes me shudder. Not a patch on Ms Noodle, my next hooman misses was a real pink poodle by comparison.

So that was my job back then. Yeah, it wasn't much, but a shag's a shag, innit? Thankfully, the fillies which I, or rather Guy, was being paid to hump... I meant that he got to keep the wad of notes, not me, and not that he, err... well, ya get my drift.

The Suit and Ms Noodle were far more civilised hoomans than Guy and his weird old misses. So when they too procured me a few sessions in return for some serious spondulix, I was initially somewhat surprised at again being touted as 'doggie dick for a dollar.' But it was a wholly different affair. Sure, I had the same old tricks to perform, obviously, but the event and even the 'prep' was way better.

Ms Noodle would pop her head around the door at brekky time on 'the day,' and say, 'Hey, just wanted to wish you the "best of luck" today' or 'I hope she's a pretty one,' followed by a giggle, but wearing that concerned mamma look of hers.

She also made sure that I was properly shampooed the night before, ya know, made to look AND smell my best; well, according to Ms Noodle at least. It was all part of the show I guess. The surroundings were always much more tasteful too, as we'd always go visit the girlie's house – all very civilised, it was.

Mostly the visits went off really well, if you know what I mean – wink, wink… but on one occasion the young lady in question really wasn't having any of it, literally too. Of course, The Suit and Mister Girlie Owner Dude were trying every trick in the book – I thought they might break out the Lionel Ritchie at one point. Thank fuck that never happened. Just imagine the embarrassment if that had got out? Still, it was a far cry from my early amateur stud life with Guy the git. On balance, The Suit and Ms Noodle certainly seemed to care more about me and less about filling their wallet by way of renting out my bits.

So, yeah, for much of my growed-up life, Timmy the Todger was a constant source of delight to others, be it financial or otherwise. Me, I didn't think a great deal about the little furry fella. He's just my todger, always there, end of, right? All I had to do was to keep him and the rest of me in trim for the girlies.

~ ~ ~ ~

Our cottage garden was a place of peace and tranquillity. Well, so went the theory, and most of the time it probably lived up to it. I mean, it wasn't particularly overlooked, that is, unless you counted the neighbour's cat who'd lay there straddling the wooden fence just to wind Taz up. Or perhaps the crows who'd look down from their perches in the big trees, or from kids who'd spend their summer evenings chatting and playing noisily at the village cenotaph, one of the only points occupying a higher elevation than us… But yes, apart from all that, it was pretty much a secluded and private garden.

It was also afforded a basic level of protection from the elements, which was a godsend for a cottage perched on top of a windy old hill. On one side of the garden was a fence, one of those six-foot affairs with larch lap panels slotted in-between concrete posts we had put in just after acquiring the place. It was functional rather than aesthetically pleasing, but a few trailing roses soon hid its blandness within a couple of short years. At the back or rather top of the garden was a traditional drystone wall that probably dated back over a century, and with parts which might have even been from the mid-1700s when the cottages were first built. The great advantage was that the garden and cottage were situated well-below wall level, and therefore acted as one heck of a solid and effective windbreak. And finally, on the other side of the garden was another stone wall, but that was largely hidden by a line of established fir trees blocking out pretty much all wind and rain, as well as any prying eyes.

Private it was, but tranquil, hmm, not always. That'd be down to me though. Penny wasn't much of an advocate of a noisy life, so rarely would she be the source of anything approaching the tag of a nuisance neighbour. That accolade was usually levelled at yours truly, albeit on a rarity of occasions I hoped. Okay, so I might have tuned the small radio in the workshop to the local retro-rock station on a Sunday morning if I was out there, but it was never what one could have referred to as loud, and it was never on for very long either. No, my misdemeanour went by the nametag of Norma-Jean, the aforementioned big V-Twin, with her rather notable short pipes devoid of much of the legally required internal baffling, and thereby rattled the windows of houses up and down the street when fired up.

I was no grease monkey though. Whilst I would dutifully put in the hours polishing the chrome to a high shine, and then of course take her out for a spin as often as time, and weather, permitted, I wasn't one to tinker with the engine for hours on end, so on the noise front it wasn't all that bad really. Trouble was, the purpose-built security shed and the back gate which led to a narrow path to the road were not remotely in line, and thereby necessitated a short uphill, five-point manoeuvre that was largely restricted to the hours of accepted civility, else it could just piss off our rather nice neighbours, one of whom was a very accommodating traffic cop, and so I never wanted to push my luck, not on home turf.

As for Taz, he mostly had the garden to himself for much of the year. Penny would busy herself with gardening in the spring and autumn, and then sunbathe during the summer months, and me, I'd take on the odd spot of gardening too, but also had a never-ending list of chores. These included clearing out the shallow lead-lined stone gutters balanced high up on the extended ladders, chopping and stacking firewood for the winter months, or humping dirty great sacks of anthracite that were also kept outside in the store that had been reduced in size to accommodate the bike shed, but was still fit for purpose and well used.

So, yes, the back garden generally belonged to Taz, and the little shit knew it. Sure, he was a decent enough pooch, mostly, but he was also an adolescent at heart his entire life, and a hormonal one at that, so, more often than not he could be described as no less than, well, a hairy little shit.

A solitary cherry tree formed the focal point of the back garden. It was situated nearer to the back wall than the sitting area, and on a slight hill offering a direct view right into the cottage and to the hills beyond if one's line of sight aligned the windows front and back. The cherry tree was also visible from the cottage windows at the back, and my guess was Taz knew that too. It was one of his favoured places to hang out, long summer days in particular, when his sole purpose in life was to top up his man-dog-tan. He may have been canine by specie, but nurture had seemingly won over nature…

Blame, if any, could therefore be placed at Penny's manicured feet. I mean, I don't know, is sunbathing considered to be otherwise 'normal' for Staffie's?

~ ~ ~ ~

Now, like any self-respecting stud-bucket, I soon realised girlies liked nothing better than the trifecta of manly attributes: those being; a) a set of rippling muscles, b) a good hairstyle, and c) a real tan not a fake tan.

Okay, so muscles weren't really an issue, them being pretty much part and parcel of the Staffie package. Upright, tall and with ripped with muscles perhaps I was not, and never would be; but short, stocky, and eminently loveable, ha, that I was — apparently, or so the neighbour's Labrador used to whisper whenever our exercise times coincided. Hairstyle, yeah right, you ever seen a groomed Staffie with a quiff? Nah, short and bristly and mostly a natural brindle colour. Nothing fancy. Didn't need it to be honest.

But keeping a healthy tan for the girlies, now that WAS something else. The undercarriage housing my prodigious tackle for hire was dark pink by nature, dappled with a few brownish patches I assumed were some genetic referencing point, or perhaps it was just engrained dirt which had been there so long that Mamma Nature just let it be. And just like you hoomans, said pink bits tended to brown off like an old turd when exposed at length to the sun's summer rays. And that's just what I did, on a regular basis I might add, subject to meteorological limitations of Yorkshire life — not somewhere famed for a climate like where the hoomans venture off to on their jollies.

In the back garden of the cottage was a solitary tree, which would sprout a shitload of pink flowers for a couple of weeks to mark the end of each winter. It was a cherry tree, apparently, yet I never saw any bloody cherries on it. Go figure. But anyways, said tree did have one unique feature that I tried my best to utilise fully to my advantage, and that was its position. It was near the top of a small hill and positioned just right to grab as many hours of sunlight as anywhere, so, for the sakes of the ladies you understand, it soon became my sunbathing location of choice.

One more check out the window, okay, okay, now was good, now was the time... I rushed over to nudge Ms Noodle's arm, and did my 'need a wee, need a wee' kinda urgent little dance. She knew the drill, and was soon heading to open the back door. Indeed, the sun was up and its first rays were about warm the grass by the cherry tree. Up the steps I raced, hotpawed quickly across the lawn stopping just before the tree, spun my butt around and firmly plonked it in front of the tree. I then slowly leant back against the trunk until my front paws lifted slightly off the ground, and there I stayed...

After maybe an hour I could feel the sun moving off centre, meaning my pink bits had moved beyond the direct glare of the sun. With Timmy acting as a sundial, it was obviously shuffle time. Gently I lowered myself back down until my paws came back into contact with the grass. I then butt-shuffled clockwise by 12 degrees, rechecked Timmy in terms of the sunlight tackle-warming effect, and leaned back against the tree, relaxing into the game once more.

Time for some more rays...

This process was repeated every hour or so for the rest of the day, and the next, and the next. By midweek it was safe to say that Timmy and the surrounding nether region had once again returned to the colour of a chocolate brownie. Timmy the Todger was beautifully tanned, back on point and ready for the ladies.

Scoffin' Granny's Dog

'We're gonna go stay with Granny this weekend,' they said. 'It'll be fun!' they said.

'As if!' I said.

'You'll enjoy it!' they said.

'Fuck off!' I said.

It was obviously a stupid idea. I mean, just why the heck would I want to go 'stay' down there? You see, Granny Suit was banging on about us 'doin' a visit' – all of us, even me!

I know the old gal was always pretty sweet on me when she came to stay up at ours, but as for us traipsing all the way down there, voluntarily leaving the comfort of my own bed. Were they serious? Couldn't get my head around such a plan, not for love nor meaty biscuits; which I hasten to add were absolutely fab, but played havoc with my rear-ended vocals.

And another thing, I'd heard it was about a billion hours to get there in the car – hah, well my sentiment was they could go screw themselves around the back of Tesco's carpark for all I cared. I mean, had they really thought I'd play ball with such a daft-as-fuck plan? Well, that's what I said to them through gritted gnashers, but alas, I guess they hadn't understood me or simply chosen to ignore me altogether as plans for said visit marched on regardless of my arsiness on said matter.

So, you guessed it. Hoomans two, me zero on that one. It was always two against one from the start, so fat chance I stood really. Brilliant. Yay... another useless road trip. To say I was displeased was an understatement. I even considered scoffin' one of Ms Noodle's dodgy chocolate cakes in the vain hope of getting a serious case of the squits, and thereby forcing an emergency rethink on the grounds of medical emergency, of the stinky kind at least. After all, they surely wouldn't be that brave or stupid to still have wanted me in the back of the car with an exceptionally dodgy bum, now would they?

I checked. 'Fuck it!' No cake left in the tin.

The next three days passed very s-l-o-w-l-y… Plans were arranged, I heard that much at least as The Suit gassed to the old girl on the phone for some 20 minutes, or 19 minutes longer than usual. It looked as if it was being planned as a soddin' full State Visit too. I mean, weren't we just driving there, doing shit and then driving back? What the heck they had to 'plan' was beyond me?

By then, The Suit and Ms Noodle had at least binned the bright blue hairdresser's vehicle. Now, don't get me wrong, from what I could gather the Japanese made some pretty mean machines of the two-wheeled variety, but that pretend baby-Jeep-like-thing? C'mon, seriously? Yeah, it was quick enough and even sounded fairly meaty on start-up, but it was still pretty much a fuckin' kids-sized shoebox on wheels, to be frank. Put it this way, if we had had a cat, and there was fat chance of that coz I'd just try and eat it, then we'd have been unable to 'swing it' within the confines of said vehicle. But by the time this monster trip 'down South' came about, we'd at least upgraded for something resembling a decent-sized vehicle. Sadly, even with the open expanse of a real Jeep, I hadn't seen hide nor hair of any cat to 'play with' let alone to attempt the swing test.

The trip had originally been planned one year previous, and thereby not long after my cottage investiture. Back then I would have been shoved in the so-called 'luggage area' of the little pretend 4x4. Well, they test-tried me, but nope, far too damned small – the car, not me. Ha ha fuckers, their dodgy plan was kyboshed at Stage One! It was great for the shops or for walkies outside of the village, and certainly a bonus for gallivanting about in the snow, but apart from standing there facing width-ways across the car, there was sod-all room, even for little(ish) old me.

There had followed an ensuing period of urgent rethinking by the hoomans, with one idea tested out that part of the rear seats could have been tilted forwards in order to give my arse a fighting chance of being seen by my own face during the planned long and arduous trek from the north to the south of Old Blighty. Of course, that would have meant being 'free to roam' at will, so next they tried in vain to suss out ways of rearranging luggage and other shit on the other back seat in order to block my being able to get too close to the front. But that was a clear failure too. I would still have been within 'dog tongue shoved in earhole' proximity, even with all their devious planning. In the end, said vehicular limitations put the brakes firmly on that trip — obviously not brave or stupid enough to risk some 18 hours of continual shoulder- and ear-based dog-slobbering.

However, with the real Jeep, all my 'car too small' excuses went right out the window, hence the trip was slapped back on the calendar.

Friday night came around all too soon, and the Jeep was all packed up, and parked on the driveway ready for some ungodly predawn mission launch hour. The hoomans grabbed a few hours kip whilst I admittedly fretted a little bit over the whole shebang. Rumour had it, on good authority too, Ms Noodle herself in fact, that we would drive for some eight or so hours… Eight or nine bloody hours stuck in the car… and then, ha, just listen to this bit, we would 'arrive at Granny's and I'd get to "meet" and to "play" with her dog.'

'Woah, slow down!' I exclaimed, 'Did you say dog?'

Then, not only did they want me to 'play' with some strange southern dog, but also the alleged plans were that we could 'sleep together'… For fuck's sake, what kind of dog did they think I was? Sleeping together, and on a first date? Didn't she know I had retired from all that? Oh and get this, the little bitch was named 'Pissy'! Or perhaps it was 'Prissy'? Whatever the heck it was, the whole plan had me worried. 'Oh crap,' I just knew it was gonna be a long, tiresome, and weird weekend away from my comfy norm.

Early hours the next morning arrived way too soon. I was escorted to the back garden first of all, and had my backend unceremoniously squeezed by The Suit so as to ensure I was running on empty. Charming. Why the heck would they have thought I might crap in the car when I would have been the one sat there with 'it'? Doh!

My efforts to cancel, forestall and otherwise disrupt proceedings had amounted to a big fat zero – as, no sooner had we returned back indoors, I found myself being bundled straight into the Jeep and with that we were on our way. Ms Noodle and The Suit took turns driving, first it was west across the Pennines on the M62 motorway before turning due south just before Manchester onto the M6, then the M5 etc. I remember sitting there nervously thinking ahead to meeting Pissy, or whatever the bloody hell Granny Suit had named her.

~ ~ ~ ~

'Please bring Taz with you,' she said.

'They'll get on just fine,' she said.

'Maybe they'll be the best of friends,' she said.

As mum's go, she's as good as they get, but the naivety of the plan that was hatched… Well, I guess I should have listened to my inner self, as it had disaster written all over it from the outset. But, had I listened? No…, not to myself, nor to Penny' clear misgivings, and certainly not to Taz either, whose antics leading up to the trip and the subsequent arrival couldn't have been more plain – he had not (!) wanted to be part of such an adventure, either that year or the one before.

The journey was long and largely uneventful. However, we made plenty of stops in order that Taz could stretch his legs, have a wee, and generally do his various disgusting 'dog things' deemed compulsory for any self-respecting hound on an adventure away from home. In addition, our lungs needed the appropriate time each and every hour to redress the oxygen to fart balance, due to Taz's trumpet solo that had gone on ever since leaving the village. I think with him it was just some automated response; any trip, any direction, any duration. He really was a smelly little git at times.

One memory of the drive down there stood out, and took place at one of our 'nature stops,' at the Gordano Motorway Services just south of Bristol on the M5. We were waiting for the four-legged friend to do his business on a grassy patch around the back of the shopping area, when we came across an old soft-top MGB GT, a classic among British sports cars of yesteryear. Although the calendar considered it to be early summer, in reality it wasn't that warm still, and certainly not at half-eight in the morning, following a very early start.

The car's soft-top was up and all stoppered in place. It appeared to all intents and purposes as an unoccupied staff member's vehicle, parked up whilst busy slaving away to pay their monthly rent. Well, to some extent that statement possessed an element of truth. It was a staff member's, and yes, he was busy inside... the car. The second I started to walk Taz by the front window it clicked. Unfortunately, the occupants had also noticed us at the very same moment... Down went the driver's side window, and a torrent of abuse was hurled forthwith in our general direction. First, the male was questioning the marital status of the moment of my conception, and then he was offering to 'tear me a new one.' How charming modern Britain had become, I thought as we calmly changed direction and veered immediately away from the car and hopefully earshot of the half-naked screaming lunatic.

Taz, however, was most disgruntled at being spoken to in such a manner, with 'Level 5 Twat' obviously having registered on his built-in 'Idiot Radar.' Normally a fairly placid dog, when it came to humans at least, he obviously took an instant dislike to the angry little person at the end of the voice. He leapt straight at the recently opened window space with a fierce growl and full baring of teeth as he vented his displeasure at the sheer existence of the 'gentleman' in the car. But whilst Taz was plentiful in his verbal muster, thankfully the short leather leash caught him mid-flight like in some Tom and Jerry cartoon scene which ended with him crashing back down to earth without being able to inflict damage to the little sportster's aging paintwork. A bit of a close call perhaps… but it did have the desired effect as the bloke, who still had his ankles warmed by his undershorts, was suddenly much less vocal.

'Okay, okay, sorry,' he said begrudgingly, 'for fuck's sake!'

And with that, we just wandered off with feint smirks across both our faces. All the other roadside pee-stops seemed to be somewhat mundane and uneventful by comparison.

After a lengthy drive down much of the western half of England, we arrived on the outskirts of Barnstable, a sizeable town in North Devon – considered way, way down south to anyone from the North. Following on from his truck stop heroics, Taz was seemingly back on an even keel, having retreated to his more usual 'couldn't give a shit' modus operandi. Arrangements had been made beforehand that we'd arrive around 11 o'clock on the Saturday morning. Of course, this was in a pre-mobile world, so stopping at a good old British red payphone box and dropping a few coins into the machine was the only way to make contact back then.

In hindsight, arranging a meeting of two diametrically opposed breeds of dog was perhaps fairly blindingly obvious as being nothing other than a proverbial can of worms, but noooo, 'It'll be fine' was all we were told on the phone, again and again. Ha ha, yeah right. Having (sort of) convinced my mother, hereafter known as Granny, coz everyone referred to her simply as Granny, that meeting up at their bungalow was perhaps inadvisable at best, the 'final approved plan' was to meet at a carpark up on the hills where said pooches could 'stretch their legs together' out in the open.

Like all plans, some are perceived idealism at best. This fact was clearly about to be established that day as, contrary to the approved plans, reality, it transpired, was about to play no part whatsoever in its execution.

Transporting a mobile fart machine had made it one heck of a long journey. The blowers had remained at full blast and windows partially open to a level that balanced necessary oxygen replacement to sustain life with the road noise and cold motorway air that blasted in. Between the lack of in-car comfort and sheer journey length, considering all the compulsory 'pee 'n' poo' stops along the way, for Taz, not us I might just add, we arrived in a state of basically relieved irritation – hardly relaxed and all happy-clappy, ready to jump out and wrap arms and paws around our extended familia.

~ ~ ~ ~

'Michael, Michael, Michael… What have you gone and done?' That was a question that went through my head a few times within minutes of our arrival.

We had pulled into the gravel carpark sometime late morning, just a bit but not overly late. Politely late, as my own mother used to say. The weather was relatively clear, but a bit blustery, so in general no problem considering clear weather was not always a given for that part of Somerset, or for any other part of the British Isles come to think of it, with rain or other forms of precipitation much the accepted 'norm.' Thankfully, that day was at least dry, if a little cool and windswept. Granny was resplendent in her rural walking garb, dressed from head to toe in a mix of 12 different shades of brown and natural tones of green. All very 'West Country.' We, of course, were in smartish jeans and shirts that were suited to a weekend away with the in-laws. Whilst not 'matching,' we were at least complementary in terms of colour and style, avoiding all the cardinal sins of the well-dressed. Overall it wasn't a bad result, even with a husband who considered fashion sense an optional extra, a box rarely ticked obviously, if ever.

The back of her nice clean Volvo estate was fitted out with a professional level of steel caging more suited to some zoological park safely transporting a pair of black bears. In reality, it was just the temporary home for one rather small and rather pampered pooch that went by The Kennel Club name of 'Prissy of Somewhere or Other.'

As the small dog it held and I eyed each other up, Taz let out the strangest of noises. Most probably it was an incredulous, 'What the heck is that?' or so was my guess.

Granny, by that point, had walked over and the usual raft of hugs and polite greetings were exchanged to mark the occasion of our state visit.

Looking at Michael, who was standing next to our dirt-covered Jeep, she rhetorically asked, 'Okay then, shall we introduce the little ones?' whilst headed straight for the handle to open up the back of her car.

It was all a bit overoptimistic in my opinion. I wasn't sure if she was genuinely excited, a tad nervous, or just cold from having waited around for 20 odd minutes after we got ourselves lost twice between the phone call and us finding the right car park.

'Why don't we keep them both on their leads, just for a short time,' I suggested.

My idea seemingly fell upon closed ears, and was met with a firm shaking of the head and a staunch reply.

'No no. No need. This is a big enough area,' she said, 'we come here all the time. I know she's fine here, and of course young Taz will be too.'

Michael, the wimp, stayed noticeably silent on the matter, having said his piece a few times. In hindsight, we had both given in with far too much ease. Whilst Granny had known Taz for a fair while, to be honest, it was only ever when visiting us at the cottage, in what was after all his home territory. The visit to the South was our first as a team, and a whole new ballgame for Taz compared to playing games in front of the wood burner back at the cottage.

And so the tailgate was duly opened, immediately reaching to its full 90 degrees with just a gentle hiss from two large gas and oil dampers bolted to the heavy Swedish steel. The canine-transportation cage was a six-sided cuboid affair, and therefore a 'cage door' had also needed to be opened so as to release Prissy, all three kilos of her at best.

Less than a minute later and Michael had opened the tailgate of our own, much dirtier and less salubrious vehicle. Our 'whoosh' wasn't bad, but not exactly impressive. The interior of our old Jeep was also cageless. A dog-guard had been self-installed, but it did the job, safely containing our canine cargo away from the driver's area. So, with no inner cage to unbolt, Taz was out and about the moment the tailgate had swung up... and then there was no turning back.

Prissy was a scruffy little thing, but of course in a rather well-groomed way that the Kennel Club had long since deemed appropriate for the discerning Border Terrier. Ours, on the other hand, was just a large mutt, complete with questionable personal habits that remained legendary long after his time. Prissy initially jumped around with obvious overexcitement. She was girlie, pink and naïve beyond measure – probably thinking something along the lines of 'Yay, another little doggie to play with. Happy, happy, happy!'

Taz waltzed over all nonchalantly like, notably putting on his most impressive tough guy, teenage swagger. I was pretty sure his fluffy bits had been inflated especially for the occasion based on their sheer size, or so it seemed, or perhaps it was the canine equivalent of adolescent young men puffing out their respective chests as they sized each other up, or when trying to impress some shapely young filly passing by on the beach during the summer.

Recklessly, Prissy then decided to make the first move. She jumped up and down on the spot whilst emitting a rather irritating howl-growl sound. However, nonsensically, she'd let rip right smack at Taz's ear level.

Unsurprisingly, to us at least, Taz didn't perceive the act to be all that friendly or innocent, and certainly not as intended I'm sure. For Taz it was just some random canine-to-canine challenge. So, not a brilliant start to the proceedings I'll admit. To put it bluntly, the whole weekend from that point on suddenly descended from congenial family visit to 'Nightmare on Canine Street.'

Staffie's are famed for many attributes, mostly for their love of children actually, which was true enough. I recall Taz being ever so gentle and protective of a two-year-old granddaughter who visited for a week. His patience seemed endless, especially as she pulled, poked and prodded him in places a little girl really shouldn't have, but, all credit to him, he just took it all in his stride and never complained in the slightest, although I'm pretty sure his eyes were watering at one stage in the proceedings.

Other famed traits of the breed include being faithful companions to a fault, whilst also mischievous beyond measure, more akin to naughty six-year-old boys but with the added bravado of a stroppy teenager playing hooky from school. Their other claim to fame relates to their raw power, and that of their oversized jaws, set into a low, wide skull made of carbon-reinforced titanium, or so one would think based on the sheer toughness of their noggin. Whilst mostly unrelated to head-butting car bumpers or busting open cat-flaps, the episode which unfolded that day was certainly a fine, if less than shining, example of how tough and utterly stubborn Staffies can be at times.

So, picture this. Petite girlie house doggie meets ruffian bloke dog from the wrong side of town in a lonely gravel carpark. Girlie-woofer makes initial playful move, but bloke-dog typically misread the moment as a challenge. Me, well, I saw it all kicking off in very, very slow motion, yet totally unable to intervene, like being stuck on the sidelines in some dream as it happened.

All of a sudden, the two dogs became as one, but not as in any poetic dance or some kind of foreplay, just as in Taz having wrapped his gnashers around little Prissy's scrawny neck, yanking her up in mid-air with her paws dangling way above the dusty gravel. To make matters worse, Taz promptly disappeared off towards the headland, leaving us all standing there quite aghast. Prissy of course went with him; kind of no option there.

'Oh shiiiiiiitttt…!' about sums up what went through my head.

'He's… He's got my baby!' screamed Granny, 'He's bloody well taken my Prissy!'

As one only prone to using even the mildest expletive perhaps once a decade, Granny's verbal exclamation triggered the desired response – Michael bolted after Taz at what seemed a suitably impressive turn of speed. Granny, meanwhile was hollering like never heard before, or since. I guess the fact that her beloved pup had been dragged forcibly off at speed, clenched firmly in the jaws of some slob of a mutt had given her ample reason to freak out it had to be said. After all, whilst she'd known Taz a fair while, it was of course just as some placid lump parked in front of the fire, back on home turf. Thereby, her reaction was hardly a surprise I suppose.

I tried my best to fulfil the role of dutiful daughter-in-law, consoling her as best I could whilst Michael gave chase like some middle-aged wannabee cross-country athlete who had obviously failed his high school sports class in some dim and distant past.

'Stop!' I heard him holler, 'Come back here you little bastard!'

It was clear Michael struggled to keep up with Taz. Regular leisurely dog walks were one thing, but sprinting after a dog on a mission was something else, especially one half likely to scoff his mother's prized pet. Thankfully, Taz obviously wasn't that intent on making an escape, it was more that his natural instincts had kicked in and he was basically running around with no idea as to where he was heading, or indeed probably why. Michael slowly gained ground on them and within three minutes had Taz cornered, figuratively speaking, between some large gorse bushes and a rocky outcrop.

Michael appeared to be trying to reassure Taz and defuse the tension, working on the notion that further hollering would just largely piss him off, and then he'd have more than likely bolted off into the distance, resulting in Prissy's future being rather short-lived. But, of course, Taz was also like 'a dog with a bone,' and quite literally too, with a small live bag of bones that kept on writhing about and howling in fear for its life.

Taz was fairly good-natured when it came to his food, but no dog owner with half a brain would attempt to remove a bone from their dog's jaws; well, not unless they intended to offer up their own radius bone as fair exchange.

Approaching cautiously from behind, Michael managed, on the third attempt, to grab Taz's thick leather collar at the nape of his neck. The next task was to set about removing the smaller dog from the larger dog's jaws, which was a fair challenge indeed.

Quickly I ushered a distraught Granny over to where Michael had settled with the two dogs.

'Do something!' Granny kept pleading, 'You've got to *do* something son!'

Prissy was still making quite a racket, and with good reason, having the jaws of a Staffordshire Bull Terrier clamped around her pretty little neck was certainly no joke. However, from what I could see, whilst there was plenty of noise going on, there was no immediate sign of blood, or even any strange air-like sounds such as might have happened if Taz's two centimetre incisors had punctured into the smaller dog's neck.

Staffie's have enormous, wide jaws, with a set of equally impressive teeth. Moreover, they have extraordinarily strong muscles working those jaws which enables them to clamp down on prey, or a rival, and not let go, never, not for love nor money, or even a handful of cheesy biscuits. Some may have heard talk of their 'lock jaw' ability. However, as far as I know, that is factual bullpoo, it's just that they have incredibly strong jaws with a vice-like grip. So, on the occasion in question, Taz had basically clamped his jaws around poor Prissy and utterly refused to let her go, no matter how much he was cajoled, sworn at, pleaded with, or requested to cooperate.

'He's killing her!' said Granny, '*Please* help her...!' she implored her son.

She was quite fraught, worried for the life of her little house companion. Both Michael and I knew that something had to be done, but that the options were limited.

A Staffie's skull is thick, very thick, and basically solid and impervious to most objects. They can quite happily head-butt their way through and out of most situations. So, first off, Michael tried slapping him firmly on the head, nope, that didn't work, Taz didn't even blink. Then he tried knuckle punching him. Now, I'm really not into animal cruelty at all, but something had to be done to force Taz to release Prissy, and so knowing how bloody tough he was it was worth a bash.

Wham! Well, he did at least blink at that, but nothing much else – head like a pile of house bricks.

My verbal reassurance continued as I tried largely in vain to calm Granny, saying how all would be resolved soon and I was sure Prissy would be fine. Perhaps it was said more in hope than expected reality, but at that point what else could I do?

Next, Michael tried inserting one of Granny's aluminium walking poles that she used when out rambling across the hills, as one does, into the gap between Taz's molars and the back of his jaw, the front half being already occupied with Prissy of course. My job was then to help by prising open Taz's jaws as Michael held firmly on to his head, but that only resulted in Taz's big bony head wobbling from side to side like one of those stupid 'nodding dogs' seen on the back shelf of cars we always got stuck behind on the motorway. All the time Taz's eyes were fixated on us; questioning what was going on as he really hadn't been able to comprehend the situation he was in, even though it was largely of his own creation.

'Ha, did ya really think that'd work?' his eyes asked.

Meanwhile, Taz's grip remained firm, his resolve characteristically resolute. Mine too for that matter, there was no way I was gonna stand there and witness doggie manslaughter, or 'doggie death by misadventure.' Michael maintained a firm grip around Taz's collar, and noted that it seemed to give him an idea. It was something we'd tried before with another dog of ours who had attempted to have the neighbour's budgie as an afternoon snack, and also similar to the hedgehog releasing trick used on Taz in the garden back home.

Michael reverse-pulled Taz between his legs, and then clamped them firmly around Taz's belly like a vice. Taz was well and truly stuck. He turned his head and his eyes spoke of disgust, and then he muttered a few veiled threats that Michael would be next on his luncheon menu if he wasn't immediately set free. But screw that, it was one battle both of us were determined would not have Taz's name recorded in the annuls as the victor.

Okay, enough was enough. Still body-trapped by Michael, and with his collar still firmly gripped, the option to invoke what Taz would perceive as a credible 'threat to life' was launched. Michael inserted the aluminium walking pole under Taz's thick leather collar and started to twist it tight around Taz's neck. After a few seconds, Taz's snorting subsided. His eyes met with Michael's and it visibly dawned on him that Michael was indeed just as stubborn as he was.

Tighter and tighter the collar was twisted. Now, I'm not kidding in that it was almost a full two minutes before Taz's resolve was slowly replaced by the realisation it was his life that potentially hung in the balance, and not just young Prissy, who was still whimpering as the minutes and seconds marched on. Taz's body wriggled between Michael's legs with a ferocity of a small grizzly trying to be force-cuddled, but thankfully his not-so-insignificant hips and his extra-wide shoulder blades helped to ensure that he remained secure if not exactly still. Michael continued to maintain a steady grip on the walking pole that was twisting the collar… all of a sudden Taz's jaws sprung open. His collar was then partially released, but only enough to permit him to take in much needed gulps of air, but was still held on to tightly as the situation was far from being fully resolved.

Prissy immediately dropped to the ground, her coat all covered in Staffie saliva, but other than that she appeared remarkably unharmed from her ordeal. I scooped up Prissy and passed her to a much-relieved, sobbing, but grateful Granny. Meanwhile, Michael frog-marched our disgraced dog all the way back to the carpark without letting go of his collar. In fact, he was almost continually on his hind legs as he was half walked, half dragged and unceremoniously dumped back into the Jeep in order to commence a prolonged period of solitary for his shameful and criminal act.

The headland walk was understandably abandoned, and so we slowly drove off in a two-car convoy to arrive at Granny's sprawling chalet-bungalow rather much sooner than expected. The next challenge was how to separate the two dogs for the remainder of the weekend, for our sakes as much as theirs. Michael employed an airlock door system between the kitchen, where Prissy was to reside in the comfort of her own bed (fair enough, it was her place after all), and the laundry room, linked to the kitchen by a short interconnecting corridor, which became the banishment room for Taz to start serving out his sentence. Barring Taz spending the weekend in the back of the Jeep, it was the only viable option.

Prissy, bizarrely, seemed none the worse for her entanglement with the rude and crude visitor from the North, complete with his large boy-dog bits, large teeth and a now established loathing for small dogs with a tendency to yap. But she bore no visible cuts, and no specific areas of tenderness were revealed when touched or gently squeezed, so we decided against incurring the financial wrath of the local veterinary, and opted instead for offering Prissy some of her favourite cooked tripe served with a generous helping of crunchy Doggie Bix. That seemed to do the trick at least.

As for ours, he was just labelled an uncouth lump of gristle that, according to Granny, hailed from way beyond the latitude where civilised folk could naturally live. Whilst not totally banished from the family, Taz had certainly done himself no favours when it came to his standing, and it'll come of no surprise when I say an invite for the three of us was not forthcoming in the years subsequent to that rather eventful weekend.

Chatting on the long and smelly drive back home, it was clear that Taz really couldn't see what all the fuss had been about. It was just some yappy little pampered intern that had been 'in his face.' Family or not, he obviously hadn't been impressed and had simply dealt with the situation as best he could – nothing more, nothing less. After all, had he chomped the scrawny thing? Nope. Had he raced towards the clifftop and flung it into the wind to see if the fluffy little pet could fly? Nope.

However, Taz's prolonged and utter refusal to play ball and release Granny's prized pet had obviously exacerbated the whole situation way beyond the realms of acceptability. However, knowing he possessed the raw power to have ended Prissy's life in seconds, but chose not to, showed heart over animal instinct. Not quite sure that Granny would have ever agreed, but still, it certainly went down as a very 'entertaining' and unforgettable weekend.

Chinwaggin' Days

One particular springtime the weather was really quite brill. I had been up to no good, as per usual, peering out the window into the back garden, and of course plotting stuff I really probably shouldn't have been. Ms Noodle had been doing some plotting of her own too, apparently, coz it was 'Ladies Day,' again, or as I used to refer to it, 'Chinwaggin' Day.'

Her mates were a mixed lot. A couple of them were sort of alright even, coz they'd do this thing where they'd bring 'something for the dog' whenever they turned up. That was cool with me, a chap could never have too many chewy bones or meaty-flavoured biccies shoved his way. But those two were clearly the minority in the gang. The other 'girls,' or 'adult females' at best, were mostly stuffy, stuck-up old bats who didn't give a flying fuck that it was my home they'd come to invade, or even that I happened to live there. I knew the type, they'd rather contemplate sniffing their own shite than come over and dare say hello, pat me on the head, bring me a toy, or even acknowledge my existence. Wankers and trollops the lot of 'em! Somewhat harsh? Nah, I woof the whole truth and nuffink but the truth.

As a result of their overall dim view of me and all my kin, you could say I lived for moments such as their gossipy gatherings. My motto was simple 'Vengeance is mine, old hags, and it tastes as sweet as pie.'

Their visits would take on a fairly regular form, come rain, snow or shine. They would arrive near enough en masse in between three and five cars, jabbering away incessantly as they drove, as they parked, as they exited said vehicles and even more so as they walked up the pathway to the cottage. I swear to you, they could have been heard gassing over a mile away...

'Aww, shut it, pleeease!' was my appeal from the moment of the first arrival until the last one fucked off. All they did was natter, gabble, chatter and gossip. And why, just why? What earthly purpose did they collectively serve? Nuffink.

So who were they? Well, Ms Noodle had retired by then, well, sort of. Basically she had left the office place to do her own thing, and these hanger's-on were, well, doing just that coz Ms Noodle was one seemingly just loved by all of hoomankind. Bunch of freeloaders in my opinion, but not that I had any say in the matter. In the good corner of the gang there was Miss Pretty Nix, real name something like Mary-Poo or summat, but I always reckoned she'd only ever wear the prettiest, boring girlie under-bits, hence her pet name. Miss Pretty Nix seemed decent enough, but God, she was just so… so bloody pink. Always so clean, so pretty, mild, and, ya know, fluffy. Basically she was just, well, just a tad boring and predictably girlie if I'm being honest. Her world always seemed rosy and cute, no matter the weather, the time of year or any other factor you'd care to mention. Saying that, however, her overly positive view of life also played to my own benefit, as it was apparently obvious that happy ladies love buying stuff for cute doggies, and she was no exception. So, Miss Pretty Nix wasn't so bad overall, coz I lost count of the number of naff toys and tasty junk food snacks she'd turned up with over the course of just a single year, so what the hell, I just played along. Play nicely, I kept on saying to myself, play nicely. Well, just for that one I suppose.

Next there was some middle-aged bint by the name of Jules, or simply Jeez as I preferred. Why? Coz every time you saw her face, you'd just go 'Oh Jeez…' This one was another former office acquaintance, but from way back, having probably eaten her way through all the office furniture and into a medically-induced early retirement, and was by then eying up an early grave too from the sheer size of her. Not saying big can't be beautiful, but in this case, a 20-seater midi-bus could have parked completely unseen behind her behind. Worse still was the old hag's general attitude, and an ego which was even larger than her butt. Yeah, never liked that one, mostly as, apart from resembling the backend of a dead dinosaur, she was one mean old bitch. She even used to boss Ms Noodle around, which in my book was one big fuckin' no-no. Ms Noodle was a doll by comparison, and deserved respect not ridicule, especially in her own home. What Ms Noodle ever saw in that one I never did quite fathom. So, old Jeez was forever on my hit list for pranks and general mayhem. Just deserts and all that, eh?

Not gonna go through all of the tribe of so-called ladies, but here's just one more example for ya. This one was simply known by two initials, H and P, like the sauce hoomans liked to splash on sausages and pies all the time. Or perhaps this one thought of herself as like some sports or music star, known only by initials rather than a proper name like other, more normal hoomans. My guess was H P stood for Horse Poo, coz that was what she mostly spouted. She had the personality of an old dry kitchen sponge. Never did find out what the H and P stood for either. She just talked all day long about absolutely sodding nothing and for no apparent reason other than to hear the sound of her own voice. Not only was her visual appeal about as close to a bag of horse doo-doo as one could get, this one really took the whole tin in fact and not just the biscuits when it came to her verbal diatribe.

Those were certainly some of the more memorable, with the others a nondescript bunch of hooman females as snooty as Tory grandees on a freebie day at the races. They were noticeably always so 'up there,' with everyone else, and me especially, very much considered 'way down there,' and I'm not just talking limitations of physical stature. But fuck 'em. Their repugnance at anything canine just played right into my paws, and carved themselves yet more notches on the cricket bat I'd always wanted to smack into their chops, given half the chance. But that said, they were also the source of endless personal challenge and entertainment to me.

So, rise to the challenge, did I? Hmm, you can bloody bet ya life I did, and rise I quite literally did I might add too!

~ ~ ~ ~

Having the girls over from the office where I used to work had become a sort of regular affair. Whilst not that often, I guess we were talking once every two months we'd get together for a girlie afternoon. We'd alternate between venues, but our place seemed to have become firmly 'on the circuit,' so to speak. Some of the girls never played host, I'll admit, but that was mostly due to factors such as them having a house full of noisy, interrupting small people, too many cats that meant there was nowhere safe to sit down, or aged in-law's in situ who seemingly knew no boundaries and would summarily invite themselves to join our gathering, thereby killing any chance of decent gossip pretty much stone dead, or just where their pad simply wasn't large enough or aesthetically pleasing to the core group to warrant the collective travel to spend an afternoon there. But, when it came to our cottage, winter or summer, well, the ladies seemed to enjoy the drive up the hill in their shiny 'never went anywhere remotely muddy' 4x4's. Fine for me, but admittedly Michael and Taz were generally less enthralled by our seeming popularity.

Michael kept right out the way on the advent of such occasions. If his timing worked out right, there'd usually be some urgent last minute task to attend to at the office, or barring that, he'd disappear into his bike shed, or just lock himself away in the spare bedroom. Taz would usually follow him around like a lost sheep, or just sit and stare at me from his armchair/bed, pleading with eyes that bore into your very soul to be taken out, somewhere, anywhere. He was a dog who visibly dreaded a Ladies Day.

One day, I was entertaining the ladies at the cottage. In fact, it was the third such gathering we'd had there that year. It had started out like any other, and should have been just so if not for 'the Taz factor' being added to the equation. Retrospectively, I'm guessing one of the girls, or perhaps collectively all, had somehow come to seriously pee young Taz off, bigtime.

Our large kitchen-diner was generally the room most favoured for such occasions. The stable door that led out to the courtyard and back garden of the cottage had the top half swung open, and my lovely deep-set, stone mullioned windows had also been flung wide open, letting a pleasant breeze waft in together with glorious sunlight that poured into the room. This had the effect of making the old oak table really shine, and reflect not only their faces, but also the time spent in preparation for the day. It was indeed a superb room for entertaining, especially in the summer, albeit only on a small scale as even double cottages were not very good at accommodating groups of more than a handful.

That particular day, Michael had elected to remain ensconced upstairs in the spare room, feebly attempting to mend the internal speaker of a portable music box which was about to give up the ghost, although in his assessment had a few more lives still to go, and thereby warranted a couple of hours of his attention. Meanwhile, Taz could be seen wandering about in the back garden, having pled his case to remain outside. So long as he kept right out of the way, he could carry on 'playing' in the garden. Little inkling did either of us have as to what he had in plan. Did I ever mention he could be a little shit at times? Well, you'd better believe it.

You see, Cherry Tree Hill was not just his favoured sunbathing destination of choice, but also for a few of his other 'pastimes,' shall we say. The first of these was skiing…

Being springtime, a sunshiny day, and then talking of skiing might ever so slightly boggle one's mind. Around an hour after our Ladies Day had reached full-on gossip mode, Jules, who was considered by most as one of life's unfortunates and eternally less amused than practically everyone else on the planet, let out an almighty shriek of utter shock and disbelief.

'What the heck is that damned dog of yours doing out there?' she exclaimed at rather near full volume, and with a chubby index finger waggling at arm's length at the open kitchen window.

It really wasn't a question, more of a statement. Being of a rather loud disposition, her booming voice soon reached everyone's ears, and naturally my eyes immediately moved to focus in the direction she was pointing, the back garden. I hardly needed to look, knowing, just knowing something undesirable was going down on the Taz front, and going down was right, Taz was bloody skiing. Oh God, not again, and not on my Ladies Day too – oh boy, this was not gonna go down well at all, that much was certain!

Starting from right next to the tree, Taz had placed his forelegs between his hind legs whilst still in the sitting position. This had the effect of tilting him back ever so slightly so that he pivoted on his hairy little butt, making his hind paws kind of hang in mid-air out front, with his tail then stretched out back and his butt crack in 100% contact with the grass. He then used his forelegs like ski poles and proceeded to 'butt-ski' down the slope of the hill. This, of course, was much to the absolute horror of the girls, who had by then gathered in front of the open cottage windows to witness an act they really hadn't bargained on seeing with their prosecco and nibbles.

Of course it didn't just end there. To make matters a tad worse, upon reaching the levelled part of the lawn, Taz acknowledged his successful 'descent' by proceeding to then 'sniff' his own trail all the way back up to the tree. What a truly disgusting creature he was at times.

Oh, and just in case the whole act hadn't been seen in its entirety by all, he only went and repeated the show for another two runs. Let's just say he didn't win any new friends that day.

Butt-ski, sniff and repeat, butt-ski, sniff... Charming! How proud was I as his 'mum'? Not a lot, I can tell you.

By half way through his third cycle I'd shot out the open back door like some escaped mad woman.

'What the hell?' I screamed, 'You absolutely horrid little cretin! You had to go and choose today of all days, huh?' I hollered at a rather bemused looking, but quite blatantly unapologetic and shameless hound.

As if he gave a toss. I should have known better. He was still half way down the hill, and whilst he'd slowed down having registered my presence, he obviously wasn't quite finished, and just continued on regardless. He really didn't have any sense of manners whatsoever, completely missing the point of my tirade on the inappropriateness of his performance.

Retreating indoors, I was of course profusely apologetic to my guests, whilst acutely embarrassed at the whole episode. My day really couldn't have gotten much worse. Oh how naïve was I… I should have known better than to expect any form to decent behaviour from Taz from that point forth. Starting to get it now? Yes, he was a little shit indeed.

Maybe 40 minutes passed incident free. The ladies and I had returned to our favourite subject matter, office gossip, this time regarding some young secretarial temp, a 20-something redhead who had allegedly scanned far more than specified in the operating manual of the A3-sized colour scanner/copier/printer.

Anyway, not content with butt-skiing and retro-sniffing said trail as a means to entertaining both himself and anyone who had the misfortune to be watching over in his general direction, for some inexplicable reason Taz decided to up the ante, going for total Grade A 'let's piss off mamma' in preference to being the root cause of any common or garden level of repugnance. On that count too, he again succeeded.

And then the gossiping suddenly stopped…

'No, no, no! What the heck this time?' I swivelled around to face the direction everyone else was staring. It was then that I lost it, 'I'm gonna kill him. I am, I've had it with him, I really have had enough!' I bawled into the air at no one in particular, and promptly stomped off towards the doorway, yet again.

Admittedly, Taz was never quite 'my dog' or 'our dog' in the early days, just 'my husband's dog,' or 'The Dog.' But at that moment in time, he was directly and meaningfully referred to as 'Michael's damned dog.' That was made very clear when I shouted at the upstairs window to Michael, who was clearly still in hiding; albeit most probably fully aware as to what 'his' dog was up to.

'What is it with you lot and your sodding willies?' I cried.

~ ~ ~ ~

Now how the heck was I supposed to answer that? More's the point, was I even supposed to respond? It was a question many husbands and boyfriends had pondered in life, for inadvertently responding to rhetorical questioning from one's better half was a dangerous game at best.

And what the heck was she on about anyway? Half knowing and half guessing the answer to my own question, I moved towards the window, knowing Taz was out there, and knowing Penny and her chums were doing their thing downstairs surely had something to do with the willies-based angle of questioning.

Out the window I looked.

Oh no, he wasn't, was he?

He was.

Taz was sat by the cherry tree, err... jacking off for all to see.

Oh shit.

With his back resting against the tree, he had somehow sussed out that placement of his left front paw at a certain angle up against his pink pencil was sufficient to perform said action by then moving his butt up and down at a predefined tempo. It may indeed have been highly efficient and workable, but I don't believe the merits of said action were quite the topic of discussion between those gathered in the kitchen – more like how many hours or days our dog had to live.

Ladies Day had indeed been a memorable event that month. Whilst almost all of Penny's friends remained thus, it later become evident the group had started visiting others' homes more in preference to ours, which was perhaps no big surprise.

Taz had certainly not done himself any favours that day. Penny was slow to forgive too, but I reckon Taz really didn't give two shits one way or the other. He hated much of that group with a vengeance, and so a bit of grief for butt-skiing and having a sly paw-job in public was no doubt part of some pre-staged plan to upset the apple cart.

Taz appeared pleased with himself all the same. I guess it was just one more tick in the box on his long-term revenge-based mission that had duly been accomplished, and with some merit too. Unfortunately for Taz, it just edged him two steps closer to the inevitable.

The Passenger

Any legislature introduced regarding vehicular safety generally deserves respect, having been founded on good moral intent and scientific reasoning. However, there are of course circumstantial exceptions when we all face the want or perceived need to break the odd rule, or two, or three...

Admit it, we've all done it from time to time, be it ditching a seatbelt on a short hop to the local shop, teaching an underage to drive in some quiet, remote spot, driving after sluggin' a larger nip than advisable or certainly permissible, or just letting the vehicle's speed nudge a little over the limit, or perhaps way more than a little. Whoever says they have done otherwise is either deceiving themselves or is that one-in-a-million saintly and rather boring individual who would likely relish joining a study group on Christmas jumper knitting styles. But come on, in reality we've all done something we shouldn't've at some point in our driving career.

Although never particularly a speed freak, I have been known over the years to partake in the odd high-speed jaunt, albeit only where space permitted, or so I always told myself. Other occasions where a willingness to bend the laws 'may' certainly have occurred, but not that I would see fit to put into print, yet other instances are worthy of sharing. Take for instance travels with a canine co-driver.

In those early days of Taz's vehicular acclimatisation, life was simply aimed at getting him used to the idea of travelling without sharing issues of a rather unpleasant nature from either or both ends of his being. We had then spent many long miles on the road as a family, that is, Penny or myself as driver, and Taz as the obligatory plus one. He would often join us on simple trips to the shops, seemingly happy to stay put in the large open area behind a dog guard in the 4x4 as we much less happily trekked the grocery aisles on the customary weekly shop.

Other than such trips of necessity, there were also dog-related ventures such as driving to and from the vets, the kennels, or just for the purposes of going for a walk somewhere outside of the village in the surrounding countryside of the Yorkshire Moors. The biggies, however, were those long-distance motorway treks that lasted for many, seemingly endless, hours. This was of particular significance as we both had familial connections to the south coast of England, which thereby meant seven or eight hours travel in each direction for weekends visiting parents, siblings, friends or more often a combination thereof.

Having taken early retirement from stressful office-based life, Penny spent her days running a one-person-did-all ironing business, whereby she would take in rubbish bags full of pre-laundered clothes from those either too busy or too rich to iron their own clothes. Usually it was the former, with 'regulars' being working mums who simply struggled to keep on top of pressing the kids school uniforms, in addition to office shirts, bedding and the like. Set up in the spare bedroom with a single large steam iron, extra-wide board, and a few boxes of hangers, it certainly wasn't a big money spinner by any stretch of the imagination, but did help keep the food cupboards stocked if nothing else.

Logistically, Penny would do 'pick ups' and then much of the ironing too, but I would often tackle a few piles of shirts or some larger items of bedding when it was too much for one pair of hands. Additionally, I also took on the 'deliveries' of freshly ironed clothes all over the area, often late into the evenings after work or at weekends.

Of course, presentation was key, so we had to devise a method of getting freshly ironed clothing back to customers in a way that worked for all concerned. Accepted in an assortment of bags, boxes, and bin liners, once ironed, the items were returned on plastic returnable hangers with clear polythene wrappers of varying lengths protecting the apparel. It was but a simple affair in many ways, but fairly professional too.

As for transportation, the family car was exchanged for a fairly recent model white panel/microvan; bit like a tall, narrow shortbread tin on wheels that was powered by a large motorbike-sized engine. Although only having 1300 cc stuffed half under a tiny hood and the rest under the floor and between the front two seats, it packed a powerful little punch as a short-haul workhorse for lightweight jobs, and was not short on character either. I had kitted it out with parallel clothes rails in the back using a homemade wooden frame knocked together over a spare weekend. Between the rear cargo tailgate and the more useful sliding side panel door, it turned out to be absolutely ideal.

But a luxurious ride it most certainly was not, and was notoriously scary on wind-blasted open roads, but with electrically assisted steering and a responsive yet economic engine, it proved fairly nippy around the hills and villages. More importantly, for driving around after eternally long days being chained to a desk, it was also hilariously fun to drive, being more akin to some coin-operated fairground ride than anything resembling the 'light commercial vehicle' it was advertised to be.

Taz would often join me on the evening rounds, particularly when Penny was entertaining non-dog-loving guests, who he, of course, loved to perpetually wind up and scare shitless. The dilemma then, where to place such a dog in a very small van. There was no way he could be set loose in the back with all the clean ironing – that would surely not impress the clientele. Instead he took sanctuary in the small passenger footwell, nestling on an old blanket.

Mostly he would sleep, not seeming to mind the continual bouncing around that the very limited suspension offered the occupants, or the general instability of the narrow-bodied little van with its very high centre of gravity. But those trips out together, though largely enjoyable, were certainly not without incident. Of course, that went without saying, with Taz involved in the proceedings.

~ ~ ~ ~

'Jeez, that sounded bloody close Mister!' I glared up at The Suit from the floor of our motorised tin can on wheels.

The Suit was out and about running errands for Ms Noodle's home ironing get-up and I was riding shotgun coz she had some 'friends' of hers over again, yawn, who I personally believed to be bags of poo, but you've heard all about that; I mean, you should have seen how they looked at me — obviously just cat people! So, nope, I was not their 'mate' no matter what was said to the contrary, and which seemingly made me canine-non-grata in my own home should any happen to 'pop over for an evening.' Therefore, I would find myself forcefully evicted on a semi-regular basis to head out 'n' about with The Suit so both they (grrr) and me would apparently feel more 'comfortable,' as Ms Noodle had ever so politely put it.

'Sod the lot of 'em!' I thought. Not that any fucker would consult me... Oh no, it was only my home, after all.

Anyway, hanging with The Suit in our funny little white baby-truck was not all bad, and even bordered on fun too. I got to sit up front, on the floor though and out of sight, but even that was marked progress from the dog-guarded area I normally travelled by. Couldn't see for shit mind, but a change is a change, right? Also, these adventures were full of sights, sounds, people, and smells which differed from being stuck home in the cottage.

Talking of smells, 'Yep, that one was me,' I whispered half apologetically up at The Suit... again. It had been my 14th apology that trip, although others less obvious I had just let slide without feeling the need for issuing any such formal acknowledgement.

Some of the road bumps were pretty bone shaking compared to being in The Suit's old Jeep, and which seemed to trigger certain intestinal processes, if ya get my drift.

Heading across to the next town, we passed via a couple of hamlets — that's a posh word for a few houses stuck in the middle of soddin' nowhere, and where I guessed some inbred disparate family members all lived in summat like a commune. In the second we dropped off ironed shirts to some arrogant twat who had Ms Noodle do what he was too lazy to do for himself each week, and all for a couple of measly quid too. Tight arse. Then we went on to visit a young mamma with three always-in-pink girls who, when I was in the van, would run out to see me and to pat me on the head, tickle me behind the ears and generally make a daft girlie fuss of me. Fine by me. But I think The Suit was always just a little bit relieved at them not being 'my type' I think. I often thought of coming up with a ruse to show some significantly inappropriate interest in scoffin' the youngest kid one day; ya know, just to freak out the 'too nice to be wholesome' mamma of theirs.

Anyway, we left Pinksville and next headed up and out of the valley and over the 'tops,' eventually hitting what was a fairly major local road that always carried a fair amount of evening traffic, even well after rush hour was supposedly over. Cold outside, and with the van's windows shut tight, the little heater was blasting away as best it could, warming my bits quite nicely as it happened. There were two sets of traffic lights on that road, and we almost always ended up stopping, either for just a few seconds waiting for green, or just slowly crawling forwards in the queue when there were just 'too many idiots clogging up the bloody road,' to put it in The Suit's own words. He wasn't wrong either. Why couldn't most of them just fuck off out of our way or just stay home altogether? We had a job to do, and more importantly grub to scoff once we got back home.

In summary, 'Sod off, we were geezers on a mission.'

A few months passed and I still hadn't eaten the Girlies of Pinksville. Might still have been lingering somewhere on my list, but I also reckoned it could have jeopardised those occasional evening trips out, so I elected to behave myself. It was early summer and even for Yorkshire, much much warmer, so much so that The Suit had dropped the windows to let some air in, and also probably to release a few farts, which were mostly mine but one or two had added a hooman twang to the air. A couple of weeks earlier,

Ms Noodle nearly passed out on us and was seriously unimpressed after blindly shoving her pretty blonde head into the van one evening just as we'd arrived back from a delivery round. The oxygen-fart mix was probably borderline lethal or explosive, and the idea of her clients' clothing having been noxiously contaminated had not sat well, hence the policy thereafter being partially-opened windows.

We reached the first traffic light a little earlier than usual, after Ms Noodle having finally dumped that arrogant twat with the shirts — yay, good riddance. Net result, a little earlier also meant a little closer to rush hour, and therefore more traffic and more delays at the lights. Whilst generally cosy, it was sometimes also a bit too warm on the floor as the little van's engine and gearbox were within centimetres of my tender bits. My butt had once again started to overheat to a point that may have induced a dangerous reaction. Something had needed to be done unless the lights turned green in less than 14 seconds!

There was only one course of action open as I saw it, so I leapt up onto the passenger seat and shoved my face out the open window and gulped a much-needed lungful of fresh air, which was way cooler than the rancid hot stuff I had been sniffing down by the transmission box. Halfway through drawing my initial breath, a piercing shriek hit my left eardrum. It was a sound that clearly belonged to some hysterical hooman female.

Having managed to draw breath and thereby averted the impending doom of anal meltdown, I opened my eyes and found myself staring straight down at a scared shitless middle-aged teacher-type driving a nondescript silver Ford.

'What the crap you lookin' at?' I indignantly woofed, taking full advantage of my comparatively elevated position.

She responded with a second scream, much like the first, and suddenly shot forward in her car just as the lights turned green. Hmm, that went well. I reckoned I could enjoy life as a sitting passenger.

Later, in the evening, The Suit attempted, with a certain level of success I might add, to retell said incident. We were both relieved at Ms Noodle's almost relaxed tolerance on the issue. Better still, no mention was made of me being grounded again either.

However, I did find I was generally told to stay 'down' whenever in the van after that, but admittedly, when we stopped at either of those traffic lights I could rarely resist bouncing onto the seat to scare the crap outta some unsuspecting fellow motorist.

Even The Suit started getting into it... with a well-timed whisper of 'Hey, here's one coming up in a mo... you ready... Now!'

Upon that command, I would leap into action and let out the biggest 'woof' going, just as I landed on the passenger seat – what an absolute blast!

I started to get the hang of it and it wasn't long before I too started to share The Suit's general love of vehicular travel.

'What's next then Boss, shall we try two-up on Norma-Jean?' I asked.

No response.

Arse. Worth a try.

Table Manners

'You have got to be bloody joking. Seriously?' Looking up at Ms Noodle, I was dumfounded at her ridiculous suggestion for what she termed my 'ultimate challenge.'

It was a few years since joining Ms Noodle and The Suit up at the cottage, and life was pretty sweet to be fair. I had even learnt a smidgeon of the protocols and manners that hoomans deemed mandatory. However, as with most things in life, there were exceptions. When The Suit was out and about, Ms Noodle would sometimes let me sneak into their posh kitchen/diner to partake in the odd snack, sat on the floor right at her side no less.

'There, now, see, I knew you could behave, given some training and a bit of trust,' she said.

It was my first, and at that point presumed one-off, occasion when I was welcomed to sit there, in their posh kitchen, tucking into some old lumps of leftover cheese and a couple of biscuits.

Slowly, this had somehow turned into a weekly ritual. Usually it was a Friday morning when I'd get to scoff some broken biscuits, sat next to where Ms Noodle was supping a tall mug of steaming cappuccino. But as to her 'suggestion,' well she was just nuts. The old gal had proposed that I, me that is, could be 'trained' to sit properly at the dining table, on a soddin' chair, and eat food from a plate.

'What the hairy turd are you on lady?' was my immediate thought.

The woman obviously had the whole meat patty missing from her burger all right. What a ludicrous thought. Utterly bonkers.

But she had insisted, and kept on banging on about it too. Not one to shy away from challenge, no matter how daft, I eventually gave in and agreed to commence training. But there was a proviso, The Suit was not to know,

194

apparently. Can't imagine he'd have been best pleased at my smelly paws getting anywhere close to where he scoffed his Sunday roast. He'd only find out at the end, once I was 'ready to present,' as Ms Noodle had put it.

The first bit, and in some ways the most daunting, was learning to put my bum on a chair made for hoomans. Now, it wasn't anything like my comfy armchair; nope, she had chosen some narrow thing called a dining chair with a straight wooden back and a funny little cushion stuck to the seat. Apparently the chairs had belonged to some king-type bloke called Edward, whoever the fuck he was. Anyway, I gotta say, trying to balance my smelly butt on just the cushiony bit was a bit tricky at first...

Of course that was just the first hurdle, coz she hadn't stopped there, no soddin' way. Next she had me lined up to learn 'how' to 'eat at the table.'

I mean, come on, as if I didn't know how to have myself a bit of scoff. Okay, so I usually dropped as much food as I ate, dribbled and drooled, and farted continuously, but so what, I'm a pooch not a puppet, right?

~ ~ ~ ~

This was my thing, a mum's thing, Penny's thing. Michael wasn't to know, well not at first. Having quit working full-time and by then doing the odd pile of ironing-at-home to earn some cash towards the weekly shop, I usually found Friday's were pretty much my own time, more or less, and as such would try and make time to grab a coffee in total peace... Well, apart from having a farting Staffie salivating in the doorway, and all because the biscuit box had been taken out of the corner cupboard and left open on the table next to my me. Yeah, well, apart from that...

It was on such a day I decided on something rather silly. Taz was, for all his disgusting habits and annoyingly adolescent ways, a pretty intelligent and trainable sort of mutt, or so I had always believed if not publically admitted. And then, I had the daft notion of table-training him. My somewhat ambitious mission was to show how that not-so-little shit of a dog could be turned into a gentleman pooch – think along the lines of Elisa in 'My Fair Lady,' and I was therefore a female Professor Higgins, well, sort of. Dippy as it might sound, that was the general plan.

My first task was to set about trying to teach Taz to come in or stay out of the kitchen upon command. After all, I didn't want Michael realising Taz even went into the room, well, not until performance day came around – if it ever got that far. But it wasn't so hard in fact. Taz was already used to staying absolutely put, right with his claws on the line separating his territory (ending in the lounge) and ours (the start of the kitchen). But once he did venture in, he was, in fact, okay(ish). Of course he had his famously vocal rear end, but apart from that, he was pretty well-behaved, well, once the initial shock and subsequent teenage hyped runaround the room.

Next was the task of getting Taz to 'sit at the table.' However, that really was easier said than done with a Staffie.

'Up you go,' I commanded.

'Why?' he'd just look back at me.

'Up you go Taz,' I tried again.

'Sod off' was the look given in return.

Back and forth we continued for longer than was comfortable, for either of us, and that was pretty much as far as training went on Day One.

On his next training day, a week later, I repeated the same line a number of times.

'Up you go,' I'd say.

And he did, eventually. But then immediately jumped back down. Up, down, up, down.

'Stay! Stay there!' I shouted at the point his bum made first contact with the chair.

He did, but then shot me a sideways glance, 'So, where's the grub?' Of course, in getting no immediate reply to the affirmative, he promptly jumped back down again.

Upon the next successful chair sit, I tried, 'Stay there, please, just for me.'

'Get real lady' he quickly retorted, 'I'm off to check out the biscuit box you left open, just over there…' – his eyes fixated as if trying to make it move telekinetically.

My hopes were somewhat dashed. That was Day Two.

Granted it wasn't an easy ride those first few days, or rather weeks, but press on we did.

'Now Taz, my little pal, let's try again,' I said, 'but I bet you can't sit there like a good boy, not a chance.'

But then, and probably just to spite me, he went and did it. And so, we had the second task under wraps. Boasting aside, that was, in reality actually the end of Day (week) Five.

The following weeks were much the same, with progress sometimes painfully slow. However, after some three months of Friday training, Taz was able to enter the room, walk over next to my chair and sit there. Then, upon command, he'd do an about turn and jump up on to the chair at the other side of me, and just sit there, good as gold. But admittedly that was after Day, err, lots and lots.

Wow, you might be thinking, brilliant achievement. Yeah, but it had cost me big time, with some six packets of my best Hobnob biscuits given away in bribes. Additionally, I also had to spend some two hours one week scrubbing one of my expensive cushioned oak chairs that Taz had ever so proudly 'skid-marked' for me – bless him, the little poo.

The diet of our esteemed mutt had developed over time. The early days admittedly bordered on hellish as we shifted him away from a diet of 'cheap as you could buy' canned rubbish that may have appeared at first to be meat-based, but had the nutritional value of an old faded tennis ball, to some special dried mix created by a veterinary dietitian specialising in canine needs we'd been recommended. A few months later though and Taz was quite a bit leaner, certainly more alert, and his coat was amazingly shiny by comparison.

But yes, unfortunately he still farted like his life depended on selling the gas in bottles to the highest bidder.

After the sweet discovery of carrots, Taz seemed more amenable to at least trying 'new stuff,' such as the brave teenage soul that he was. His second most favoured snack had become the Granny Smith's apple, and he soon came to love an apple in the garden. In that, Taz perfected the 'chuck 'n' scoff,' whereby he'd pick it up in his jaws, and then promptly hurl it as far as he could across the lawn, then 'wait,' to see it drop, then 'attack,' bounding over and devouring it like some invading species from Mars that had to be destroyed at all costs in order to protect civilisation from immediate extinction.

So, you've guessed it. The Granny Smith's apple became his new Friday table snack, or so the plan went... But that took too many more weeks than I cared to admit, but we did eventually get there.

'Taz, relax, it's not going anywhere,' I'd say to his panicked face, 'now eat it s-l-o-w-l-y...,' I'd repeat over and over and over to his seemingly deaf ears.

Yes he'd sit, and yes after a while he'd even wait for my command to eat... but the inner lunatic would immediately take over and he'd attack the plate like some half-starved velociraptor. At least once or twice a pre-cut chunk of apple landed on the floor, followed within half a second by a 20 kilo eating machine, so the standard flat-type plate was swapped for a vertically-sided serving dish. This reduced the risk of 'apple breakout' and as a result, kept Taz more or less in place for the ensuing final part of the act.

More weeks passed by, and progress was made, step by painfully frustrating step. Eventually I knew, 'this was it' and so I talked the plan through with Taz, who of course just stared back at me like I was some mad old biddy, and instead went about looking in every direction possible in search of where the biscuit box had been moved to, ignoring almost every word that passed my lips. Best I could do was to trust the training had sunk in – as the saying goes, time would tell.

Later that day, Michael arrived home for the weekend, and was 'busy' relaxing by the fire with a booklet on discount hardware, screws, nail guns, and bath fittings. I guess it was interesting to him anyways.

Going for broke, I said… 'Michael, listen up. Don't be alarmed, and you must promise not to say anything about what you are going to see until after we've finished. Deal?'

'Err, okay…,' he replied cautiously, but with a worried look.

'Taz and I have a surprise for you… Are you ready?' I asked.

I'd used my kindest but wifely 'non-negotiable' voice. He relented of course, he wasn't stupid. We'd been married long enough that he knew it was safe to make a challenge, and when to, err, not. He walked over to the kitchen doorway somewhat intrigued, yet relaxed, having just half-stepped over Taz, whose front paws had seemingly been glued to the carpet gripper that demarked the territorial boundary at the entrance to the 'forbidden kitchen.'

I sat there at the table and Michael stood with his back to the kitchen sink. I waited for a full one minute, and then said…

'Taz, sweetie,' I started.

You should have seen Michael's face at that bit alone – sweetie!

'Now, are we ready to show Daddy our new party trick?' I asked.

Taz had become solid, not moving one bit – just his usual motionless sat-in-the-doorway self. Oh crap, I thought, was he trying to wind me up, after all that hard work, week in, week out? Or was he just trying to see how much he could embarrass mum, just for a laugh?

On my second request, thankfully, it registered. Amazingly, he sat up on command. Michael continued to look on, albeit by then somewhat intrigued.

'C'mon then, shall we have a snack then Taz?' I asked casually.

At that, he stood and walked over the golden line, and deep into enemy territory, or the kitchen at least, which was, after all, normally a land outlawed.

Over to my side of the table he came, and then sat down. Michael was amused, yet still unimpressed. Fair enough, we hadn't really started.

He asked, 'So what, he's gonna eat a biscuit? Yeah, wow.'

Ignoring the jibe, I looked down at Taz and gently spoke, 'Up in your chair then,' I instructed.

Taz turned, eyed up Michael for a long second and then promptly vaulted onto what was, after all, a polished oak semi-antique cushioned Edwardian dining chair. Michael's coffee mug stopped five centimetres short of his mouth – ha, we finally had his attention.

Rising from my chair, I walked over to Taz, who was sat patiently on the dining chair as if butter wouldn't melt, and then slowly proceeded to tie a large white cotton serviette around his furry, muscular neck, just above his thick leather and metal spiked 'don't mess with me' dog collar.

Michael had become frozen. Taz too was still, although I thought I had detected a cheeky little smirk resting on his face.

I then walked to the fridge, opened the door, and carefully extracted the vertically-sided dish with which we had practised. It had already been pre-prepared with neatly cut chunks of fresh Granny Smith's apple. I then walked back to the table and set the dish right in front of Taz, whose snout was hovering about eight centimetres above the plate.

Taz looked at me with begging eyes, as if to say 'Mum, can I scoff it now? Aww, please mum, please!'

Michael gave us a 'What the...?' kind of look.

This smelly, generally disobedient, boisterous, dirty-habited mutt was now sat bolt upright at the dining room table, wearing, of all things, a freshly ironed Egyptian linen serviette tied around his neck. As he sat there, he was drooling over a plate of neatly sliced Granny Smiths. To apply the term 'surreal' would be a clear understatement in describing the moment.

'Wait please Taz,' I said.

Taz did just that, same as we had practised over and over in the preceding weeks. One full minute passed… not a muscle moved in the room, not from anyone, canine or human.

'Go on then,' I whispered.

Taz looked me straight in the eye, as if, 'Ha, didn't expect that, now did ya lady?'

He then ever so nicely ate the apple slowly(ish), piece by piece, like a trained canine from Hollywood itself.

And that was that, challenge complete.

I was personally quite amazed, and a little shocked to be honest. Michael was, well, he was just speechless. Taz had surprised everyone, and probably himself included.

But then, to round off his triumphant achievement, and just to prove beyond doubt he was indeed Taz and not some actor-imposter, he let rip with one of the loudest trumps he'd ever released, whilst looking me dead straight in the eye. Cheeky git.

He then hopped down, shook his tail and waltzed off out of the room with just a nonchalant sideways glance at Michael. Then he walked back across the lounge and jumped back up into his armchair and promptly went straight back to sleep. It was a truly memorable moment, a one-off and never to be repeated.

Barking to a Higher Octave

In general, Taz was never a particularly boisterous hound. But like all dogs, and especially those with a personal history of abuse, torment, captivity or having just been routinely unloved, he certainly provided a sack load of memorable moments to test the patience of any true saint. Notwithstanding the odd moment, he was a loveable rogue at best. A pet with many revolting habits, yet he possessed the soul of a true and loyal four-legged friend. Yes, he could be a total arse at times, very often in fact, but he also boasted such a huge heart that you'd just wanna hug him, well, sort of, maybe. However, that largely depended on how smelly such an encounter threatened to be, and whether or not he had recently discovered and part digested a heap of cat poo or worse, like some unwanted gift left behind by the local vixen who often seemed to pass through the garden in the early hours.

Good or bad, lovable or loathsome, Taz was one of a kind, but at the same time, just a typically adolescent Staffie – rowdy one minute and capable of endearing civility the next. Take his uncanny ability to become the master of decadence, grasping the delicacies of banquet hall etiquette, or scoffing sliced apple sat at a table complete with an elegant serviette worn stylishly around his fat neck. But, admittedly, he was mostly a total nut-job, one who managed to wreck a cat-flap and half a door in just a few seconds, and all because the neighbour's cat happened to saunter pass outside beyond his immediate field of vision. Stranger still, he could transform from a beast happily about to devour the precious domesticated companion belonging to one of our most senior family members (yeah, good move there matey, not!), into a fun-loving pup who appreciated nothing better than to play tricks on car drivers queued at the traffic lights when sat bolt upright on the passenger seat of a small white utility van.

But ultimately, for Taz, it was his antics of a more carnal nature that secured his widespread fame, if not fortune, and also led to his eventual downfall from whatever grace he'd managed to notch up over the years. It was certainly true that the boy's tackle had raked in a wad of cash over the years for extending Taz's bloodline, however, there were also many somewhat less appealing and nefarious applications of said apparatus, that of being forever known as 'The Hillside Wanker' for starters!

However, instances of his sexually-inspired antics became, unfortunately for us and for anyone else that dared visit or peek over the garden wall, more and more frequent. Perhaps it was just unfortunate timing that we'd often caught him 'in the act,' but perhaps not given the regularity of said events. Or, maybe he was just Taz being a total git of his own volition, exercising his dog-given right to bash the candle at will… We were never quite certain, but nevertheless something clearly had to be done if we were to preserve any more than one or two distant friends who would still dare to visit us. Whilst not an unreasonable chap on the whole, our dog-owner relationship had reached a natural limit. By that I mean due to our obvious language barriers, we may not have been able to adequately explain to him the reasoning behind our displeasure, and that he really had to stop showing off his dog-hood to all and sundry.

Conversational attempts at behaviour modification didn't go well…

'Look Mister,' I once said to Taz, 'Ya just can't just spend your days tossing-off under the cherry tree. It's just not on mate!'

Taz had stared blankly back at me.

'Too much of that'll make ya go blind, you know that, right?'

Still he'd stared blankly.

'And you must realise what you did the other day really upset your mum' I said with some earnest.

But I was met with that same old blank look.

'We all know you used to "do it" for cash, but seriously, nobody wants to actually see it mate, not when they only popped in for a cup of coffee and a chat,' I had said dryly.

More blank stares.

Lowering my voice, I then eyed him up, man to dog, and slowly but resolutely said, 'You just don't give a crap, do you?'

Well it was progress, his head tilted three degrees to the left. So you can see, it was forever a struggle to get our point across.

It was also painfully obvious nothing was or ever likely get through his thick skull, and that his habits were more than just a passing phase; it was a way of life for him. Discussions were held at length between Penny and me, but the upshot was simple, his good old days were well and truly over, it was time to consider the benefits of canine orchiectomy.

~ ~ ~ ~

Blank stares, my arse... I was stunned at the raft of accusations being thrown in my general direction. Stunned I was. Cheeky old codger.

In ending the so-called conversation, I woofed, 'Yeah whatever mate, bite me!' After which I just farted and walked off, leaving him to deal with that instead.

Personally, I never did quite understand what all the fuss was about. Back in the day when a fair bit of cash was being wafted about when 'doing my thing' with some young filly, nobody seemed right bothered about the morals involved, nor what I did with my own bits 'after hours.' Money talked, or so it seemed. So what the heck they were all fret-up over, just coz I perhaps did more than my fair share of 'doggie-daydreaming' with Timmy the Todger under the cherry tree? I could never quite work it out. I was a bloke dog, so deal with it. But no, the crux of the matter was that I had apparently appalled, shocked —and perhaps secretly enthralled— one or two of the, err, ladies with one of my jolly good adventures with Timmy the Todger.

Ah well, stuff 'em, I thought. They'd soon forget about it anyway. I was pretty sure of that, well, almost, and then they'd move on to some new obsession over which to chat endlessly of an evening. I was fairly convinced they'd just put it down to my boyish tendencies.

Me thinks I could have been a tad wrong on that score.

About a month after 'Treegate,' the now infamous Ladies Day event from which my fame had spread like wildfire, there was much hushed talk, both between The Suit and Ms Noodle, and also between Ms Noodle on the phone with, well, a fair number of her mates, and all about some upcoming event that I was clearly not privy to.

Not content at being kept in the dark, I tried asked her out straight.

'Oi, lady!' I said, 'What you up to? What you been plannin' with the old fella and yer mates on the phone?'

She stared back at me with a blank expression, yet still loaded with contempt.

'C'mon,' I challenged her, 'I know you've been plotting summat, and that it obviously involves me, coz ya keep staring at me when you're gassing in hushed tones?'

Another blank stare.

By then I was becoming a little fucked-off to be honest. Now I like surprises as much as anyone, but for the life of me I couldn't quite suss out what they were up to. Was it to be a good surprise, or a not so good one? Buggered if I knew.

That week had comprised of two lengthy 'conversations' between me and my hoomans. In one they had gabbled away some shit at me, over and over, but I had just stared blankly back at them like some village idiot. Later, I had been the one doing the interrogation, but then I also found myself on the receiving end of a pack of blank stares. Cheeky sods, blank stares were supposed to be my thing, not theirs, and I didn't take too kindly to the tables being reversed and shoved back in my own face.

Arse.

At the end of the day, I was no nearer uncovering what the chuff was about to go down. Bugger 'em, that was my plan. I decided to just carry on regardless and shove my head in the sand.

The next day had seemed like the ideal opportunity to put said plan into action. It happened to be a lovely sunny autumnal day and what better way to pass the time than a quick visit to Cherry Tree Hill and a spot of 'woof woof' with Timmy.

This time I was witness to wild hand gesticulation and raised voices from behind the triple-glazed windows. This time, both of my hoomans were banging on the windows, and then out they marched, in unison, and both looking like they'd just lost a month's pay on the gee-gee's. They were seriously not happy bunnies, a notion confirmed after feeling a moment of slipper-to-butt contact. So, I guessed a quick wank was probably off the menu for that day at least, or perhaps just not in front of the windows at any rate. Hmm, I would have put some effort into researching alternative venues.

~ ~ ~ ~

A week or so passed on by. It was a Saturday, and whilst waiting for my weekend morning walkies, I was most put out to find both my water bowl and my food bowl had both been removed the night before. Not overly bothered, I guessed they were in the washer-machine thingy, but it was strange that there was no water at least.

'Oi,' I called out, 'Hellooo… where's me water and, while you're there, where's me brekky?' with a follow-up of, 'I'm half-starved down 'ere.'

'We are going out in a minute Taz, one sec…' was the response shouted from Ms Noodle, who was still upstairs.

Strange, very strange. It had gone well past normal walkies time. It was then that I noted them both near the front door putting on their trainers and grabbing their normal 'going to town' jackets, so not wellies or walking jackets, normal garb. Hmm. What the heck were they up to? Joint walks were practically unheard of, and so the change in get-up was a trifle disturbing, especially when it was looking like a 'front door' job too.

'Just give us a drink before we go then, will ya?' I tried.

Silence… Okay, was this like verbal 'blank staring'?

'I get it. This is some sort of punishment for too much pocket billiards without the pockets?' I offered, half-jokingly, having referred to that personal habit of mine that was still the general discussion point when it came to me and them.

More silence.

But, then they both appeared, and then oddly looked at each other. I then heard The Suit say something weird to Ms Noodle.

'Okay, let's get this done. We'd better leave now or we'll be late for his appointment,' he said to her.

Noticeably, it had specifically been 'his appointment,' not 'ours' or 'my' or 'yours' – The Suit had definitely said 'his,' meaning mine. But that made no sense, not to me at least.

Oh crap, it could only mean one of two things. Either I was being dragged off for my nails to be clipped by that redhead bimbet who called herself a 'pet manicurist' – some daft cow she was. Or, and this was by no means certain, but things were starting to fall into place – it was potentially an appointment for the bloody vets, which meant seeing that tortuous white-coated old twat who last time saw fit to jab a fucking great needle up my butt. Looked like there wasn't gonna be any walkies that day.

After a short drive of eight or nine minutes I found I was right on Count #2, a soddin' vet's visit it was.

I was part dragged, part pulled, and part pushed across the small carpark and into the overly clean, painfully bright, white-walled waiting room of the town's premier veterinary surgery. Other victims had already been lined up, each with their respective owners, and each looking as scared shitless as I probably had to them.

A couple of real old dogs looked well-fucked too. They were obviously past it, probably smelled of wee and were obviously there for *the* big injection… Whoa! Suddenly question after unanswered question flew about my brain. Was that it? Was I gonna sample the afterlife that day, up there floating about on my own personal doggie-cloud? Perhaps I'd get to meet a pink poodle at last? But it was all too soon, wasn't it? Could it really be 'my time'?

I let out a howl, 'Nooooooo…'

They then proceeded to drag my sorry arse out of the waiting room and into Treatment Room Three, which was second on the right down a narrow, but of course also very brightly lit, corridor.

Sure enough, that masked devil was waiting for me, as was Assistant Vet Girlie, who as usual smiled a completely false smile. In my book, she was probably a tad scarier than Doctor Death himself.

'Come on then boy, you can relax now, we are all here to help you,' said Assistant Vet Girlie.

'Fuck off!' I spat back, 'I'm too young to die!'

She smiled her most weird and insincere smile.

The bastard vet only then went and smiled too, even more scary.

Half a second later and The Suit slowly smiled too, sort of, and then even Ms Noodle managed a half smile.

That was it. The sand in my hourglass was almost up. But why? Was it really all because of a few good shoofties with Timmy under the damned cherry tree?

I tried whimpering out some belated apology, as begrudgingly as it felt, or I was about to when a fuckin' red-hot poker of a needle went up my bum… again.

Within seconds, weird images started to float through my mind, like I was sort of floating around in space… there were big dogs and small dogs, fat dogs and thin dogs, scrawny dogs and even a few sexy poodles too… but all were somehow joining me up on that hill; some were applauding, some were staring, but some were, err, shall we say, joining in!

I felt all fuzzy…

Hmm…

'Fuzzy Wuzzy was a bear,'

'Fuzzy Wuzzy had no hair,'

'Fuzzy Wuzzy wasn't very…'

…and then time stood still.

~ ~ ~ ~

– SOME TWO HOURS LATER –

~ ~ ~ ~

'…fuzzy, was he.'

'Whoa, what the fuck?' I blurted out, 'Where am I?'

Those were my only recognisable thoughts that seemed to be swimming very slowly around my brain as if it were full of steamin' hot porridge.

Was this doggie heaven? That was my next thought. Had it happened, had my clogs been popped for me?

Then, all of a sudden, 'Oh shit, what are YOU doing here?' I asked, but looking at no one in particular.

I was lying there all weird and pissed-like, sat on my heavenly cloud, but there right smack in front of me was none other than The Suit and Ms Noodle…! Had they slipped me something rather special as I went through them Purly Woofin' Gates?

'Welcome back Taz… It's all over now,' came the not-so-reassuring voice of Assistant Vet Girlie.

209

'Hmm, so I'm NOT dead then?' I voiced, but reckoned I was talking more to myself than anyone else.

For some reason I then looked down my body, and did a quick count; one, two, three, four legs (phew), but then…

'What the fuck?' I screamed.

There was a huge white bandage covering the nether region where my Timmy lived, but could I get a decent look, could I as heck as like – I was wearing one of those sodding stupid plastic radar collars.

'Oh shit, what have ya gone and done?' I hollered.

A sly smile slowly spread across Ms Noodle's face as it all became rather too clear. I had finally sussed out the purpose of the trip to the vets, and of all those phone calls and secretly-laid plans.

'Nooooo… not the crown jewels!' I cried out.

I knew instantly life from that moment on was on a collision course for some pretty big changes. Suddenly thrust into a life without my boy tackle, was I going to start knitting classes? Would I have to, or even choose to, wear a fluffy pink collar? Would I enjoy talking about holiday plans with my manicurist, and other sorts of girlie shit? To say that sheer terror seared my veins in nanoseconds would be no gross exaggeration. I was in full-on panic mode.

~ ~ ~ ~

Days dragged into weeks, and slowly I found myself having recovered from that bastard op. Life had indeed changed, albeit perhaps not quite as I or others had expected.

After a few more weeks I was running around like new, well almost… minus me knackers of course. Great relief though, happy to report, as I hadn't become suddenly interested in pink stuff, knitting, toy dolls, cookery or daytime telly, and therefore perhaps I still could be the one to have the last laugh after all…

I found myself going and sitting under the cherry tree, but fucked if I knew why. Nothing seemed to click. What was it I used to do when sat up there? Memories were really, really foggy on that front. C'mon brain, think!

Hour upon hour I sat on that hill, trying to recall. Nope, nada.

Tired of trying to kick-start the old grey cells, I laid back against the tree and sighed a not-so-contented sigh to myself. As I did so, my front right paw gently rubbed against Timmy the Todger, which by the way seemed pretty bored with life following the forceful eviction of his two bestist pals.

But, then… whoa, what was that? Hmm, something felt kinda nice down there. I wiggled around just a bit more… and then I looked down…

'Oh my, hello Timmy!'

Nurse Pooch

'Okay Taz, I'll be there in just a minute. Show some patience for once!' I semi-begged my stroppy old dog.

In actuality, he wasn't that old. Like all of us, his years had started to advance somewhat, but unfortunately not his adolescent view on life. On that score he was, somehow, still very much a hormonal youth, with his habitual predilection for recklessness he really should have grown out of long ago. And if not for age alone, his partial lack of masculine tackle should have at least calmed him down, if not stopped his carnal urges altogether. But no, on that score too he was still very much one of the lads, and very much a regular cause for embarrassment whenever the opportunity presented.

Likewise, I wasn't old either. Yes, my years had also started to inevitably advance somewhat too, but I was by no means an old lady, or even much past a middle-aged one. Partly, thanks to the career situation Michael had found himself facing at the time, I had managed to escape from office life early, or 'let out on good behaviour' as I called it. But life was never dull, not with Taz around. I continued to have friends up to the cottage, although the office girls did seem to come over with much less frequency following the debacle when my beloved pooch had done his level best to show us and himself up big time. Taz might have attempted to gloss it all over as some 'do about nothing,' but neither we nor many of my friends shared his viewpoint.

Putting all that aside, Taz was, with all his rough edges, still a big kid, but he was our kid all the same. Knowing that, he still played on our good nature at every opportunity, just trying to see how far the rope would stretch, and with it how far our patience would go. I guess you could write his résumé one-line header as something along the lines of, 'Taz, a loud, proud, and lovable little shit.'

~ ~ ~ ~

The old lady was, well, being 'old' that day I guessed. Ms Noodle didn't seem quite herself again, sort of not as blonde 'n' bubbly. On the other hand, perhaps it was more to do with my continued laddishness. It was true, the hoomans had won the recent Battle of Cherry Tree Hill, having ganged up on yours truly and done away with my knackers, but that hadn't stopped me being, well, me.

'Woss up wiv yer then?' I enquired, 'You's walking around like ya got the squits.'

Never quite sure to what degree the hoomans understood my accent, the look on Ms Noodle's face indicated a significant level of comprehension, and it didn't sit well.

'You cheeky little sod,' she exclaimed!

So my guess was pretty much on the mark, either that or she might have just been taking my collective woofs the wrong way, thinking I was trying to hurry her up. Yes, maybe that was it. Either way, I decided it was best to keep my trap shut on that occasion, recent memories of them stitches and my own funny walk for a while having forced aside some of my more hastier acts of bravado.

But yeah, summat wasn't right with the boss-lady. She seemed to wince far too much to blame it on her recent girl's night out in those pointy shoes with heels taller than my food bowl. Guess she needed a trip to the hooman's vet.

~ ~ ~ ~

213

Being home-based, Taz went most places with me. Most days he'd pull me down the road to the local shops, which then meant he'd be tied to the railings outside – his lead I meant. I tried to refrain from literally tying my dog to the railings, although it had certainly crossed my mind at times. Meanwhile, I would grab whatever supplies were needed from the shelves on my own after Taz found himself unceremoniously banned by Cyril the shopkeeper for his excessive farting; Taz I mean, not Cyril. Other days I would take Taz in the car and go to shops further afield. The weather was rarely hot, and he had two car window security grate things that meant I could leave him in the car with a decent opening in both rear windows. It perhaps wasn't ideal in terms of vehicular security, but I went on the notion that what sort of idiots would attempt to break into a locked car with a 20 kilo Staffie staring back. If they still managed to nick the car, well, good luck to them.

Often I'd elect not take Taz out with me, such as when visiting friends or cities some distance away. As much as he enjoyed our trips together, he had all the creature comforts back at home, and to be honest seemed quite a settled pooch when it came to cottage life. The other trip type he never accompanied me on were those of a medical or personal nature. It always seemed somewhat inappropriate, and the only time I did try it, he seemed really put out by my visiting the doctor's surgery, transforming into the likes of a fully trained 'medical support dog' crossed with a wannabe nurse whose training consisted of nothing more than watching the entire series of St Elsewhere on telly.

But Taz, like most dogs, was inherently able to key into my physiological state. He knew when I felt happy, he knew when I felt sad, he certainly knew when I was angry, and also when I just felt like crap or needed nothing more than a good hug. When I was not so good, Taz would generally, although not always, temporarily trade in his usual boisterous ways and go all nursey on me, putting on his imaginary doggie nurse's uniform, after which he'd remain very much by my side like some ankle-worn security monitor. I guess in a way it was similar to how he reacted when my elderly mum would come to stay. Without need for any prompting, Taz would cease all jumping and running around indoors, never once banged into her legs, didn't throw toys in her general direction or nudge her arm forcefully to incite play, or even try to clean out her inner ear canal when sat bolt upright beside her on the sofa. Most dogs have a highly developed system for health detection in others, and usually a wonderful bedside manner too, irrespective of their normal behavioural traits.

Medical check-ups and doctor's visits never appeared high on my list of life's priorities. Generally I considered them somewhat of an interruption to the normal grind, and would therefore be greeted like almost a new patient whenever I visited the local medical centre, although that was probably more down to the wit and sarcasm of northern British humour. But, like all of us, there comes a time when one knows that professional support from the system should really be sought.

An almost constant lower backache had plagued me for some time. But whilst it hadn't really been all that noticeable or disturbing during a January trip made in search of tigers and leopards in Northern India's national parks, by early summer it had become more than just a nagging ache, and had even stopped me cycling very far on what was a regular trip to rural southwestern Turkey. Sofa sitting had certainly lost its appeal, as had driving my car more than just locally, as it was seemingly impossible to find myself anywhere close to a comfy position for more than a few minutes at a time. Taz, of course, had picked up on this and donned his 24x7 healthcare uniform, then opted for a life glued firmly to the calf muscle of my left leg.

Leaving the boy at home, I popped down to the medical centre to show my face, reintroduce myself yet again, and seek some much-needed expert opinion about my back. Nothing untoward was brought up, and armed with a few nondescript pills, off I went.

But, with no positive outcome from that particular course of treatment and symptoms having progressively worsened over the subsequent seven days, I returned once more, and that time came away with an appointment to see a back specialist – in 10 weeks' time. Marvellous. To cut a needlessly long story rather much shorter, a quick money-up-front trip to the local private hospital had me sat in an orthopaedic surgeon's clinic within less than a day. As much as it didn't sit well with me to take that healthcare route, not sitting well was also becoming a serious issue by then, and the prospect of a 10-week wait versus reduced spending power in the short term meant it was a no-brainer, as they say.

Then, to add to that, being informed by the surgeon of a further 12-week wait for a free, but necessary, Magnetic Resonance (MR) scan when you're in constant discomfort and pain was also a pill too harsh to swallow, and so a small fortune (not kidding) was cobbled together from our reserves in order to get the scan at the same private hospital just two days later. The good news was that at last we were getting somewhere, diagnostically speaking; the bad news was that it showed multiple metastatic spinal tumours.

Bugger. Well, at least I knew I hadn't been imagining it, and nor had Nurse Taz.

~ ~ ~ ~

Ms Noodle was startin' to hobble around like a bit of an old goat with two of its legs tied together. She had been down to see the hooman's vet a few times I think, or that much I had guessed coz she went out on short trips, and didn't take me coz I tended to freak out a bit waiting in the car as I could smell sick hoomans nearby – a weird and uncomfortable feeling, I can tell ya.

Me and Ms Noodle started to watch a lot more daytime telly together too, and much of the rest of our time was spent sat in the garden in the sun, or even if it was cloudy but still warmish. But she seemed to have a real problem getting comfy, sitting awkwardly on a bunch of cushions piled on the park bench under the back window. Sometimes I would stay indoors, coz

I could still keep an eye on her as my armchair was just the other side of that very same window.

At other times I would go all full-on nursey and crawl on to the bench beside her, and then drool on her leg whilst she chatted on the phone. I guessed she was a bit crook coz she'd just stroke the back of my ears rather than give me a clip around them for messing up her nice clean jeans. But hoomans seemed to like being fussed over, and it seemed only proper after all to return a cupful of the fuss she'd given me for the years I'd lived with them. I won't mention the arse kicking's in that equation, nor having been hollered at incessantly when I'd pissed her off big time for having a wank or three under the tree in front of her so-called mates. But nah, on balance Ms Noodle was worth fussing over – she was my hooman mum after all.

~ ~ ~ ~

Taz, he was my buddy whenever I was ill. He was my friend, confidante, snack partner, TV critic, knitting companion, and general all-round supporter during daylight hours. Admittedly, at the time we were talking about, I slept a fair bit too, but of course that matched well with Taz's own lazy-bum lifestyle. We were probably quite a sight, both of us snoring in unison from our respective places in the lounge, him sprawled out on his old armchair and me usually similar on the sofa.

Driving had started to become really uncomfortable, so I'd spend most of my days watching the box or sat on my garden bench soaking up the Yorkshire sun, in what was arguably a rather decent actual summer; quite a rare treat for this south coast softie. Other than Taz, the telephone was my lifeline, and enabled me to keep in touch with those dear to me, have a gossip or three, and generally escape into the worlds of others. I knew things weren't looking good for me, a few years working in a hospital haematology laboratory had taught me perhaps more than I needed or wanted to know.

Medically speaking, things progressed very rapidly. From the initial MR results, the emergent necessity for a Computerized Tomography (CT) full body scan at least meant not having to shelve out all our savings on that. But unfortunately, luck doesn't always run true, and I never personally got to hear the results of that particular scan, having been hospitalised the same day the results came back. Timing was never my strong point, I guess.

~ ~ ~ ~

Bugger. Arse. Poo.

I had a tonne of notable experiences in my short doggie life, some pretty cool, others bloody horrid. This latest one definitely fitted into the latter. I had to sit there staring through the glass door from my doggie room at the back of the cottage as two hunky-chunky paramedics lifted Ms Noodle over the front doorstep in a special wheelie chair thing. They'd slapped a funny-looking Darth Vader mask thing on her with tubes hanging out, and she was all wrapped up in a big fluffy blanket, which seemed a little at odds with such an otherwise lovely sunny Friday morning.

And then the door was shut.

That was that.

Silence.

I waited for The Suit to come home later in the afternoon with Ms Noodle, but he didn't. It was indeed very strange.

Instead, much, much later, after it was proper dark even, Parker, the next door geezer popped in to see me. That wasn't that unusual in itself, coz he had a key of his own and had come to put some lights on, draw the curtains, give me some much-needed nosh and of course to let me out for a wazz and a whoopsie. He was always a decent fella to me, so I was, of course, still happy to see him.

But, weirdly, there was still no sign of my own hoomans though.

A couple of nights later the front door opened. This time it wasn't Parker, but The Suit. Poor sod, he looked well-fucked. He then sat down by my bed on the floor and started to tell me all sorts of stuff about Ms Noodle. Dunno quite whether he was really talking to me or just ramblin' on for his own sake.

'So when's Ms Noodle comin' home?' I enquired.

'Tomorrow...,' he started.

My eyes lit up.

'Tomorrow, I'm gonna take you to see her, okay?' he added.

I didn't really understand, but knew The Suit well enough to know he wouldn't jerk me around, and that I could trust him with all things Noodley.

~ ~ ~ ~

Sure enough, the next morning The Suit was true to his word. We had been up and out early for our usual walkies and bunny chasing, although that kinda came to an abrupt halt when one little shit darted across the field, and yours truly hadn't seen the little thin strand of electrified fencing wire which made Timmy the Todger instantly tingle like crazy when I ran straight into it. Bunny features had just run off laughing. Bastard. Next time I swore, next time.

After brekky and a bit of clearing up, The Suit drove me in the car to somewhere I hadn't been before. It was only about 20 minutes away. The place was huge, like a massive vet's clinic. And just like my vet's place, there were lots of snooty gits strutting their stuff in white coats. The only difference being the complete absence of guys like me. Yep, no dogs allowed, apparently, as was even spelt out with a crude and rather politically vindictive nasty sign by the front door I noted. Guessed it must have been a 'hooman's only' type of vet's surgery, just a really big one.

The Suit spoke to someone on his little mobile telephone thingy, and then we walked all around the outside of the buildings. With such an enormous place, I reckoned the local hoomans must be a pretty sickly bunch to need that many vets to look after them.

'So, what we doin' then Mister?' I asked up at The Suit as we walked. Guessin' his 'dog' was improving when he looked down at me.

'We are off to see your mum,' he began. 'You know she's been poorly, right? Well, she has to stay here to see if the doctors can help her to come back home soon. But, because you have been such a good dog and looked after her so well, the chief doctor here has agreed for you to visit her quickly. Okay?'

Hmm, okay. Best behaviour time. I knew what these hooman vets were gonna be like, and any farting or silliness would only get me kicked right back through the door, so yes, I was about to put on my very bestist behaviour, just for Ms Noodle.

~ ~ ~ ~

The Suit met some white-coated young lady by an open door at the side of one of the buildings. She seemed nice enough, good legs too, for a hooman. She led us quickly along a white corridor to the third door on the left, which she opened and then we all walked in.

'Whoa. Fuck me!' I murmured.

Lying there in a really cool looking bed with cables and pipes and chunky big white wheels was none other than Ms Noodle herself. She had about 63 pillows on her bed too, and lotsa white sheets. Everything was white, apart from Ms Noodle, who appeared a bit grey and looked very pooped to be honest. On both sides of her bed were some small televisions, but the programmes they showed were like maths stuff, with numbers, and lines, and graphs all moving about. Then, she looked over at me, slowly made eye contact and gave me her lovely Noodley smile.

'Taz, my boy,' she whispered, 'Come give your mum a hug.'

I went over, and knowing the routine, smartly jumped up onto the chair beside her bed in a single clean bounce and proceeded to nuzzle my favourite hooman. She petted me slowly with her soft and beautifully manicured hands.

Looked like her absolute bestie had very recently been in to 'do her nails,' which was summat Ms Noodle placed above many aspects when it came to her personal presentation to the world. She might've looked like shit, but I knew that with fresh sparkly posh nails, she was gonna be feeling pretty groovy on the inside at least, so that was summat positive.

The nursey vet lady seemed overly nervous at my being there though, especially as I was sat on the chair, and repeatedly she examined her special nursey watch, then whispered something to The Suit whilst slightly nodding her head over in my direction. She was being fairly obvious, 'better make it quick coz your dog best not be seen in here.'

Me and Ms Noodle hugged for a really long couple of minutes. She then looked at me and said, 'Be ever so good for daddy now, won't you. Oh, and no more wanking in public, you little horror, okay?'

Poor nursey vet lady. I don't think she'd have understood anyway, even if The Suit had bothered to attempt an explanation, which he notably didn't. He seemed content to let her make of that statement what she would. I liked his style. Good man.

Ms Noodle then squeezed my right paw and ever so softly said, 'Goodbye lad, I'll see you soon.'

With that, me and The Suit trudged back to the car, retracing our steps around the collection of buildings, and then drove back to the cottage. He didn't say a word. Me neither. Come to think of it, I didn't even fart once. That was another weird thing about that very weird day.

Epilogue

That visit to the big building with the hooman's vets had been the last time I ever saw or spoke with the lovely Ms Noodle. You see, she never did get to come back home with us. The Suit was well-sad, so I think Ms Noodle must have become one of those special angels in the night sky, coz I know that's what happens when hoomans get really sick, or as old as dinosaurs, right?

Then, after a prolonged stay of a few weeks at the hotel with Misses Mary and Mister Tom, I came back to the cottage to learn that everything in my life was about to change once again. My time as 'Taz the Rural Rascal' was coming to an end too; and life had another new fresh start in store for me.

The Suit had plans for a move overseas, that much I knew. The cottage, the hill, and the cherry tree changed hands to owners who would no doubt install their own four-legged friends, so what was to become of me? Well, as it happened, life had, yet again, dealt me a whole new twist of the cards.

~ ~ ~ ~

The Suit had sat down and attempted to explain how things were going to be. He'd assured me that my new life would be just as cool, although of course different in many ways. And with that, the two of us got into his car and left the cottage behind for the last time. Also in the car went my doggie bed, a bag full of towels, my food and water bowls, all 19 of my raggers, as well as the leftovers of a bag of Granny Smiths, half a kilo of carrots, and almost a sack full of the birdseed that kept me so trim 'n' slim.

The drive was over after about an hour, and we pulled up in front of a small terraced townhouse. I hadn't been there before, I knew that much, so I was surprised when the person who opened the front door was none other than the lovely Misty!

Of course, I'd known Misty for years; just didn't know she happened to have lived where we had driven to visit that day. Her mum was none other than Aunt Gina, my lovely Monday mate who helped clean and polish the cottage for Ms Noodle and then took me for walkies afterwards, whilst her dad was Mister George, that stand-up farmer bloke who'd ridden off into the sunset, or to the other side of the village at least, on that old black bike The Suit had flogged him many moons ago.

Most importantly here, Misty always seemed pretty comfortable with my errant ways; probably coz she was well nearer my own age too. Yeah, I know, I had a bit of a dodgy rep by that point and, as a consequence, not all the hoomans I encountered could somehow 'get me,' whatever that quite meant.

She waltzed over to me and immediately gave me a sloppy snog right on my left earlobe.

'Tazzy baby! Welcome to your new home!' she blurted out.

Somewhat embarrassed I let out a sly one, and then did my level best to grin back at her, while of course holding my breath as it really wasn't a nice one I'd dropped. Hmm, I really ought to have tried harder – you know, a time and a place, and all that shit.

She then led me further into the little house to 'show me around.' There was a naff little back yard, but no garden, and no hill, and no cherry tree. However, Misty then took my bed from The Suit and plonked it on the floor, right by a new gleaming big fat white radiator.

'Now Tazzy, that was fitted just yesterday, especially for you,' she explained. 'I'm afraid you don't have your own room here, but this is your very own corner of the living room, and so yes, that is your own personal radiator,' she proudly announced. She then went across to the window, 'Come see, Tazzy, see over there, that's a huge park where you can run around every single day with me. You see, I work from home so you'll never be lonely here. So, how does that all sound to you, okay?'

I looked at Misty, then across to The Suit, and then back at Misty.

'All looks pretty bonza to me, Misty. Now, shall I unpack before or after we head to the park?' I asked, but then something caught my eye.

Misty had obviously noticed my concentration drift out the window.

'What is it Tazzy? she asked.

'More like, "who" not what? Don't tell me that little minx of a poodle that just strolled past is my neighbour?' I asked with a gleam in my eye and a twitch in the Timmy region.

~ ~ ~ ~ ~ ~ ~ ~ ~ ~

Printed in Great Britain
by Amazon

36096122R00139